Elm Tree Road

By Anna Jacobs

Cherry Tree Lane
Elm Tree Road

Elm Tree Road

Anna Jacobs

First published in Great Britain in 2011 by
Allison & Busby Limited
13 Charlotte Mews
London W1T 4EJ
www.allisonandbusby.com

A CIP catalogue record for this book is available from
the British Library.

10 9 8 7 6 5 4 3 2 1

13-ISBN 978-0-7490-0997-7

Typeset in 11/16 pt Sabon by
Allison & Busby Ltd.

Paper used in this publication is from sustainably managed sources.
All of the wood used is procured from legal sources and is fully traceable.
The producing mill uses schemes such as ISO 14001
to monitor environmental impact.

Printed and bound in the UK by
CPI Mackays, Chatham ME5 8TD

Elm Tree Road

Chapter One

The night before, Nell slept only fitfully. She kept waking with a start, terrified her father had found out what she was going to do and was coming to drag her back and beat her. In the end, the sounds from other houses in the terrace told her it was time to get up. She lay for a moment or two longer, feeling desperately sad, then got out of bed and lit a candle.

That woke her sister Mattie, who didn't say anything, just lay staring at her from the far side of the bed, looking as miserable as Nell felt. At twenty-nine, Mattie knew how serious this was and that only desperation would have driven them to it.

It was strange. Mattie was running away to avoid marrying the man Nell's father had chosen for her, and Nell was running away so that she could get married.

They had to shake their youngest sister awake, as usual, and Renie was excited rather than sad. To a sixteen-year-old, this seemed like an adventure.

Today all three of them were running away from their

bully of a father. Nell was leaving with Cliff, and they were going to get married as soon as they could. Now she was twenty-one, she didn't need her father's permission. He wouldn't have given it, she knew, even though she was expecting Cliff's child. Her father said it was his daughters' duty to support him in his old age.

Renie was going to live with them but Mattie had to make her own way in the world. Nell didn't know where her sister was going – anywhere away from *him* – and was upset that Cliff wouldn't let both her sisters come and live with them. But he could get stubborn sometimes and he'd put his foot down about this. Mattie was too old to get married now, he said, and she'd be on his hands for ever. What's more, she'd want to rule the roost and he wasn't having that.

Any other morning she and her sisters would have chatted quietly as they got dressed, but today they were too sad to talk. Nell managed to squeeze into four pairs of drawers, three shifts, three petticoats and two blouses, then rolled up stockings and other bits and pieces and crammed them into a shopping bag. She had to take as much with her as possible without *him* realising.

Renie and Mattie's clothing was similarly bulky, and Renie also had a shopping bag full of bits and pieces. They thought they could get away with taking that to work without anyone realising what they were doing.

Even if they'd been able to leave openly, there were no suitcases in the house because their father didn't approve of going away on holiday. He'd only once gone on the annual trip put on by the Railway Works for its employees and their families, and after that had refused point-blank to waste his time or let his family go on it. Nell had cried about that several times as a child, seeing all her friends looking forward to Trip Day.

Any other father might have noticed their sudden plumpness today, but not Bart Fuller. He shovelled down the breakfast Mattie put in front of him, then left for work without so much as a thank you.

Only then were the three of them free to hug one another and whisper final hopes and wishes. After that Mattie stepped back and said harshly, 'Go on with you. No use drawing it out. And make sure you get your wages today. You'll need every penny.'

Nell couldn't hold back a sob and a final reminder. 'Remember, Mattie, wherever you are, be sure to get in touch with Cliff's family in two years' time. We'll do the same, Cliff's agreed about that. We'll let them know where we are, too.'

Renie said nothing, just looked at Mattie, her eyes brimming with tears, then gave her eldest sister another crushing hug and rushed out of the house.

Nell followed more slowly, catching up with Renie and telling her sharply to stop crying. She automatically greeted other women they met as they walked to the laundry where they both worked. It was a cold morning with rain threatening, and she got teased about wearing extra clothing to keep warm. They noticed. *He* hadn't.

After they'd clocked in and were heading towards their workstations, Renie whispered, 'I'm frightened. He'll find out, I know he will.'

'No, he won't. It'll be all right, I promise you. We've planned it very carefully. I like your new idea of pretending to be sick. It'll be more convincing. *He* won't catch us.'

But Nell was afraid too. She knew their father had no idea what they were planning to do, but still, fear of him churned inside her.

At quarter past eight, Renie put their plan into operation, doubling up as if in pain, then rushing to the outhouse. She didn't come back and the chargehand sent Nell to see what she was doing. When she got back, she reported that her sister had a bad stomach upset.

When the chargehand went to check up, there was no trouble persuading her to let Nell off for an hour to take her home, Renie looked so white and sickly.

'Your sister shouldn't have come in today. I could tell the minute I saw her that she was sickening for something. And you hurry back, Nell Fuller. I'll have to dock your pay for every hour you're away, you know.'

But when the chargehand had gone back to work, Nell slipped along to the office and begged for their pay up until yesterday. 'If I have to get something for Renie from the chemist, I'll have no money at all. You know what my dad's like.'

'Why do you both need your wages?'

'In case I can't get back here. Dad'll kill us if we've no money for him this week.'

And because everyone knew what a bully Bart Fuller was, they let her have the wages owing up to the previous day. She sighed in relief as she put the money in her purse.

Not much to run away on, less than two pounds, but better than nothing.

They got to the station with several minutes to spare before the nine o'clock train, finding a place to wait behind a pile of luggage, hoping no one they knew would notice them.

'What if your Cliff doesn't come?' Renie asked, shaking the raindrops off her scarf and settling it more comfortably round her neck.

It was Nell's greatest fear too, but she wasn't going to admit that. 'He will come,' she insisted.

But at five to nine Cliff still hadn't arrived.

'He's not coming.' Renie clutched her arm. 'Dad'll kill us for coming home from work.'

'Of course Cliff will be here.' Surely he wouldn't let them down?

At three minutes to nine, he rushed into the station, carrying a suitcase and a canvas sack with a drawstring containing his toolbox, as they'd planned. Without his tools, how would he earn a living for them?

He gestured to them to go to the platform where the train was already waiting, and went to buy the tickets. He came running to join them, only just in time. After he'd put his suitcase in the overhead net, he sat down, still clutching his toolbox.

He didn't say a word, just stared at her, then looked out of the window. Nell had expected him to comfort her, put his arm round her. He was supposed to love her, but he hadn't acted lovingly ever since she told him she was expecting. And that wasn't fair.

As the train whistled and began to puff slowly out of the station, Nell saw a shawled figure standing watching near the entrance. In spite of the shawl being pulled down over the woman's head, she recognised her sister Mattie instantly. That was the final straw. She began to sob.

'Be quiet!' Cliff snapped. 'I don't know what you've got to cry about.'

Nell tried to control herself but the odd tear was still escaping when the train pulled into Wootton Bassett, where they were to get off.

'Hide in the waiting room till the other passengers have left the station,' he ordered.

He kept watch near the door, then beckoned them. 'Right. It's clear.' He hurried them across to a low wall at one side, boosting Nell and Renie over it, then passing them the bags. Finally, he scrambled over himself.

Nell hoped he would give her a hug now that the first part of their escape was over, but all he said was, 'Hurry up.'

He set off walking away from the centre of the little town. 'I told my cousin we'd wait by the side of the road.'

Renie shivered. 'I hope he comes quickly. It's going to rain again soon.'

Nell nudged her. Cliff seemed on edge, so it was best not to chat and disturb him.

Only a few minutes later one of the new motor lorries that were starting to replace horses and carts came into view, moving far more quickly than a horse ever could. Nell had never ridden in a motor vehicle before and felt a bit nervous about this part of the journey. She didn't like the smell it made but the faster they got away the happier she'd be.

'Here's my cousin,' Cliff said unnecessarily as the lorry drew up next to them.

The driver got down from his high seat at the front, grunted something that could have been a greeting, and came round to lift the back edge of the tarpaulin covering the goods. 'They can shelter from the rain under it,' he said to Cliff. 'You come in the front with me.'

'We should have gone on by train,' Renie said, scowling at the dirty floor of the truck.

'How many times do I have to tell you? My cousin's giving us a lift so that your damned father won't be able to trace where we've gone from Swindon. He's taking this load to Gloucester and from there we'll go by train to Manchester.'

'Are we still going to Rochdale?' Nell asked. Cliff hadn't wanted to talk about details.

His voice was sharp. 'Why do you keep asking that? You know I've got relatives in Rochdale who'll help us get started. That's better than going among strangers. My mother's written to them. In between crying her eyes out because I have to leave.' He looked at her as if that was her fault.

Nell shut her mouth with a snap. They'd never agree about his mother, who had spoilt him rotten and would never consider anyone good enough for him. The few times they'd met, Mrs Greenhill had looked down her nose at Nell. She hadn't liked visiting them. It was a dark, mean little house and his mother set a poor table, even when guests were invited.

Cliff helped her up into the back of the lorry, where she and her sister had to squeeze in uncomfortably between two crates.

As he got Renie settled, Nell couldn't stop another tear tracking its way down her cheek and didn't bother to wipe it away.

'Damned well stop crying!' he yelled suddenly. 'What

have *you* got to cry about? I've given up my job and family for you. You're getting a wage earner to look after you and the baby, aren't you? That's what you women want, isn't it? All I can say is, it'd better be bloody worth it. Make sure you give me a son.'

She stared at him in shock, never having seen him like this. As if it wasn't his baby too. As if she could do anything about whether it was a son or a daughter.

Scowling, he yanked the edges of the tarpaulin round them and went to sit in the front next to his cousin.

She exchanged quick glances with Renie, but didn't make any comment. What could you say? Done was done.

Nell felt lost today, not her usual self at all, and to top it all, she was worried sick about Mattie, who still hadn't recovered from a bad cold and shouldn't be out in such weather. To her surprise, she was also more than a bit nervous of this new Cliff, who'd just spoken to her harshly and looked at her as if he hated her. When they started courting, he'd been so nice, so loving, but he'd changed.

She got annoyed with herself for being so timid. He might have had to give up his job, but that was more his fault than hers. He was the one who'd forced himself on her, so why was he blaming her for the baby? And once he'd done it, he'd expected her to let him use her body every time they could steal an hour together.

She couldn't understand what he saw in it. She found it an uncomfortable business and it must look so silly. No wonder people did it in secret. But it was what men and women did together when they got married, and it seemed to please him, so she'd just have to put up with it as other wives did.

Renie reached out to take her hand, and as rain began to fall more heavily, the two sisters pulled the tarpaulin right over themselves and huddled close to one another for warmth.

'We'll be all right now we've got away,' Renie whispered.

A little later she said, 'Your Cliff's grumpy today, isn't he? Is he often like that?'

'No, he isn't. He's worried about getting away from Dad, that's why he's so bad-tempered. He's not a big man, like Dad, would never hold his own in a fight.'

But Nell wasn't nearly as sure as she pretended that they'd be all right. She wasn't sure of anything today, not even the man she was going to marry.

The industrial parts of Lancashire came as a shock to the two girls, so smoky was the air and so grimy were the buildings. It was far worse than the centre of Swindon and the railway works. Whole towns seemed to be wreathed in black smoke as you passed through them by train.

The station in Manchester was crowded, but they were lucky and found a train to Rochdale ready to set out.

The railway station there wasn't even in the town centre, so they had a long walk to get to Cliff's relatives. The man they were going to was some sort of second cousin and had sent a letter telling them how to get there. Cliff had never met him before, but family helped one another in times of trouble.

By now, Nell felt so weary she could hardly put one foot in front of the other. Even Renie, usually full of energy, was quiet and pale. And it was raining again. Would it ever stop?

Cliff's cousin George and his wife Pauline looked at Nell disapprovingly and hardly said a word to her. She wanted to yell out that it wasn't her fault she was expecting a baby, but was afraid of being shown the door if she upset them, so kept quiet.

Lodgings had been found for the two sisters a few doors away, and Cliff was to sleep on the sofa at his cousins'. Before they knew it, Nell and Renie had been taken along the street and left for the night, even though it was only half past eight.

'I'm not doing food at this hour,' the landlady said as the front door closed behind Cliff. 'I don't serve meals after half past six.'

'But we haven't had any tea!' Renie protested.

'Nothing to do with me. You should have come earlier if you wanted tea. Won't hurt you to go without food for one night. I went to bed hungry many a time when I were a little 'un.'

Nell shook her head at her sister, who looked at her incredulously then snapped her mouth shut. After the landlady had left them, she said, 'I'm sorry to have brought you to this.'

'It's not your fault.' Renie came to sit beside her on the bed. 'Shall we nip out and buy something from the corner shop?'

'No. We'll manage tonight and she'll feed us in the morning. We need to save every single penny of our money.' She hadn't given any of their wages to Renie, who always spent any coins she got straight away, buying sweets, magazines or other rubbish. Not that any of them had had much chance to treat themselves because their father took nearly all of their wages. 'We might as well go to bed. It's cold and damp in this room.'

'But I'm thirsty.'

'There's water in the bathroom tap.'

In spite of her complaints, Renie was soon asleep but Nell lay awake worrying. If this was an example of how Cliff kept his promise to look after her, what was the rest of her life going to be like? He hadn't even asked the landlady about their evening meal, and had gone quickly back to his cousins' for his own tea.

Only, what could she do but marry him with a baby on the way?

She didn't cry, was beyond tears now. She'd expected to feel happy at escaping from her father, but instead she felt apprehensive about the future.

Before she went to sleep, she murmured a prayer for her eldest sister, hoping Mattie had found somewhere better than this for her first night.

She was woken next morning by a nearby mill hooter, which was nearly as loud as the one at Swindon's railway works. It was soon followed by others, then the clatter of clogs on pavements. She was so tired, she dozed off again, and of course Renie never stirred till someone shook her awake.

There was a knock on the door and the landlady yelled, 'Get up, you two! Everyone else has gone to work and I want you out of the house.'

'What about breakfast?' Renie asked when they went down.

'What about it? You've missed it. I cleared the table

half an hour ago. It's up to the Greenhills to feed you now. Don't take long. I want to clean the house. And remember, no lodgers are allowed inside during the day, so don't come back till teatime.'

'But we need something to eat,' Nell protested. 'We didn't have tea last night, either.'

'Well, you're not getting anything from me now. I don't usually have your sort staying here. I only took you in for the sake of poor Pauline Greenhill.' She looked at Nell's stomach suggestively.

Nell could feel herself blushing, and as soon as the door had closed behind the landlady, she said, 'Hurry up. We'll have to buy something to eat.'

She staggered as they went out into the street and Renie caught hold of her. 'Are you all right?'

'Just a bit dizzy. I don't feel well in the mornings at the moment.'

They went along the street and knocked on the door to find Cliff waiting impatiently for them. 'You're late. I have to go and see about a job. It's not looking like rain, so you might as well walk into town with me and start getting to know your way round.'

'What time will we meet you?' Nell asked, feeling as if she was talking to a stranger.

'Come back here at twelve.'

'What about food?' Renie asked. 'We haven't had anything to eat since you bought us those sandwiches yesterday. That landlady didn't give us anything last night and not this morning, either. She said we'd missed the time for breakfast. But no one called us down, did they? She's just trying to cheat us.'

He looked at them in surprise. 'I thought tea and breakfast were included in the board. She's certainly charging enough.'

'She told us to clear out and said the Greenhills would have to feed us.'

'Just a minute.' He went along the street and knocked on the door of their lodgings.

They could hear the sounds of an argument but couldn't make out the words.

Nell was still feeling faint, so leant against the wall.

Suddenly their bulging shopping bags were hurled out on to the pavement, spilling clothes all over the place. Renie ran along the street to help Cliff pick them up, but not before some of them got wet and dirty. Nell was feeling so queasy she didn't dare move for a minute or two.

Cliff came back with her bag, still looking angry. 'She should have given you meals. I'll ask my cousin for something. You can't go without food.'

He left them standing outside, and when he came back, said, 'There's some bread you can have. Don't use too much marge on it. They've not got a lot of money, not with five children. We'll buy them another loaf while we're out. You can leave your bags here in the front room.'

Five children, Nell thought with a shudder. She didn't want that many. Just this one was causing so much trouble. She felt more tired than normal and sick every morning.

When they left his cousins' house after being given one thin piece of bread and scrape each, he said, 'You'd better come with me and wait outside the upholstery place while I go and see about the job. We'll get something else to eat after that, then go and look for some other lodgings for you. If I get this job, you can start looking for work as well. It'd make a big difference to have us all bringing something in.'

After they'd waited a few minutes outside the upholstery factory, Cliff came outside again. He looked so downhearted, Nell could tell at once that he hadn't got the job. She didn't like to remind him they were still hungry. Renie had wanted to buy a loaf, but she'd told her to wait. They weren't spending a penny unless they had to, because who knew what they'd need their own money for? Cliff had far more than them. He'd been saving for years. She'd heard his workmates tease him about being tight-fisted.

He looked at her. 'I didn't get it.'

She went to pat his arm. 'I'm sorry, Cliff. What shall we do now?'

'The foreman said there might be a job in somewhere called Milnrow. I have to go there by train, but I think you'd better stay here in Rochdale. I don't want to pay three lots of fares for nothing. I'll see you later at my cousins'. Don't go back there till teatime, though.'

He was gone before they could do anything. He seemed quite desperate to get a job, and she could understand that, but it was only their first full day here, so if it took him a few days to find one, it wouldn't be the end of the world. It clearly meant a lot to him, though. When she thought about it, he'd had a job right from school, working for Great Western, first as a lad who did anything asked of him, then as an apprentice, then as an upholsterer, one of the better jobs in the railway works.

This must be the first time in his life he'd not had a wage

coming in and he was panicking. That would explain why he was so . . . tense.

But he could still have given some thought to them, and he hadn't. Not even one minute's consideration.

She linked her arm in her sister's and they started walking along by the river in the centre of town, which was crossed by several bridges. One of them was quite new, and when they stopped to look over the edge at the muddy shallow river, an old woman passing by stopped to chat and told them the Esplanade Bridge had only been finished the previous year.

'Why is the water red?' Renie asked.

'From the dyeworks, love. It often changes colour, depending on what they're using there.'

Renie wrinkled her nose. 'It doesn't smell very nice.'

The woman laughed. 'Where there's muck there's money!' She moved on, and as it started raining again, they followed her to the more sheltered Yorkshire Street, with its rows of shops.

It was a long cold day and they didn't always find shelter from the showers, so got wetter and wetter. At noon, Nell bought a stale lardy cake, cheap because it'd been baked yesterday. It gave you quite a lot for your money, and they shared that, finding a drinking fountain to wash it down.

The next time it began to rain hard they went into the library for a while. Nell read the newspapers while Renie found a book about a maid who fell in love with her mistress's son.

They kept quiet, trying not to be noticed, but after a while a man came over to them. 'Are you members of the library?'

'Er . . . no. We've just come to live in Rochdale and we're waiting to see if my . . . husband gets a job. I thought I'd see if I could find a job too.' She indicated the newspaper.

'Well, you can stay another hour till you've checked out the jobs, but we can't have every Tom, Dick and Harry using the library as a shelter when it rains.'

Nell remembered to keep her hand hidden inside her skirt so that he didn't see her lack of a wedding ring. When he looked at her as if expecting a reply, she nodded and said, 'Thank you.' What a mean fellow! She went back to looking down the columns of jobs. Many of the job names meant nothing to her, because they were in the mills, and what did she know about mill work?

Anyway, once she and Cliff were married, she'd have a house and husband to look after and wouldn't be able to work full-time. That left jobs like cleaning or doing people's washing privately, which didn't pay much. She sighed. Cliff wasn't the only one who'd come down in the world. The supervisor at the laundry in Swindon had said she was a good worker and might be put in charge of two other girls soon. She'd lost her chance at that now, as well as everything else she'd dreamt about. And it was all his fault.

After an hour, the man who'd spoken to them before came to stand nearby, so they left the library, to find it still raining steadily outside.

'We can't just walk the streets,' Renie said. 'I'm soaked already. Surely Cliff's cousin will let us wait in the house?'

They went back, but when Pauline opened the door, she didn't invite them in, just kept them standing on the doorstep.

'I wonder if we could shelter in your house?' Nell asked. 'Cliff's gone to somewhere called Milnrow and we've nowhere else to go.'

'You should have been more polite to your landlady.'

'Polite? She refused to give us any tea or breakfast. And it was Cliff who quarrelled with her because of that, not us.'

'She told me you'd turned up your nose at bread and marg.'

Nell drew herself up and said quietly, 'Not one crumb was offered, and she didn't give us a cup of tea, either. But if you'd prefer to believe her, I can't stop you. Don't let us prevent you from getting on with your housework.' She turned away and put her arm round Renie, who was shivering. 'Come on, love.'

'I suppose you'd better come in.'

'Not if we're unwelcome.' Nell began walking away, calling over her shoulder, 'We'll be back at six. Cliff should be home by then.'

'You should have gone in, even if she was unfriendly,' Renie said. 'I'm so c-cold.'

'Not when she thinks we're immoral and liars. And she hasn't called us back again, has she? She's just let us walk away.'

'What are we going to do for the rest of the afternoon?' Renie asked.

'Find shelter, if it's only at a bus stop. Cheer up. Things will get better once Cliff finds a job.'

'He looks at us as if he hates us.'

'He's worried about money, isn't himself at the moment.'

'We've lost our jobs too.'

'It's different for a man.'

'I don't see why,' Renie muttered.

'Because he's the breadwinner.'

'We all have to buy food. And I'm starving hungry again.'

'Don't let's argue, love. Now, keep your eyes open. There must be somewhere we can shelter.'

Chapter Two

Cliff found the upholsterer's shop he'd been told about and stopped in dismay. It was an upholsterer's all right, but it was small and looked run-down. There was a roughly written sign saying, 'Man wanted, must know the trade', so he went inside.

An older man shuffled out from a door at the back. 'Yes?'

'I've come about the job.'

'Know anything about upholstery?'

'Yes. I've served my apprenticeship.' He pulled his papers out of his inside pocket.

The man barely glanced at them before handing them back and saying, 'Got your own tools?'

'Of course.'

'Come through, then.' He led the way into a much larger workshop at the back, which was in chaos. 'Sorry about the mess. I've been without help for weeks, except for my grandson here, and he's not up to much, poor soul.' He tapped his head and indicated a spotty youth with a dopey expression, who was sweeping up half-heartedly. 'I'm Don Rayner.' He offered his hand.

'Clifford Greenhill.'

'Where have you been working?'

'On railway upholstery for Great Western in Swindon.'

'Good job, that. Why did you leave?'

Cliff hesitated, then decided on the truth. 'I got a girl in trouble and her father's a brute. I had to leave town quickly.'

Rayner frowned at him. 'Nay, I don't want someone working here who'd leave a lass in trouble.'

'I didn't leave her. She came with me. Her father would have beaten her senseless if he'd found out she was expecting. Me too. He crippled a fellow who was courting her older sister. We're going to get wed as soon as we find somewhere to settle.'

'Oh. Well, I suppose I could give you a try.'

Cliff looked round. 'It's mostly domestic work, I suppose?'

'It's all domestic, but I don't expect it's much different from what you did.'

'How much are you paying?'

'Thirty shillin' a week.'

'I was earning two pound five shillings a week in Swindon.'

'Well, thirty's all I can afford. Take it or leave it.'

Cliff hesitated, then said, 'I'll take it.'

'You can start this afternoon, then. I've got a rush job on.'

'All right. But I'll have to leave at five o'clock. I'm meeting Nell at six in Rochdale.'

Later, as they were working together on a button-backed sofa, Cliff had a sudden thought. 'Know any houses to let near here?' That'd mean he'd not have to waste money, time and shoe leather on travelling.

'There's one close by in Willow Court. It's not much but it'll give you a start. I'll send the lad to ask for the key and you can nip round and have a look at it when we've finished this.'

A couple of hours later Cliff nipped along the back alley and found his way to Willow Court, stopping at the entrance to look round in dismay. No wonder the house was cheap. It was a very low form of housing, though at least it wasn't the worst of its type.

Five narrow dwellings clustered round a tiny oblong courtyard with an old-fashioned water closet near the entrance. Inside the empty house, he found one room and a scullery on the ground floor, two small bedrooms upstairs. 'Cheap' was the only good thing you could say about the place, and the fact that it was close to his work.

His mother would go mad to think of him living here. Still, it was only four shillings a week rent and they'd need furniture and everything, so Nell would just have to put up with it for the time being. They could move somewhere better later. And her cheeky sister should be grateful for anything.

Late that afternoon Cliff got off the train in Rochdale, feeling miserable in spite of having found a job and having earned three shillings that day. It was raining again and he shivered as he tramped across town to his cousins'. He'd come down in the world and no mistake. Women! They weren't worth it. And now he'd be saddled with a child *and* a sister-in-law.

He'd heard there were ways to stop more children coming, and by hell, he'd make sure he found out about them. If he and Nell had more than one or two children, they'd be poor for the rest of their lives.

Why did he have to fall for a girl with a father like that? He'd been set for life at the railway works, might even have managed to buy his own house one day, and now look at him.

Renie and Nell walked on in the rain, sheltering in an occasional shop doorway for a few minutes. But each time they lingered, someone from the shop came to ask them to 'Move on, please'.

There were two main streets leading upwards from the town centre and there were plenty of shops along them. They even went into one or two of the bigger places to look at the goods, pretty dress materials that Nell could have made up easily. She was starting to like sewing, or rather, to like the clothes that came from it.

After someone had asked yet again, 'Can I help you, miss?' Nell had had enough. 'Let's find somewhere else to shelter, Renie. The rain's eased off a bit.' She turned off along a narrow side street and followed it aimlessly.

The wind suddenly started blowing hard and yet another squall sent rain driving in their faces. They were passing a small chapel, the door of which was open. 'Let's try inside there,' Nell said. 'Surely *they* won't turn us away.'

They ran for the porch and she nearly bumped into a

thin, slightly balding man standing under it near the door. 'Oh, sorry.'

'Do come in. You look soaked through.'

She stared down at herself. She hadn't realised quite how wet she was, but her skirt was actually dripping on the floor. 'Can we . . . shelter here for a bit?'

'Of course you can. The Lord's house is open to everyone. Have you no home to go to?' His voice was gentle, his accent posh, but his eyes were kind.

'Not at the moment, no. We've just arrived in Rochdale and my young man's looking for work.'

'Then you're very welcome to stay here out of the rain. I could make you a cup of tea. I have a small spirit stove. Your poor friend's shivering.'

'That's very kind of you. If it's not too much trouble.'

He smiled at them. 'I'm Septimus Garrett, by the way. I'm the minister here.'

'Nell Fuller.' She realised she should have said Greenhill, but it was too late now. 'And this is my sister, Renie.'

They sat on hard wooden chairs in his private room, their outer clothes draped over other chair backs, even their indoor clothes steaming from the heat of the fire. He asked a few questions and was so sympathetic about their plight that the whole story came tumbling out.

When she'd finished, Nell looked at him apprehensively, cradling her second cup of tea in her hands, enjoying its warmth as much as its taste. 'I know I've done wrong,' she faltered.

'Let he who is without fault cast the first stone,' he said quietly. 'And if you're still homeless at the end of the day, you can sleep in here tonight, as long as you don't mind sharing a rug on the floor and using another rug as a blanket. My home is just across the street, the house with the blue door. Just knock if you need help. This is quite a poor area and we haven't any proper beds to offer you, I'm afraid, but others have sheltered here.'

Tears came into her eyes. 'Thank you. You're very kind.'

'It's my calling to help others.' His smile was warm and made him look much younger. 'Now, what time do you have to meet your young man?'

'About six.'

'Then I suggest you stay here until then. I can even lend you a newspaper to read. I have to go and visit a woman from our congregation who's sick, but I'll be back before you leave.'

When he'd gone, Renie sighed. 'It's horrible being homeless, isn't it? I never thought it'd be as bad as this, though.' She gulped and scrubbed at her eyes with one hand.

Nell didn't have the energy to comfort her. 'It's no use crying. It won't do any good. Things will get better once Cliff finds a job, and in the meantime, we'll just have to put up with things.'

She hugged her knees and sat soaking up the warmth, too weary to read or chat. What was there to say that hadn't been said a dozen times already?

When Cliff got back to his cousins' house, he expected Nell and Renie to be waiting for him there and was surprised not to see them.

'They wouldn't stay,' Cousin Pauline said.

Something about the way she avoided his eyes as she said that made him feel suspicious. 'On a rainy day like this? Where else would they go?'

She glanced at the children and gestured to him to follow her, leading him into the chilly front room where he'd slept the night before.

'Have you seen them? Do you know where they've gone?' he pressed when she stood twisting her apron hem, still seeming reluctant to speak.

'How would I know where they've gone? Women like that usually find somewhere, I'm sure.'

He looked at her in shock. 'What do you mean, "women like that"?'

'Well, your mother wrote that your . . . young lady is expecting. Your parents are very upset about you marrying this Nell Fuller, you know. You weren't even engaged to her, apparently, till this happened. I suppose that's why you're in such trouble with her father. And her sister's a bold piece, if you ask me. Cheek the King, that one would.'

He held back his indignation only because he had nowhere else to turn for help. 'My Nell's not like that. She's never been with anyone but me.'

Pauline sniffed as if she didn't believe him.

'I know she hasn't,' he repeated.

His cousin George came home just then, slamming the door and stopping in the doorway of the front room. 'What are you doing in here? Is my tea ready? I'm starving.'

'It's nearly ready, love. We were just talking and I didn't want the kids overhearing.'

31

She tried to move past Cliff but he barred her way. 'You do believe me about Nell, don't you?'

She shrugged. 'If you say so. We won't wait for them two, though. My George needs his food after a hard day's work.'

George rubbed his hands together briskly to warm them. 'That smells good, love.' He turned to Cliff. 'Why aren't them two back yet? What can they be doing out on a rainy day like this? I warn you, I'm not having any immoral behaviour from anyone who comes into my house.' He turned to go through to the back.

'Just a minute, George!' Cliff looked from one to the other. 'It seems my mother's given you the wrong impression about Nell. She's a good girl.' He could see that they didn't believe him and added, 'I forced her, if you must know, and that's why she's expecting.'

'Oh.' Pauline went bright red.

'I'm not proud of what I did. And . . . I've not treated her well since we left Swindon, either, because I was upset at having to give up my job. Her father's a brute. He nearly killed a man who came courting her older sister.'

George clapped him on the shoulder. 'Right, lad. I'm glad she's not that sort. Pale little thing, isn't she?'

'She isn't usually pale. She's usually very pretty. I'm worried about what Nell and Renie will do tonight, now they've been thrown out of those lodgings down the street. That woman's a right old cheat. She didn't feed them so much as a crumb, and they only had a piece of bread and scrape here this morning, so they must be starving hungry as well as wet and cold. I'm not paying that landlady the full amount, whatever she says.'

They stared at him open-mouthed.

'She told me they turned up their noses at what she offered this morning,' Pauline said.

'No, they didn't. Would you, if you hadn't eaten since the day before?' He wasn't finished because a man had his pride, even when it was going to cost him money. 'If we're not welcome here, just say, and we'll find lodgings somewhere else.'

George shrugged. 'I'm glad we've got that sorted out. We'll let 'em sleep in the front room tonight if they've nowhere to go, eh, Pauline, but we've no blankets to spare.'

His wife nodded. 'They can cover themselves with the rag rug from the back room. It's the best we can do.'

'Thanks.' Cliff let her pass, watched them both walk towards the warmth of the kitchen and went to look out of the front door, feeling guilty about Nell being out in the cold and rain all day. He stayed on the doorstep with the door nearly closed behind him, stubbornly watching for them, suddenly desperate to be sure they were all right.

When the two of them came into view, there was a man with them and Nell was smiling up at him, which annoyed Cliff after the conversation he'd just had.

Her smile faded when she saw him scowling at her and she looked at him uncertainly. He was reminded yet again how tiny she was, how fragile she felt in his arms.

'Where the hell have you been?' he demanded. 'I've been worried sick to think of you out in the rain all day.'

'Mr Garrett kindly let us shelter in the new chapel. Mr Garrett, this is my betrothed, Cliff Greenhill.'

The stranger held out his hand. 'Pleased to meet you.'

Cliff could do nothing but take his hand, but he was suspicious about why a man that age would fuss over two bedraggled young women.

'He's the minister there,' Nell said.

'Ah. I see.'

'Actually, I'm the minister there *and* at a new chapel we've just opened in Milnrow. My wife and I will be moving there soon because we want a garden.'

'Milnrow, eh? We're going to be living there too.' Cliff felt himself relaxing a little. 'I've just got a job at Rayner's.'

'Don and his wife are members of our congregation, though he hasn't been to chapel as often lately because he's been snowed under with work, though I can't approve of toiling on the Sabbath. Iris will be glad he's found someone to help him.'

'Good. Then my job should be safe for a while.' Cliff could hear how bitter he sounded, but couldn't help it. He saw Nell wince and felt guilty all over again. He'd been feeling guilty ever since she told him, but angry too. He didn't *want* to get married yet, not even to her. 'I'm pleased to have met you, Mr Garrett. Come inside out of the rain, you two.' But the man didn't take the hint and still lingered.

'I hope we'll meet again, Mr Greenhill. Are you chapel-goers, by any chance?'

Cliff hesitated, but he knew employers usually preferred their men to go to the same church as they did, so nodded. He'd never cared much about going to church, let alone which one he went to, though his parents attended the parish church in Swindon every Sunday and had done all their lives.

He didn't like Christ Church, though, so he'd stayed away when he could. The gentry sat at the front still, like in the bad old days. They acted as if they were better than anyone else, expecting you to wait for them to lead the way out. He wasn't even sure he believed in God anymore. Why would a loving God do this to him?

It was Mr Garrett's turn to hesitate. 'From what your young lady has told me, you'll be setting up house from scratch. I'm sure our congregations, small as they are, will help you find some bits and pieces of furniture. They can be very generous to those in need, true Christians. And if the things they find for you need mending, well, I'm sure a man with your skills will be able to do that.'

Cliff hated to need charity, but he'd been dreading having to spend his savings on buying a whole houseful of furniture. All they had at the moment were his toolkit, the clothes they stood up in and the few things in their bags. 'Thank you. That'd be very . . . kind. We're going to be living in Willow Court.'

'You've found us a house already!' Nell exclaimed.

'It's not very big, but it's cheap and close to where I work. It'll do to get us started.'

She flung her arms round his neck and stood on tiptoe to plonk a quick kiss on his cheek. 'You've done so well, Cliff. All this on your first full day here.'

When she looked at him like that, so trusting and admiring, he felt a bit better. 'I said I'd look after you, didn't I?'

Mr Garrett smiled at him from behind Nell. 'If you come to the morning service at the Rochdale chapel tomorrow, I'll introduce you and ask the congregation for help. Now,

I'll let you get these young ladies into the warmth again, and I'll go home to my wife.' He tipped his hat and strolled away.

Pauline was still a bit stiff with Nell and her sister that evening, but she wasn't quite as sharp and scornful as she had been, especially when Nell made Cliff give her the money to nip out to the corner shop and buy a few bits and pieces of food.

The following day, since it was a Sunday, she even suggested they come to church with her and her family.

'Thanks, but I think we'd better go to Mr Garrett's chapel,' Cliff said. 'My new employer goes there and the minister's promised to ask his congregation for help with finding furniture. I've paid this week's rent, so we can move into Willow Court as soon as we have beds and a few other bits and pieces.'

The scornful look returned to Pauline's face. 'We don't have anything to do with that lot. We go to St Chad's and always have done. And our family's never had to accept *charity*.'

Cliff's expression became thunderous but it was Renie who answered them.

'Neither had we until one of *your* family got my sister in trouble.'

Pauline's sharp intake of breath echoed round the room.

'Let's go and get ready,' Nell said hurriedly into the frosty silence that followed. In the front room, where they'd passed an uncomfortable night, she turned on her sister. 'Don't you *ever again* say anything cheeky like that to people who're helping us!'

'I never heard of such grudging help.'

'That doesn't matter. At least we had somewhere to sleep last night. Just keep your mouth shut, for once. You're too quick to say things, you are.'

Renie burst into tears. 'I wish I'd gone with Mattie. She'd have found us somewhere better than this.'

Cliff came into the front room just then, glaring at them.

'I've told her to mind her manners while we're guests here,' Nell said quickly.

'Good. See that you listen to your sister, who has more sense than you, Renie. Now, are you two ready for chapel?'

'Nearly.' Nell went to look into the mirror that hung over the mantelpiece, shivering in the chill damp room. She looked terrible, exhausted and pale, and she was feeling nauseous again. No wonder he wasn't acting fondly towards her.

All she had to put on her head was the scarf she wore to go to work. She couldn't afford to give in to her sickness, though, so she took a deep breath and went across to Cliff. 'It'll get better than this,' she whispered.

He clasped her hand and for a moment she saw the old Cliff looking at her lovingly. Then he shook his head and turned back into the sharp new Cliff, with the tight expression on his face. 'At least it isn't raining at the moment.'

The small chapel had a few chairs at the front, not matching, and behind them rows of benches. It was nearly full, and people smiled a welcome as the three of them sat down on an empty bench at the rear.

The service was more vigorous than the one in the parish church in Swindon, with people singing hymns as if they meant something, not just droning them out tonelessly. There wasn't a choir in such a small chapel, but two women in one corner sang a descant to the hymns, and they had lovely voices.

Then Mr Garrett went to stand by the lectern to deliver his sermon. It was short and to the point. 'I take as my theme today loving your neighbours in deed and truth, from John chapter one, verse three, line eighteen.' He paused, then went on quietly, 'Yesterday I met a young couple who'd been driven away from their home by a violent man. They're here today, new to our congregation, and I'm sure we all welcome them.'

There were mutters of agreement and more people turned to smile and nod at them.

'These young folk are about to get married and set up a home, without any friends or family to help them. They're in desperate need of furniture and everything else, and I'm sure you'll help them if you can. They're going to live in Milnrow and attend our new sister chapel.'

He left it at that and gave out the number of the final hymn.

Nell blushed to think they'd been singled out as needing charity. She could see that Cliff's knuckles were white on the edge of his hymn book, so didn't try to catch his attention. Still, it would be worth the embarrassment. The sooner they could find furniture, the sooner she could leave Cliff's cousins' grudging shelter and then surely he'd be his old self again?

And if people helped them now, well, they could help

others in return once they were on their feet again, couldn't they? That way they'd regain their self-respect.

After the service, Mr Garrett came across to speak to them. 'I'm so glad you came today.'

Cliff nodded, hesitated, then said, 'We'd like you to marry us as soon as possible, if that's all right. I'll get a special licence. I think it'll be money well spent, because we want to start off as we mean to go on here.'

'I shall be very happy to marry you.' He turned. 'Ah, Mrs Lambden. May I introduce you to Mr Greenhill and Miss Fuller, who are soon to marry and are just setting up home? And this is Miss Fuller's sister, Renie, who is to live with them.'

An older woman stopped beside him, studying them, then smiling as if she approved of what she saw. 'Welcome to our congregation. I've got an old bedstead that I've no use for. You'll have to mend the webbing, but it's got years of use in it yet.'

'Thank you,' Nell said. 'We'd be very grateful for it.'

Others came across and she kept a count in her head of the bigger items they'd been offered. Cliff's face was grim and he clearly was hating this, but she didn't care. She just wanted to get into her own home.

Mr Garrett whispered to them not to leave yet and went to speak to others. Once the last people had left, he came back. 'I'll mention you in my next service today in Milnrow. Oh, and I'm sure I can organise the loan of a horse and cart to take the things to your new home.'

'We're very grateful for your help,' Nell said. She'd repeated those words several times but Cliff seemed not to find them easy to say, so she was doing it for them both.

As they walked back to his cousins' house, they smelt bread baking and went round to the back of a bakery to find the man selling loaves, even on a Sunday. They bought two loaves and some scones and took them back to Cliff's cousins', which brought a near-smile to Pauline's narrow face.

'I'll buy some more margarine tomorrow,' Cliff told her.

But the night again seemed long and uncomfortable to Nell, cuddled up to her sister on the thin rag rug, which hardly softened the hard floor.

She'd never slept so badly in her whole life, never felt so miserable. She was getting married soon, ought to be happy, but how could you be when life was so uncomfortable and the man you were marrying looked at you sometimes as if he hated you?

On Monday Nell gave Cliff her birth certificate in case he had time to get a special licence, then she waved him off to work. She looked down at the money he'd given her to buy some margarine and another loaf. Two shillings. Not exactly generous, but even so, she'd spend as little of it as she could. She and her sisters had had a lot of experience in being careful, with a father as stingy as theirs.

She glanced up at the sky and was relieved to see that though there were patchy clouds, it didn't look like being a day of constant rain, at least. They'd be able to stay away from Pauline and her sour face. There were three small children at home in the house, and two had gone off to school. The two toddlers were sent into the corner of the kitchen to 'play quietly', and were smacked if they made a noise. The baby was laid in a shabby high pram, not even sat up so that it could look round, poor thing.

Five children! thought Nell. And so close in age. No wonder Pauline's grumpy. Nell intended to persuade Cliff not to give her too many children. There were ways of preventing them, she'd heard. She did want two or three children, of course she did, but not a whole gaggle of them, and not close together, either.

As she and Renie were getting ready to go out, there was a knock on the front door.

Pauline went to answer it and came to the door of the front room. 'It's for you.' She went back to the kitchen without a word of explanation.

Nell hurried to the front door to find Mr Garrett standing there. 'Do come in!' Thank goodness she'd cleared away their makeshift bedding from the front room!

He stood there beaming at them. 'We had a lot of offers of help from the Milnrow congregation as well as the Rochdale one, and my wife has found you a few bits and pieces too. The thing is, I have the chance to borrow a horse and cart today, so we could take the things out to Milnrow without you incurring any expense.'

'Oh, that's wonderful! Thank you so much.'

'I know where Mr Greenhill works and I know where Willow Court is, but perhaps it'd be best if you and your sister came with me, because I doubt his employer will want him to take time off work to help me take the things into the house.'

He gave one of his jolly laughs. 'I'm a good driver, I promise you. I grew up on a farm with horses.'

Once again, being with him lifted her spirits. 'That'd be

wonderful! I can't believe you've got things organised so quickly.'

'We try to help one another in the chapels, and I regard it as part of my job to organise that, when people are in need. One day, perhaps you'll be the one to offer help to another soul in trouble.'

'Oh, I will. I'd already decided that.' She smiled at Renie, who had been listening to them. 'Won't it be wonderful to have a home of our own?'

'I can't get away from here soon enough.'

Her voice was loud and no doubt carried into the kitchen through the half-open door. 'Shh!' Nell whispered.

Renie tossed her head, scowling.

'If you can come with me straight away, we'll start collecting the things,' Mr Garrett said.

It took most of the morning to collect the donations, and, as he'd said, many items needed repair. But there were household utensils too, bowls and dishes, an old knife, worn thin with sharpening, all sorts of small useful items.

When they got to the upholstery workshop, Mr Garrett led the way in to ask Mr Rayner about giving Cliff just a little time off.

'He's not here,' Mr Rayner said.

Nell's heart sank. Had something gone wrong already with the new job? If so, this would all be in vain.

'He's gone into Rochdale to get a special licence to marry his sweetheart,' Mr Rayner added. 'He couldn't settle to work, so I told him to get it sorted out.'

She had to lean against the wall because she felt wobbly with relief.

Mr Rayner looked across to where the two young women were standing. 'Which one of you is Nell?'

She moved forward. 'I am.'

'I wish you well with your wedding, lass.'

'Thank you.'

'Can we get into the house?' Mr Garrett asked. 'We've got some pieces of furniture that people from the two chapels have donated and I've brought them across.'

'I heard you'd been asking for stuff on Sunday. I've a piece or two I can let you have as well, but your man will have to fix them. The chair frames have nothing for you to sit on at the moment.' He laughed. 'Hard work, that's what I'm giving him.'

'We're very grateful and we don't mind hard work,' Nell said quickly.

'I know where the house key is. Willow Court is only just round the corner.' He nodded to her again. 'The lad can give you a hand with carrying things in, Mr Garrett. He's strong in the body, even if he is weak in the head.'

As Nell walked out of the untidy little shop, she felt a tiny thread of happiness start to unfurl inside her. But it withered the minute she saw the house they were to live in, smelt the stinking water closet near the entrance to the little court and saw the filthy walls inside the house. She wanted to turn tail and run then.

Only she couldn't run, could she? Not from the baby growing in her belly and not from her new life, either. The child would probably be with her for the next twenty years, till it got wed and left home, and probably there would be other children to look after too. Only she intended to love her children, not drive them away. She was determined this one should have a happier life than she'd had, however much trouble its creation had caused.

She felt as if she'd grown years older in the past few weeks, but there was no use moaning. Taking a deep breath, she turned to the minister. 'Let's start carrying the things in, then, shall we?'

He gave her a gentle smile, as if he understood what she'd been thinking. 'You won't be on your own here, my dear. You'll make friends and you'll be able to turn to people at chapel if you need help. We pride ourselves on being practical Christians.'

That kindness nearly made her weep, but she forced back the tears and nodded. 'I know. It's all been . . . a bit rushed.'

She tried to move and couldn't. Things blurred round her and she knew nothing more until she came to, lying on the ground, with Mr Garrett's coat under her head and Renie kneeling beside her.

'What happened?'

Renie took hold of her hand and gave it a squeeze. 'You fainted. Mr Garrett caught you or you'd have bumped your head. How do you feel?'

'A bit dizzy.' She sat up and waited a moment or two until she was sure her head wasn't spinning, then she let Renie help her to stand up.

Footsteps heralded the return of Mr Garrett with a cup of tea and a scone provided by Mr Rayner. 'Here. Drink this. Did you eat any breakfast?'

'No. I feel a bit sick in the mornings and dizzy sometimes.'

'My wife's the same. It usually passes after the first three or four months.'

'I hope so. I need to get a job and earn some money.'

He looked at her consideringly. 'Doing what?'

'Anything that pays. I worked in a laundry before.'

'I could give you a day's work each week helping my wife with the washing. It's a bit much for her, and our previous washing woman just left town. My wife's also expecting, as you must have noticed. She's further along than you and is quite big now. We hadn't expected to be blessed again, but the Lord has decided to give us another child.'

'I'd be happy to work for you.'

'Good. Now, drink the tea and eat the scone. We need to get this furniture in place, so that the lad and I can go and collect the things offered by the congregation here in Milnrow.'

'There are more things?'

'Oh, yes, quite a lot more.'

'I can't thank you enough.'

After he'd gone, she and Renie walked round the house. They had been given two bed frames, both needing rewebbing. Three threadbare blankets. Some ragged old towels, which would only be usable for cleaning, so full of holes were they. Still, you needed rags. There were odd spoons and knives, but no forks. Two plain white cups in perfect condition, another without a handle. The teapot had a chunk missing from the end of the spout, but it was all right otherwise. There were two drinking glasses, one badly chipped.

She studied a sagging armchair and two stools, the latter

rough pieces clearly made by an inexpert hand. She tried one stool and sat there for a moment, gathering herself to continue.

Renie giggled suddenly and sat on the other stool, which wobbled to and fro on uneven legs. 'Which one do you think is the master's seat?'

'The armchair, of course.' She smiled back. 'I wonder if there's a corner shop nearby? We could buy some tea and maybe a loaf and some margarine, and leave them here. We've got a bread bin, so even if there are rats, they'll not be able to get at it. I'm quite hungry now.'

'Jam too?' begged Renie.

'Yes, why not? But we'll use it sparingly.'

She stared round, assessing it all, feeling determination rise within her. 'I want to move in here as soon as possible, even if I have to sleep on the floor. But before we do, it'll need scrubbing from top to bottom and the walls distempering. You and I can do that, but you'll have to climb the ladder – if we can borrow a ladder, that is. I don't want to risk it, not with me getting so dizzy.'

By the time Mr Garrett came back, they had a cup of tea to offer him – Nell was using the cup without a handle – and had met a neighbour, who had come in to see who was moving in. Peg wasn't the sort of person Nell usually associated with, but she was good-hearted and had offered to lend them a scrubbing brush and bucket.

It was greatly needed. She looked round, hands on hips. Before she'd finished this place was going to be sparkling clean. She might be poor, but she could afford a bar of soap, and water and elbow power were free. And for all her flightiness, Renie was a good worker.

They would manage.

Cliff turned up just as the minister was bringing the second load of donations back. He looked round and grew very tight-lipped at the sight of the battered furniture they'd been given. 'This is rubbish! My mother wouldn't have it in the house.'

Nell went to thread her arm in his. 'It'll do to give us a start. And if you could let me have some money, I'll get us the bits and pieces we're lacking, then Renie and I will scrub the whole place down.'

He looked down at her in a more kindly way than recently. 'I'm sorry I can't give you better than this, Nell.'

'We don't need to stay here for ever and it's a start.' She hated to see the shame on his face and tried to distract him. 'I've met Peg next door and she says there's a big market in Rochdale where you can buy blankets, sheeting and towels really cheap if you get the seconds. That'll save us a lot of money. She's offered to take me there on Friday, but I'm going to need money to buy the things.'

'I'll give you some. By then you'll be Mrs Greenhill.' He patted his pocket. 'I've got the special licence here. If Mr Garrett will oblige, that is.'

The minister and the lad came in just then, carrying a rickety table with a scarred top. 'If I'll oblige with what?'

'Marrying us.'

'You've got a special licence already?'

Cliff nodded. 'Better not to wait, I thought. Could you marry us tomorrow, do you think? We could come to the chapel here in Milnrow during my midday break.'

'Of course I can. It'll be my pleasure. Um . . . you don't want to invite any of your family to attend?'

'I have no real family now, except for Nell, of course. My cousin won't want to give up a day's work and his wife is . . . busy with her children.'

Nell kept a smile on her face somehow. It seemed a shameful way to get married and she didn't even have anything pretty to wear, but she wasn't going to say that. Cliff was upset enough about the whole situation.

Once they were in their own home, things would surely improve.

When she thought about it, Nell decided that she might have to get married in this shabby way, but she wasn't wearing a headscarf to her wedding, not for anything. She found a second-hand clothes shop on the way home and bought a hat for her wedding, a plain little straw one with a stained ribbon round it, for a shilling. She bought a yard of navy-blue ribbon to match her dress and coat, then realised she'd need needles, thread and scissors, so bought them too. She trimmed the hat up quickly after she got back.

'What will Cliff say about you spending money on the hat?' Renie asked.

'I don't suppose he'll even notice.'

But Pauline had noticed and pretended to tease her that evening about vanity and spending.

Cliff looked at her very sharply.

When Nell and Renie went to get ready for bed, she thrust her own money at Renie. 'Look after this for me, will you? And don't spend a penny! I'll just keep a few shillings in my purse. He might ask for my money, but I don't want to be totally without some of my own, not ever again.'

Renie nodded and gave her a quick hug before wrapping the coins in her handkerchief so that they wouldn't clink.

When Cliff tapped on the door and asked if they were decent, Nell told him to come in. He closed the door and stood staring at her.

'Did you really spend money on a hat when we have nothing but rags and broken furniture to our name?' he demanded, keeping his voice down, but still sounding furious.

'I bought it second hand. It only cost a shilling.'

'You shouldn't buy anything you don't need.'

'I did need it! I only had a headscarf. I'm not getting married in a headscarf.'

'What does that matter? Anyway, *I'll* decide what we need in future. Give me the rest of your money.'

And though she'd expected him to want that, planned to give him a few shillings just to keep the peace, something in her rebelled.

'No.'

He gaped at her in shock.

'If you don't trust me with money, you shouldn't be marrying me at all. I'm not having you treat me like Dad did, taking everything I earned and doling out money a penny at a time. I'll work hard. I'll find a job and I'll keep your house clean, but I won't ask you for every penny I spend!'

49

He took a jerky step forward, one hand twitching as if he itched to slap her.

'If you ever lay one hand on me, Cliff Greenhill, I'll leave you, married or not,' she said loudly. 'I won't put up with beating, not now, not ever.'

He looked down at his hand, and even in the dim light, she could see a flush stain his cheeks. But it seemed a long time before he apologised.

'I'm sorry, Nell. Of course I won't hit you. I'm just . . . worried sick about money.'

She moved across to him. 'I know. But I'm not a waster or a fool and you shouldn't . . . treat me like one.' Her voice wobbled and she clapped one hand to her mouth, wanting to cry.

He repeated what she'd been saying to Renie. 'It won't always be like this. I promise you it'll get better, Nell.'

That comforted her as little as her own assurances had comforted Renie, but at least he'd spoken to her more gently. She glanced across the room to see her sister already lying on their makeshift bed on the rug, with the three thin blankets they'd been given piled on top and her back turned to them.

Cliff smiled at her briefly, then moved to extinguish the lamp and go to his temporary bed which was now in the kitchen, because Pauline wasn't having him sleep with the girls.

He didn't try to kiss Nell, didn't even give her a quick hug. She wished they could be alone. They'd not had a real chance to talk since they'd left Swindon. You needed privacy to make up your quarrels, she thought as she got into bed with her sister. Only then did she let the tears fall.

She made no sound, but Renie must have known, because she reached out to brush away the tears with her fingertips, then hugged Nell close.

But that only made it worse. It should have been Cliff hugging her.

Her last thought before she fell asleep was that it was her wedding day tomorrow and her oldest sister wouldn't be there. Mattie had been so much a part of her life, a second mother to her and Renie.

It had all gone so wrong.

And why had Cliff told the minister he had no family? She'd wanted to ask that, but he'd looked so unhappy, she'd not spoken out.

Tomorrow might be her wedding day, but she'd never been so unhappy in her life.

As Nell and her sister got ready for the wedding, which was to take place in the afternoon, she had to concentrate hard on self-control or she'd have wept. Her wedding outfit consisted of a navy serge skirt and a rather crumpled white blouse, with her everyday navy coat over them. It was three-quarters length and showed off the mended tear in her skirt, which had been good enough for work, but oh, she wished she had something better to wear today.

The chapel in Milnrow was just off Dale Street, and was even smaller than the one in Rochdale. In fact, it looked more like a small warehouse than a chapel, and perhaps that's what it had been originally.

They were the first to arrive, a bit early, but she'd been too nervous to wait any longer. They found the door open, so went inside, standing just inside the double doors. The place was so empty that when Nell moved forward, her footsteps echoed. She walked slowly to the front, past the six rows of benches, to stand by the plain table which served as an altar. Turning, she laid one hand on the roughly made lectern and looked back at her sister.

'This chapel's only five minutes' walk from our house,' she said, trying to be cheerful. 'It'll be very easy to come here on Sundays.'

Renie was still staring round. 'It's very plain and shabby, isn't it?'

'So am I.' Nell cast an anguished look down at herself, then put one hand up to check her hat. 'Is it straight?'

'Yes. And you look nice. That hat really suits you.'

Nell sighed and looked at the shabby leather-bound bible on the lectern. 'The chapel's just starting up, like me and Cliff. But oh, I wish we'd been able to afford a photograph!'

There was a sound to one side, a door opened and Mr Garrett came out. 'Hello! Nice to see a bride arrive early.'

A woman followed him out. She was heavily pregnant and looked tired, but had a very sweet smile.

'This is my wife, Dora.'

Mrs Garrett came over to shake their hands, then looked from one to the other. 'It's very obvious you're sisters.' She focused on Nell. 'I wish you happy, my dear.'

'Thank you.'

She produced a box camera. 'I wondered if you'd like me to take a photograph of the wedding? It won't be very big, but my dear Brownie takes excellent photos.'

Nell burst into tears.

Renie put an arm round her sister and smiled reassuringly at Mrs Garrett. 'Nell was just saying she wished she could have a photo to remember the day by.'

'I often take them at our weddings. It's my hobby, photography. I take photos of babies and children too. You'll have to wait till I've finished this roll of film, though, to see how the photo turns out.'

Nell pulled herself together. 'Sorry. I'm a bit . . . weepy lately. And thank you. Thank you so much.'

'It's the baby,' Mrs Garrett said confidently. 'I was just the same with my first.'

Mr Garrett glanced up at the clock on the wall, a plain affair with a scratch across the glass covering its face.

The second hand was broken off, but Nell was close enough to see its stump moving jerkily round the centre of the dial as the seconds ticked past. She kept glancing towards the door and then up at the clock.

'He's just been held up,' Mr Garrett said soothingly. 'I'm sure he'll be here in a minute or two.'

Renie said nothing, but she was scowling.

Mrs Garrett fiddled with her camera.

Another four minutes ticked slowly past.

In the corner of Mr Rayner's back room, Cliff washed his hands carefully and knotted his tie more neatly, leaning both hands on the sandy-coloured slopstone as he stared into the fly-specked mirror on the wall.

He shook his head and closed his eyes in anguish. He didn't want to get married. Not this way and not yet. He felt too young for all that responsibility.

A wild desire to run away seized him, not for the first

time. Hadn't he proved that he could find a job easily? He could still get away if he really wanted. He'd only to collect his tools and put them in the box, then pick up his case which he'd brought over today from his cousins' house. He could take a train to Manchester and it didn't matter where he went after that. No one need ever find him.

But if he did run away, he'd never dare see his parents in Swindon again. They might not approve of this marriage, but they'd be shocked if he didn't give his child a name by marrying the mother. And Nell . . . Nell would be on her own, bearing a child in shame. And it *was* his fault. She'd been right about that. Only she was so pretty and fresh-looking, how could a man resist her?

He left the house reluctantly, then passed a public house. On a sudden impulse he went inside and ordered half a pint of bitter. He stood at the bar sipping it. Not many people were here now, because most of the lunchtime drinkers had left.

He stared down at the glass in surprise. It was empty.

The barman came up to him. 'Want another?'

Why not? 'Yes, please.'

He paid over the money and stared down into the thin layer of foam on top of the beer. Could he do it? Did he dare say *to hell with everyone* and run away?

Nell felt panic begin to rise as the clock hands ticked slowly on.

Five minutes.

Ten.

No sign of Cliff.

She stared down at her clenched hands. She wouldn't look at the clock again for a while.

What would she do if he didn't come? She knew only too well that he wasn't happy with the thought of getting married, but she refused to take the blame for that.

Fourteen minutes late now. Drat! She'd looked up again.

Seventeen minutes . . . and twenty seconds.

The street door opened and Cliff came in, looking stiff and angry. 'Sorry I'm late. We had a rush job on.'

But when he came to stand beside her, Nell could smell the beer on his breath. She shot him an angry look.

He stared back at her, his expression hard and unfriendly.

He didn't seem like the man she'd fallen in love with. If she wasn't carrying his child, she'd have left the chapel that minute and found somewhere else to live and work. But a baby changed all that, took away your freedom. You had to give it the best start in life that you could, and that included a father – even if that father didn't want to be married. You couldn't allow your child to be born a bastard.

Mr Garrett's deep voice interrupted them. 'Shall we begin? My wife has offered to act as a witness because you need two of them, you know.'

'Thank you so much,' Nell said automatically. Cliff, she noticed, didn't say anything. Lately, he seemed to have forgotten how to thank people for kindnesses.

'If you'll come and stand here, Nell, and you here, Cliff. Renie, to this side and Dora to that. There, that's fine. If you're ready? *Dearly beloved . . .*'

Automatically Nell made her responses and so did Cliff, in a dull monotone.

'. . . *I now pronounce you man and wife.*'

The minister waited, and when Cliff didn't move, said to him gently, 'You may now kiss the bride.'

Cliff gave Nell a peck on the cheek but there was no warmth in his eyes, and he was still staring at her as if she were a stranger.

'We'll go outside for the photograph,' Mrs Garrett said.

'We can't afford photos,' Cliff said at once.

The minister's wife looked at him in shock. 'I don't charge for them.'

'Mrs Garrett has offered to do it for nothing.' Nell could hear how sharp her own voice was. Two could play at that game. If he wanted to speak curtly, so would she.

'Oh,' was all Cliff said.

They stood just outside the double doors while Mrs Garrett lifted up her box camera and took two pictures of them. 'A second one, just to be sure. And now, a photo of the two sisters. I'm sure your older sister will want to see that.'

When she'd finished, she looked at her husband.

He took over again. 'Do you have somewhere to go?'

'Yes. Back to work,' Cliff said. 'Mr Rayner's letting me have an hour off, but he might dock my pay if I stay away for longer and we can't afford that.' He turned to Nell. 'I'll see you back at the house, later.'

She nodded, but he wasn't looking at her. She could see the minister and his wife glancing at her with pity, so squared her shoulders and said, 'Renie and I will get on with the whitewashing. We've got some old clothes there.'

She'd bought them from the second-hand shop. 'Thank you so much for marrying us, Mr Garrett. Oh, just a minute. Has Cliff paid you?'

The minister looked embarrassed.

'How much is it? I don't have the money, but I'll make sure he pays you on Sunday.' She knew the minister wasn't a rich man.

When they'd walked back into the chapel, Renie looked at her as if uncertain what to say.

She had to tell someone. 'Cliff had been drinking. I could smell it on his breath.'

'No! How awful.'

'It's upset him to leave his job in Swindon.'

'Ha! Doesn't he think it's upset us too, having to leave Mattie and everything we knew? But you and I didn't go shouting at people and boozing before the wedding, let alone arriving late, did we?'

Nell sucked in a deep breath, suddenly feeling older. 'I suppose men are different. Come on. Let's get on with distempering the downstairs again. I'm glad we've finished the bedrooms and don't have to go back to his cousins' house tonight.'

'Me too. That Pauline is a spiteful cat. She didn't even wish you well this morning.'

'I didn't want her good wishes. She's less than nothing to me. I'll never willingly go near her again.'

Nell was glad they still had work to do on the house because it took her mind off her worries. She was married, but she didn't feel married. She had a husband who could hardly bear to look at her and who boozed on the way to his wedding.

But at least she had some purpose in life now, to make a home for her coming child.

She linked her arm in Renie's and laid the other hand on her belly. She had her sister and child, at least. She'd love them and they'd love her, she knew.

And perhaps, once he was settled, Cliff would be more like he used to be.

Chapter Three

Nell looked round the little house as she and Renie carried the last of the things back inside. The whole place was clean now, at least, and freshly distempered. All white, she'd decided. It made it look much brighter.

She could do nothing about the occasional stink from the WC at the entrance to the little courtyard, but she'd see the other tenants and work out a roster to keep it clean. Thank goodness it wasn't a privy, which had to be emptied weekly. You couldn't do anything about the way they smelt in between visits by the night soil men, however much ash you sprinkled down them.

There was a knock on the door, and when she opened it, Mr Rayner's lad stood there, holding Cliff's suitcase and some packages.

'Bring them inside,' she said, and he mumbled something and did as she asked.

'Take the suitcase upstairs. Careful! Don't touch the wall there, the distemper is still wet.'

When they came down, she sent him back to work.

Normally she'd have had biscuits to offer or a scone, but the pantry only contained the raw ingredients and they'd had to make do with shop-bought stuff today.

'I'll unpack Cliff's things later,' she said. 'I'm tired now. Let's have a cup of tea.'

'He ought to have helped with the painting,' Renie commented sarcastically. 'Do you think he'll even lift a finger in the house?'

Nell sighed. 'I doubt it. Most men don't, so why should he be any different? Why do you say things like that? It doesn't change anything and you never know who'll overhear. I keep telling you to speak more quietly. You have a very carrying voice.'

Renie came to put an arm round her. 'Sorry. I didn't mean to upset you.'

'You seem to forget that I had to get married, and at least my baby will be legitimate now, whatever happens.' She didn't let herself think about what the 'whatever' might mean. Strangely, she couldn't seem to think of the baby as Cliff's, because he'd never shown the slightest interest in it.

'Did he really force you the first time?'

'I don't want to talk about that.'

'But did he?'

Nell nodded.

'I'm never getting married,' Renie said. 'Cliff might not be as bad as Dad, but he still expects to rule the roost. I don't want some man ordering me around and forcing me to do things I don't want to.'

'You'll change your mind. Women can't seem to help falling in love, and anyway, women don't earn enough to live on their own. You have to live with us to manage now,' Nell said tiredly. She finished her cup of tea then went upstairs to the bedroom to unpack. At least Cliff had mended the webbing on the bed base and bought a new mattress, though he'd grumbled at the cost of that.

Was he short of money? She didn't have the faintest idea how much he had in his savings account, though he'd once boasted to her that he had quite a bit behind him. He locked his bank book in a tin box. She'd seen him take it out when they needed to buy furniture and other items, so that he could take money out of his bank account. Afterwards he locked it away immediately.

She didn't know what else he had in there, but he guarded the box just as jealously as he'd guarded his toolkit on the way here. She'd seen inside his toolkit, which was immaculate, with everything well cared for, but whenever he opened it, he made sure she couldn't see inside the box.

The bedding she'd bought at Rochdale market lay folded on the mattress. She still had to finish hemming the sheets, because there hadn't been enough light at Cliff's cousins' house.

How wonderful it'd be not to have to sit and look at Pauline's sour face in the evenings, or listen to the crying of one or other of the children, who seemed an unhappy bunch. She would join the library and get books to read, or just sit and chat to her sister or husband. And later, there would be the baby to cuddle.

In the meantime, she was putting together a home, however humble. The chest of drawers was still balanced on two bricks where the feet had come off at the left side, and one of the drawers was missing its handle, so had two big screws poking out to open it with. The wooden chest which she'd found in a junk shop for a few shillings was a godsend. It had been filthy inside and out, the wood scratched and scarred, with one hinge wonky, but she'd scrubbed it out and it would hold all their household linen quite easily. Even Cliff had agreed it was a good buy when she'd taken him to see it.

There was a small old-fashioned gas stove in the scullery kitchen at the rear. She'd cleaned it, poking out all the jets with one of her two hatpins, but still didn't trust the stove, because sometimes the back burner just went out, for no reason that she could tell.

Cliff said if it was easy enough to relight and if it was working well enough to cook their meals, there was no need to waste money on getting the gas repairman to check things out. She didn't dare go against him on that, because there were so many more important things to sort out.

When he came home that night, he smelt of beer again.

'You've been drinking!' she said.

'Mr Rayner bought me a pint after work, to celebrate the wedding.'

'How am I supposed to celebrate it?'

His voice took on an edge. 'You're married. You've got what you wanted. Be content with that and leave men's things to me. I'll make sure you don't wear the trousers in this house, by hell I will, and if I want a drink I'll have one.'

She stifled a protest at this and hoped he hadn't seen the tears in her eyes. She dished up the stew that had been waiting for him. There was a nice crusty loaf to go with it, followed by sponge and custard with jam. She didn't tell him these were stale sponges that she'd bought cheaply, and he didn't seem to notice. He ate everything she put before him, but didn't thank or compliment her. For such a small thin man he had a huge appetite.

Afterwards he sat down to read a newspaper a customer had left in the shop, leaving her and Renie to clear up.

'Don't forget, I'm going to work for Mrs Garrett tomorrow,' she reminded him later as she gave him his nightly cup of cocoa. 'I'll pick up a pie or something on the way home.'

'I don't like spending money on baker's foods. My mother says it's wasteful.'

His mother didn't have to go out to work. 'I can't be in two places at once, Cliff. Renie's going out looking for a job tomorrow, so she won't be here. I won't have time to cook anything when I get back, and anyway, I'll be exhausted. Would you rather have bread and ham? Only I thought you liked pies. Washing is hard work, you know. Mrs Garrett says it'll be easier when they move to Milnrow, because they'll have a bigger house there with a garden and proper laundry equipment in the scullery.'

He muttered something but let the matter drop.

When she went up to bed, he was waiting for her, his eyes gleaming. She knew what he wanted and tried to resign herself, but he hurt her again and she couldn't help crying out.

'What the hell's the matter with you?' he growled when he'd finished.

'You hurt me. It's always uncomfortable. Isn't there . . . a better way of doing it?'

'What do you know about other ways?'

63

'Nothing. You know I don't. That's why I'm asking you.'

'Well, I don't know any other way, and this one suits me well enough, so you'll just have to do your duty as a wife, won't you? A man's at least entitled to some bed play.'

She heard him turn over and soon he was asleep, making that little whiffling noise, as usual. It was beginning to irritate her, that silly little noise was.

She let the tears escape then. If this was marriage, she didn't like it. He'd been kind to her and been fun to be with when they were walking out together, but since the baby had been made and they'd come to the North, he'd become grumpy and selfish.

Did all men change once they got what they wanted?

Did women always have to take second place?

With Mrs Rayner's help, Renie found a job working in the canteen of a local mill, doing any kitchen job required, helping to cook and serve the lunches, then cleaning the tables and mopping the floor in the big room, where workers could either bring their own dinners or buy food cheaply. It had to be made ready for the night shift, and then mopped again in the morning, after the men who worked at night had trampled dirt in. But at least this job ensured she ate well and didn't have to provide her own lunches, because they could eat the leftovers.

'Renie should hand over her wages to me, now she's living in my house,' Cliff said at the end of the first week.

'She'll pay us enough for her keep, and what she does with the rest is up to her,' Nell said at once.

He glared at his wife. 'Do you always have to contradict me?'

'When you're not being fair, yes.'

As he turned to her sister and opened his mouth to continue the argument, Renie said sharply, 'If I have to give you all my money, I'm moving out into lodgings. Some of the girls at work share rooms in a good place. I'm not working for nothing. I want to have my own money saved for when I marry.'

As her eyes challenged his, he half-opened his mouth, made an angry little noise in his throat, then said to Nell, 'Well, see she pays her way, and a bit more for the trouble. And as far as I'm concerned, the sooner she marries, the better.'

Afterwards he went out for a drink with a fellow he sometimes met at the pub. He didn't come home drunk, so he couldn't be spending all that much money – well, she guessed he wasn't – but he went out regularly.

Renie glanced at her sister, as if uncertain whether to speak.

'Give me half your wages. That'd be fair.'

'All right. And Nell, one of the women I work with thinks I can get a job washing glasses and helping in the kitchen of the King's Head hotel on Saturday nights. Do you mind if I do that?'

'Is it a respectable place?'

'Oh, yes. Very. Go and look at it. Rich people eat meals there, or stay the night. Working men don't go in there at all. It's lovely inside, all shining brass and velvet curtains and dark polished furniture.'

'Have you been there already?'

'Mary took me. I had to go and meet the housekeeper to see if I was suitable, and she wants me to start tonight because they've just lost a kitchen worker. I can walk home with Mary afterwards. She lives just round the corner from here. They'll pay me three shillings a night, so that's more money for my savings.'

'What are you really saving for? You told me you didn't want to get married.'

Renie hesitated, then said with a toss of her head. 'After Dad, and seeing how Cliff is to you, I want to make sure I'm never dependent on a man.'

There was a pregnant pause, then Nell said, 'Very sensible. You should put the money in a savings bank account, though, so that no one can pinch it.'

Renie came to put an arm round her. 'I'll do that. We've both learnt the hard way to be careful and sensible about money, haven't we?'

Nell nodded, her throat clogged with unshed tears. She didn't say how much she envied her sister that freedom.

'I keep wondering how Mattie's going on and hoping she's landed on her feet.'

'She'll be all right, Renie. There's no one as capable as our Mattie.'

'You're very capable too, these days.'

Nell looked at her in surprise. 'Do you really think so?'

'Yes. And you stand up to Cliff, which you never used to do. I'm glad of that. One day, when I'm older and know more about the world, I'm going to make a life of my own, so I'll be glad to know you won't let him bully you after I've gone.'

'I was hoping you'd marry and settle down near here, so we'd still be together.'

'I'm sorry, love, but I meant what I said: I'm never going to marry. Never, ever. I want to see a bit of the world, London for a start. All I know is Swindon and this part of Lancashire.'

'You'll change your mind about marriage once you meet a fellow, and London sounds to be a dangerous place to me. I don't want you going there on your own.'

She could see Renie's chin tilt upwards in that stubborn way she had, and sighed. Her little sister could be very headstrong at times. It'd got her into trouble with their father, and it'd get her into trouble again before she was through, Nell was quite sure.

She just hoped life didn't give Renie the sharp lessons she'd had to face herself.

When Renie brought home her first pay, Nell took half and put it in the kitchen drawer. 'I want to talk to Cliff about this money.'

Cliff came in and ate his tea, saying nothing about giving her the housekeeping money. When he'd finished, he stood up.

'Just a minute,' Nell said. 'I need my housekeeping money if you want to eat next week.'

'I've decided that you can pay for the food from Renie's money, and you should join a clothing club too. I'll pay for the rent and gas from mine, plus any big household items.'

She didn't hesitate. 'No.'

He stared at her in shock. 'What did you say?'

'I said no. You need to give me a pound a week and I'll make that stretch to cover food and rent for all three of us, together with my money from Mrs Garrett. You're a hearty eater, Cliff, and that takes far more money than Renie gives me. What I want to do with this extra money is open a savings account and put Renie's money in that, saving for a rainy day.'

'Very sensible. I have a savings account already. We can put it in there.'

'We need an account for both of us.'

'It's for the man to manage the money.'

Suddenly she'd had enough of trying to be tactful. 'All right, then. If you don't want to give me the money, you can manage everything, the housekeeping *and* the shopping. I'll wait for you to bring the groceries and the market stuff home to me, then I'll cook them for you.'

After a nervous glance from one to the other, Renie slipped out into the back scullery, something she'd done last time they argued.

Cliff thumped the table. 'I'm the man here and I'm not putting up with that.'

'And I won't put up with being treated as a stupid nothing who doesn't know how to handle money.' Nell folded her arms, which she hoped hid the way she was shaking. 'We're married, so we should be working *together*. I want a savings bank account with money that both of us can withdraw from, just in case. What if you had an accident? I'd have nothing to tide me over because it'd all be in your bank account. It won't be easy to manage without Renie's money, even so, but I'm prepared to try so that we can save, and one day,' she cast a scornful look round, 'get a better place to live than this. Maybe some weeks I'll need a shilling or two of her money, but I promise you I'll put most of her money away every single week. But I'm not blindly handing it over to you.'

'Then I'll take it from her.' He made as if to go into the scullery.

She rushed across to bar the door. 'You said you'd not thump me, but you'll have to do that to get past me.' She waited, feeling sick with fear, but she was *not* going to back down about this.

He moved from one foot to the other, as if uncertain what to do.

'Are you going to manhandle me, in my condition?' She jutted her stomach out as much as possible and he looked down at it in distaste, something he'd done a few times now. It had upset her greatly.

'I'm not starting another savings account!' he yelled and flung out of the house, banging the door behind him.

More good money wasted on beer, she thought angrily. She had to skimp and scrape to make her money last and she resented every glass of beer he bought.

The week was filled with rows and accusations from him of her being unnatural and unwomanly, wanting to boss him around. She ignored them.

On Wednesday afternoon she had no tea waiting for him.

'Where's my food?'

'You didn't give me any housekeeping money. I've run out.'

'I'll get myself some fish and chips, then.'

'Are you going to get some for me and Renie as well, or do we have to go hungry and watch you eat?'

He hesitated, then slapped some money on the table. '*She* can go for the fish and chips.'

When Renie had left, Nell said quietly, 'I'll need money for food for tomorrow, Cliff, if you want your tea waiting for you after work and sandwiches packing to take to work.'

He closed his eyes. 'Heaven help a man with a wife who wants to wear the trousers!'

But in the end he gave in and they went and opened a savings account together, with both of them able to put money in or take it out.

'I'll want to see that bank book every week,' he said as they walked home. 'And if you take money out without my saying so—'

'I'll have to when I buy the baby things – or are you coming shopping for those with me?' Nell knew he'd never do that, because his so-called friends from the pub would mock him.

'You always have to have the last word,' he yelled. 'No wonder your father kept a firm hand on things. I'm too soft with you, I am.'

He stormed off, going to the pub no doubt, and she took the bank book home. She put it on the mantelpiece.

She didn't show him the other bank book, which had a pitifully small amount in it, but which only she could access. She made a special pouch for it and stitched it to the bottom of the canvas bag she carried her purse and bits of shopping in. He never even noticed it, because, of course, he never went near the shopping bag.

As time went on, she added the odd shilling from the family housekeeping pot to her own money, telling him she couldn't quite save all Renie's money that week. But as the amounts she took away from it were small and the joint savings kept mounting up, he didn't quibble.

She resented it bitterly that he continued to go out drinking three or four nights a week. But there was nothing she could do about that. She knew she'd pushed him as far as he would go. He sat at home reading a library book the other nights. They both used the library a lot. This wasn't what she'd expected from marriage! She'd thought they'd do things together, make plans for the future, talk about their baby. He hardly ever spoke to her these days except to order her to get him something like a cup of tea. And he certainly didn't suggest they go for walks at weekends any longer, however fine the weather.

Renie had made friends and went round to their houses sometimes. As a married woman, Nell couldn't go out in the evenings on her own. If she hadn't been able to get books from the library too, she'd have gone mad.

It'd be better when the baby arrived. She'd have someone of her own then.

Chapter Four

Like her sister, Renie had become very careful with money, but with the help of her friend Carol, who had a sewing machine, she'd worked hard to improve her dressmaking skills, so still managed to dress decently.

One night, a lass she worked with said, 'Why don't you come out with us to the variety show in Rochdale tomorrow night? We go up in the gods and it's only threepence midweek.'

Renie had a quick think. She worked hard on Saturday nights and hated it when she had to stay home other nights, waiting for Cliff to come back from the pub or sitting opposite him on a hard stool, watching him read in comfort in the armchair. He still expected to be waited on hand and foot, tossing orders at Nell, who was growing bigger and more awkward now.

You'd think there was something wrong with having a baby, to hear him taunt her sister with how ugly she'd become. Renie didn't think she was ugly. Renie thought she had a lovely soft glow in her eyes – when he was out, at least – especially when Nell cradled the jutting stomach with one hand and got that dreamy look.

Him calling her ugly didn't stop him pestering her after they'd gone to bed, though, did it, because Renie could hear them through the thin wall between the two bedrooms.

One day she asked Nell what it was like in bed, but her sister only grimaced, so she knew it wasn't as good as some people said it was. Was that because of Cliff, or was it always like that? Why did no one ever tell you these things?

When she told Nell she was going to a variety show, her sister encouraged her to go out.

Cliff immediately said she was to be back by ten sharp.

'I'm not leaving before the show ends,' Renie said. 'That'd be a waste of money.'

'I'm not having another sister on my hands with a big belly,' he threw back at her.

'You won't have. I'll take care not to go out with the sort of man who'd force a girl.' She was sorry for that the minute the words left her mouth, because the look he threw at Nell said he was furious.

'Oh, Renie, when will you learn to think before you speak?' Nell said after he'd gone out.

'I'm sorry. Will he . . . hit you?'

'He'd better not.'

But he was still angry when he came home, pot-valiant after his night's drinking, and Nell had to pick up the rolling pin and threaten to hit him with it if he so much as laid a finger on her. It was a close thing for a minute or two. He seemed to have fallen in with a rough crowd, who encouraged him to treat his wife like a slave.

Well, he could push her only so far, as he'd found out once or twice. And if he dared to hit her, she'd wait till he was asleep then hit *him* with something. Hard. Even if he hit her again, he'd soon learn that she'd bide her time and get back at him.

Nell went into labour at the end of September. She prepared for the birth calmly, looking forward to having her body to herself again afterwards. She'd been so dreadfully tired lately.

She arranged for Mrs Totting, the local midwife, to come and deliver the baby. She knew they'd passed an act making it illegal for women not certified as midwives to attend mothers in childbirth as a way of earning a living, and counted herself lucky that they had a certified midwife in the district. She'd not have liked a male doctor attending the birth.

She had a chat to the pleasant older woman about what to expect and what to have ready, and also how to prevent other children when your husband wouldn't take the necessary care.

'I've helped a few women that way,' Mrs Totting said. 'Too many babies would wear anyone down. I had three and that was enough for me.'

'Thank you. Cliff says he's going to use one of those rubber things, though.'

'Don't rely on that. When they get randy, they forget to take precautions. You take care of yourself as well, like I've told you.'

'I will.'

'I reckon you'll go all right with the birth,' the midwife said. 'You're small but you're healthy.'

'How can you tell that?'

The midwife shrugged. 'You've a good colour, your hair's shiny not dull, there are all sorts of little signs. Who'll be helping you afterwards?'

'I don't know anyone, really. We've not been here for long.' And the other women in Willow Court weren't really her sort. They spoke to her pleasantly, but they were a bit rough.

'Can you afford to pay for help? I know a couple of women who'd welcome a day or two's work.'

'If you tell my husband it's needed, he may agree. He'd not do it just to spare me, though. It'd be a waste of beer money, wouldn't it?' She couldn't help feeling bitter about that.

The midwife grinned, suddenly looking much younger, in spite of her grey hair. 'I'll warn him to let you recover properly if he wants other children, not to mention a wife who can keep up with the housework for years afterwards.'

Cliff grumbled, of course, but he agreed to have someone in for a few days.

'My mother never needed pampering like that,' he complained after the midwife had left. 'She didn't have relatives nearby to look after her, either.'

'And she never looks well, does she? Sometimes your father has to pay one of the neighbours to do the rough work.'

He looked at her and frowned, but didn't complain about the coming expenses again.

She'd feel happier if he'd occasionally say thank you for what she did. She was a good wife to him, she knew. The house was as neat and clean as hard work could make it and they'd settled into a way of life that ensured that Cliff, as breadwinner, was well looked after.

But he took that as his right.

The pains started on Sunday morning and Cliff went for Mrs Totting, who came to check and said the baby wouldn't be born for some hours. 'First babies usually take their time,' she said cheerfully as she prepared to leave. 'I'll check you tonight, but I reckon it'll not arrive till tomorrow.'

Nell looked at her in horror.

'You'll be all right, love.'

The pains went on right through the night and Nell began to get worried. Cliff left her to it and went to sleep downstairs in the armchair. She sent Renie to bed, because her sister had to go to work the next day.

Cliff came up for clean clothes in the morning and she looked at him in dumb misery.

'I dare say you'll have had it by the time I come home,' was all he said. 'I'll be glad to get this fuss over with.'

She heard him downstairs, ordering Renie to get his breakfast, then he went off to work as usual, without even calling a goodbye.

Renie came upstairs with a cup of tea and some toast. 'Are you going to be all right?'

'Yes. You eat the toast, though. I'm not at all hungry.'

'Do you want me to stay home from work?'

'No. I'll manage.' She felt embarrassed at the thought of her seventeen-year-old sister seeing her give birth. What if she screamed? What if the neighbours heard? The walls were very thin in these houses.

Mrs Totting came back just after breakfast, still as cheerful as ever. 'It's moving along now. It'll be born early this afternoon, I should think. Get up and walk around.'

'Is it all right to do that?'

The midwife looked at her sympathetically. 'Haven't you had anyone to talk to about it at all?'

'No.'

'Eh, you poor thing. Well, you're not sick and it helps the baby if you move about. I know what I'm doing. You'll be all right. I can't stay, though. I have other women to check on. I'll come back in a couple of hours.'

Nell listened to the door shut behind her and got up, walking round the house, feeling terrified, for all the midwife's assurances. What if something happened before Mrs Totting came back? What if she had a fall on those narrow stairs? Who would hear her cries for help?

About eleven o'clock there was a knock on the front door and she found her neighbour Peg standing there.

'It's not arrived yet, then?'

'Mrs Totting says this afternoon.'

'She's usually right. I wondered if you wanted anything from the shops.'

'Thanks. A loaf would be a help, and some scones. I'll get you the money.'

'I'll make you a cup of tea when I get back.'

But she must have lingered at the shops because Mrs Totting turned up and in the nick of time too, because the pains had suddenly got much sharper.

Pride alone kept Nell from screaming, but she couldn't

hold back the groans. It hurt. Dear heaven, it hurt so much.

'Soon be over,' said that calm voice which had guided her through it. 'Push hard now.'

Suddenly the pain eased and Mrs Totting chuckled. 'Eh, it's a little lass. She's got red hair. Anyone in your family got red hair?'

'My sister Mattie's hair is reddish – not as red as this, though.'

'Here, put her beside you while I finish up down below.'

As Mrs Totting cut and tied the birth cord, then started pressing on her stomach to encourage the afterbirth, Nell looked in wonderment at the tiny baby, who was waving her arms around and giving a few mewling cries, as if in protest about the world she found herself in.

And just like that, love twined around Nell's heart. 'She's beautiful!'

'They all say that. But yours *is* beautiful. Not big, but got all her fingers and toes. She'll be like you, not a big woman. What are you going to call her?'

'Sarah.'

'Nice name. I've always liked it. There. That's done. Now, let's get you and the bed cleaned up. Have you got someone to cook your husband's tea tonight?'

'My sister will do it.' What about *my* tea? Nell wondered. Why do people think only of the men?

There was a knock on the front door and someone yelled, 'Mrs Totting? Can you come. Mrs Bray's started.'

'Two babbies in one day! And Jenny Bray always delivers quickly. Will you be all right? Put her to the breast if she seems hungry.'

Nell was left alone with her daughter. She picked the baby up and watched as the infant slumbered, then moved restlessly, as if nervous of the new world, then slumbered again, with such soft little breaths.

She didn't want anyone there, just herself and little Sarah.

All too soon Peg from next door got back with the loaf and offered to bring her up a cup of tea. Suddenly Nell realised she was both thirsty and famished, and asked for some bread and cheese to go with it. Why should she keep that for her husband? She needed decent nourishment too.

By the time Cliff got home from work, she'd fed Sarah for the first time, with Peg's help, and was sitting up in bed, feeling proud of herself. She'd done it, had a baby, and managed just fine.

He came upstairs. 'What is it?'

'A girl.' She beamed at him, waiting for him to praise her for producing such a lovely little baby.

'Trust you. A man wants a son. What shall we call her? You choose.'

'Sarah.'

Contrary as ever, he scowled and said, 'I told you I wanted to call her after my mother.'

'Sarah Margaret, then.'

'We'll call her Margaret.'

'We'll call her Sarah.'

He glared at her. 'You're doing it again. You always have to go against me, don't you?'

'I'm the one who bore this baby and I'm the one who'll

be looking after her, so I'm the one who chooses what to call her every day.'

He walked round the bed to stand looking down into the drawer they were using as a cradle, letting out a grunt of disappointment. 'Red-haired too. They'll call her "Carrots", whatever name you choose.' He turned round. 'What've you done about my tea?'

'I've not done anything. I've been busy birthing your daughter. Renie will get it, if you ask her nicely.'

'She's late and I'm hungry. I'll go and get some bread and jam to put me on.'

Nell didn't cry when he'd gone. She was beyond tears now, as far as he was concerned. Everything she did seemed to upset him and it had, she thought sadly, totally killed any love she'd once felt for him. Had it ever been love? Or had she just been pleased to have a fellow courting her, like the other girls, even if she did have to see him in secret.

All Cliff was to her now was the breadwinner, the man who would ensure that her daughter didn't go hungry.

She was going to buy one of those little sponges from Mrs Totting. Although she loved her daughter, she didn't want any more of Cliff's children, because she didn't think he was going to make a good father. His parents had spoilt him rotten and he was more like a child himself most of the time.

Renie came rushing in, running up the stairs to look at her niece. 'Aw, she's like Mattie as well as you.' She lowered her voice. 'She's not much like *him*, is she?'

'I don't know. And keep your voice down.'

'Can I cuddle her?'

'Get Cliff's tea first. He's hungry and in a bad mood.

There should be some ham left. Fry it up with an egg.'

Renie rolled her eyes but didn't complain. Later she brought Nell a fried egg and some bread, and stayed upstairs all evening chatting.

Cliff went out 'to wet the baby's head'.

'As if he's done something clever,' Renie whispered scornfully. She waited until his footsteps had stopped echoing round the little yard, then began to draw patterns on the sheets with one fingertip. She opened her mouth to speak, then shut it again.

'What's the matter?' Nell asked.

'I've had an offer of a better job.'

'Oh? What as?'

'A waitress. They're going to train me properly, and if I do all right, I can work at it full-time and leave the canteen. Mr Jackson says I've got a nice manner with people. I've helped out in the restaurant a couple of times now when they were short-handed.'

'That's good news, then, isn't it? Will you be earning more money?'

'Not at first. They've got to train me, so I won't be earning as much. I'll still pay you the same, though, so dear Cliff won't have any excuse to throw a fit.'

'Shh,' she said automatically, even though she knew he'd gone out. But the window was open and she didn't want anyone overhearing and reporting back to him. The men round here certainly stuck together. 'Well, how much you save is your own business.'

'I'll be making more money later, if I do it well. Posh folk sometimes give you tips and you can keep them for yourself.'

She sounded so excited. Nell was pleased for her. 'You seem really happy about the job.'

'Yes, I am. I'm fed up of cleaning that canteen. I'll make sure I give satisfaction at the restaurant.' She giggled. 'I'll have to learn to talk more posh. They don't like my Wiltshire accent. *This way, sir, madam. I hope you're happy with your meal.*'

Nell laughed, surprised at how well her sister could speak when she made the effort. But Renie had always been a good mimic.

'I have to buy myself a black dress and some aprons, but they'll launder the aprons for me, so that won't give you any extra work. When I go full-time, I'll need two black dresses in case of accidents and spills, but I can buy those out of my savings.' She sighed happily. 'It's a good job, Nell. It's got prospects. The owners are from a family who have hotels in other places, London and Bath. I might get to work there one day.'

'Women don't need prospects. They get married.'

'Not all of them. Not me.'

'Then you'd better be very careful. You're pretty enough to turn men's heads. You don't want to end up like me.'

Renie reached out to hold her hand. 'I will be careful, I promise you. Maybe I'll get rich, then you can leave *him* and come to live with me.'

'And pigs might fly. People like us don't get rich.' And they didn't leave their husbands either, not only because they couldn't afford to, but because if they did they'd lose their precious respectability – and might even lose their children. The law sounded to be on the men's side, from what she'd read.

She felt sad as she lay in bed, waiting for Cliff to get

back. Renie had so much to look forward to and what did she have?

A small snuffling sound from across the room seemed to answer her question. She had Sarah, that's what. And whatever Cliff said or did, her child was going to have a happy life and all the chances Nell hadn't had. She'd make sure of that.

Sarah was a model baby, not crying much, gurgling with laughter as she grew older and looking round alertly. Nell loved being a mother, loved her little daughter.

She missed her sister's company in the evenings, though, and had to make do with her library books instead. She found herself reading about her own country. She'd seen so little of England and wished she could travel and explore other parts.

The librarian told her there were books about travel, so she took some of them out, reading them voraciously, dreaming she'd gone to the Cotswolds and seen the pretty villages in the photos for herself, or visited Cheshire with its black and white houses.

She read everything she could find about Wiltshire, wanting to know about her own part of the country. All she knew was Swindon with its huge railway works. Maybe one day she'd manage to visit the nearby countryside. It looked so beautiful in the photos.

She was counting the days off till two years had passed, at which time Mattie had agreed to contact them via Cliff's parents.

To her surprise, Cliff didn't want to contact his family yet. He looked at her in disgust when she suggested it again.

'I've told you before, I'm not going to get in touch with them till I've something to be proud of here. I've not got a decent job yet and we're living in a hovel.'

'I'd have thought you'd have told them about your daughter, at least. Isn't she something to be proud of?'

'They'll not be able to see her, so it won't matter. And don't you go talking to people about my parents. As far as folk round here are concerned, I've not got any close family left. I doubt I'll see them again, unless I get lucky suddenly.'

She stared at him aghast. 'But if you don't get in touch, how will I find out about my sister Mattie? You know we said—'

'You'll just have to manage without her. And she's no loss, I can tell you. She was a right old bossy breeches, that one was.'

'I'll write to them myself, then.'

He came to loom over her, where she was cuddling a sleepy Sarah. 'If you do, I'll walk away and leave you, then who'll bring home the money to feed your brat?'

His face was red and he had that ugly expression on his face. She couldn't think what to say to him, was afraid for her little daughter.

'I mean it,' he said more quietly, stepping away from her again. He looked at the clock. 'Time to go out. I'm thirsty tonight.'

Her heart sank. That meant he'd come home and start pawing her. He always did after a drinking night. She'd better put the little sponge in. So far she'd managed to stop herself getting pregnant again, even though he'd caught her without the sponge a couple of times and refused to wait.

Chapter Five

The old King died on the sixth of May and his son, George V, come to the throne. It caused a lot of talk that Halley's Comet blazed across the skies on the eve of King Edward's funeral. The passing of an era, some said. Bad times were coming.

At the time, Nell had been too busy settling into her new home to worry about what the new King was doing. What did she care about who was on the throne? And as far as she was concerned, the bad times had already arrived in her life.

As the first year of Sarah's life passed, news came that King George's coronation would take place on the 22nd June 1911. That was to happen in Westminster Abbey, of course, with only the nobility and important people attending. But all over the land there were celebrations and street parties with bunting strung between the houses and tables brought out for a special meal.

This time Nell took an interest, and when the people in the court arranged a small tea party, she joined in, providing a cake, causing a row with Cliff who hated to see her spend money on others.

He didn't attend the party, preferring to drink his loyal toasts in the pub with his mates. It was better without him, and for once Nell really enjoyed herself.

There had been some warm days in the spring, but the summer was far hotter than usual. Nell escaped from the stuffy little house as often as she could, taking Sarah for walks in the pram she'd bought second hand, walking on the shady side of the street.

It took her some time to gather her courage together to broach the subject closest to her heart to Cliff. She made sure she'd prepared his favourite meal and as he pushed away the plate after a second helping, she said quietly, 'Isn't it about time we looked for somewhere better to live?'

His hand stopped dead in the air and he looked at her sourly. 'No, it bloody well isn't! This place suits me just fine. It's close to work and close to my friends.'

Which meant close to his pub, she knew. He seemed content to continue working for Mr Rayner, which puzzled her, and though his wages had been raised to thirty-five shillings a week, he hadn't given his wife any of the extra money.

She tried to speak reasonably. 'But it's not good for Sarah here and I find it very stuffy and hot. And you know how bad the lavatory smells.'

'There's strikes going on and all sorts of trouble. Just be glad my job's safe and we have a roof over our heads.'

'But it needn't cost much more. I've asked around and—'

'Look, Mrs Finicky, we'll find a new house when *you* find

the extra money to pay for a higher rent. Isn't it enough that the damned government makes me pay National Health Insurance? As if I can't manage my own money.'

'But, Cliff—'

He gave a sneering laugh. 'I'll just thank you to remember that I'm the wage earner here and you should do what I want and be grateful for the money I give you.'

She blinked to drive away the tears but he noticed.

'Selfish bitch! You only think of what you want. You're a rotten wife, you are.'

She didn't bother to argue, could only hope that the heat and smells in the small square courtyard the houses were built round would make him change his mind.

But one hot day followed another and they didn't seem to have any effect on him. They drained her of energy, though.

She missed Renie's company desperately during the long, quiet evenings, and often wished her sister didn't work at night. Was this going to be the pattern of her life? An increasingly grumpy husband and an aching loneliness.

For the first time she began to think seriously of escape for herself and her daughter. If she could earn enough money to support the two of them, she'd leave him without the slightest hesitation. Was there any way of doing that? She puzzled over it for hours, but couldn't see how she could support them on a woman's wages. And who would look after Sarah while she worked?

No use discussing it with Renie, because her sister might be seventeen, but she was still prone to blurt things out like a thoughtless child. Anyway, her sister had her own dreams and Nell would make very sure Cliff didn't spoil them.

* * *

One day Renie came home from work looking flushed and happy.

Nell had waited up for her, because her sister had been working extra hours and they'd hardly caught up with one another for days. Sarah had been restless, so in the end she'd brought the baby down so as not to wake Cliff. 'I'll get you some cocoa. Just hold Sarah for a minute.'

When they were seated on either side of the fire, Renie said abruptly, 'It's happened.'

'What has?'

'What I hoped for. They've asked me to go and work in their London hotel. It's called The Rathleigh.'

It was hard not to beg her to stay, but Nell had already prepared herself mentally for this. 'That must mean they're happy with your work.'

'Yes. I'm a good waitress. I'm quick and I don't forget orders, and I get really good tips. Of course, I'll have to live in if I go there. Most of their London girls do.'

She hesitated, then added softly, 'I'm sorry you'll be left on your own, but in a few months it'll be two years. We agreed to write to the Greenhills about Mattie and then—'

'Cliff won't do it. He's not contacted his parents because he's ashamed of where he's working, and he's not going to. He says if I write to them, he'll walk out and leave me.' She took comfort from her little daughter's warm body curled up on her lap.

'Oh, Nell, no! It was the one thing that consoled me about leaving you, that you could find out about Mattie.'

'I daren't go against Cliff.'

Renie sat quietly for a few moments, then said, 'I'll tell

90

them I can't go to London yet. You can't live like this, with him stopping you doing things and leaving you on your own more and more. And if he had any decency at all, he'd get you and Sarah out of this hovel.'

How she found the strength to say it, Nell would never know. 'Don't refuse. This is your big chance for a better life. One day things will be better for me, I'm sure. Go to London, make a better life for yourself, only . . . don't lose touch. Write to me as often as you can.' She lifted her mug of cocoa and swallowed the tears with the warm comforting liquid.

'I will. I promise. Every single week. And you'll write back?'

'Of course I will. When do you go?'

'They want me to leave next Monday.'

'So soon?'

'I'm sorry, Nell, but they need the extra staff for Christmas. I'll have to learn new ways before then, because it's a much fancier hotel, with really rich customers. Lords and ladies, even.'

As her sister still looked doubtful, Nell said firmly, 'Don't lose this chance to better yourself. You won't get many opportunities like this. Only . . . don't let any man talk you into . . . you know, doing it. Even if he says he loves you.'

Renie reached out to squeeze her hand. 'I won't. And if I ever get rich, I'll come back and take you away from all this.' It wasn't the shabby little room she was thinking of as she raised her eyes to the ceiling, where Cliff was sleeping.

* * *

Nell told Cliff the following evening, after Renie had gone to work. Naturally he created a fuss. 'I'm not letting her go. It's not safe in London.'

'She's nearly eighteen now, old enough to decide for herself. And anyway, the Carlings will look after her. They gave her a piece of paper with all the information, and it shows how caring and careful they are of their staff.'

'But *we* need her money.'

'We'll manage perfectly well without it.'

'Why should we? No, she can't go. And this time, you'll do as you're told, my Lady Muck. I'm her guardian and she's under twenty-one.'

'This is her big chance and I'm not letting anything stand in her way, Cliff. Anyway, you're not her guardian. Mattie is. So you don't have the right to stop her.'

He flung his book across the room at her, just missing the baby and hitting her on the shoulder.

She stared at him in shock, then said in a voice so harsh it didn't even sound like hers, 'If you ever hurt this child, I'll make you sorry you were born.'

He had the grace to look a little ashamed. 'It was an accident. I never touched her and I never will. But I don't know how I keep my hands off you, you disobedient bitch. You're all alike, you women. No gratitude. And don't think I'm giving up my spending money when you're struggling without her money.'

'I just said we'd manage. We've got money saved, after all.'

But he wasn't listening to her. He continued to grumble and threaten, gradually running out of steam and scowling at her for a few moments. After that, he picked up his library book and settled down to read. She put Sarah to bed and got her own library book out.

That night, the words she read might as well have been gibberish, for all she took in of the story, but she took care to turn the page every now and then because she sensed him looking across at her occasionally.

She didn't know what she'd do without Renie to cheer her up. She'd be totally on her own then. Alone with him. And he was right about one thing: it would be hard to manage without her sister's money. But she'd do it somehow.

After all, she still had Sarah, the best little love in the whole world.

But after this incident she was definitely going to find a way to leave him one day. There had to be a way. You were supposed to be married till death parted you, but she didn't want Sarah growing up in this uncomfortable atmosphere; didn't want to waste her own life putting up with it, either.

A letter arrived from Renie within two days of her departure, giving the address to write to. She was bubbling over with enthusiasm about her new job and the excitement of being in London. She was going to spend her first day off walking round the nearest sights with one of the girls who slept in her dormitory.

Nell left the letter on the mantelpiece and mentioned it casually when Cliff came home from work. She wished she didn't have to show it to him, but it'd only cause trouble if she tried to keep her sister's letters secret.

'There's a letter from Renie. I put it on the mantelpiece, if you want to read it.'

'Where's my tea? I've been working all day and I'm hungry.'

If she'd been Renie, she'd have asked him what he thought she'd been doing all day, but Nell had learnt life was easier if she held her tongue and just thought a sharp answer to him.

Cliff waited till after tea to pick the letter up and read it. 'Hah! After all we've done for her. Out of sight, out of mind. Ungrateful bitch.' He threw it into the fire.

Nell rushed across the room, but it was too late. He'd thrown the letter on to the hottest part of the fire and it caught light immediately. He smiled and that was the final straw. She turned on him, seizing the nearest object and hurling it at him. The ugly ornament someone had given them caught him squarely on the forehead, then fell into the hearth and smashed on the tiles.

She followed it with a big piece of coal and snatched up the poker as he clenched his fist.

'You stupid bitch!' he yelled, rubbing his forehead and taking a step towards her. But when he saw the poker he stopped dead.

'You burnt that to hurt me,' she said. 'You actually wanted to hurt me.'

'I treated it like the rubbish it was.' He winced as his fingers encountered the bruise she'd caused. 'You'll pay for that.'

Up came his fist again, so she brandished the poker. 'If you lay one finger on me, ever, I'll wait till you're asleep and hit you with this or anything else that comes to hand. And if you *ever* burn or damage one of my sister's letters again, I'll cut up all your clothes. See if I don't.'

He gaped at her. 'All this for a stupid letter?'

'No. All this because of your cruelty. That letter was the only contact I have with my family now, the only contact with someone who loves me. Because *you* don't care about me, that's obvious.'

His face went very still. 'I'll let it pass this time because you were upset, but if you ever throw anything at me again, I'll chastise you good and proper. Even the law says I have the right to do that, as your husband.'

'I'll fight back. I won't put up with being knocked about. And I meant what I said: you'll get thumped once you're asleep any time you touch me.' She slapped her free hand down on the tattered Bible that sat on the mantelpiece. 'I swear that.'

She heard him suck in his breath and wondered if she'd have to prove she meant it. Their eyes met, but she was so furious she wouldn't have been surprised if sparks were flying from hers, literally. She'd never been able to stand people who were needlessly cruel to others.

He was the first to look away, then he walked across to the mantelpiece, and as she tensed, expecting him to hit her, he took a shilling out of the housekeeping pot and walked out of the house.

He'd be going to the pub. Any excuse these days. But he'd never touched the food money before. He liked his food too much.

She went across to the pot and took the remaining coins out, putting back two pennies and a halfpenny. She'd make sure he was the one to go short of food this week, and she'd keep most of the housekeeping money on her person from now on. She'd make a pocket and tie it round her waist under her skirt. Her child wasn't going to go hungry to buy him booze and nor was she.

Sarah began to whimper as if she'd felt the anger beating through the house. Nell went across to pick her up and comfort her.

It'd have been hard to say which one was comforting the other most. Nell rocked and wept, then rocked some more. Sarah whimpered and nestled against her, then fell asleep.

She didn't put the baby to bed for a long time, she needed her too much.

When Sarah was just over a year old, she contracted diarrhoea and nearly died. Nell, who had been nearly frantic while her daughter was so ill, swallowed her pride and begged Cliff to consider moving to a more salubrious area.

'The baby's all right, isn't she? It toughens them up, being ill does, them that recover anyway, and she wouldn't dare die, the way you dote on her.'

She ignored that gibe, one often repeated. 'Please, Cliff, let me look for a better house. It needn't cost much more.'

'This place suits me. It's as close as you could get to where I work, and where I meet the lads for a drink. Besides, I haven't the money to waste on paying extra rent.'

'I thought you might look for another job, a better paid one. We could move to Rochdale, even.'

'Are you deaf, woman?' He raised his voice. '*I don't . . . want . . . to move.* I'm suited where I am, and I get on well with Don. He lets me practically run the place now.'

'Well, he should pay you more, then.'

He tried not to smile but didn't succeed.

'He's raised your wages again, hasn't he?'

Cliff shrugged. 'What a man earns is his own business.'

'You didn't think to give me a bit more money? You know it's a struggle to manage on so little housekeeping.'

'Shouldn't have let your sister go to London, should you, then we'd all be comfortable. Well, we would be all right if you'd give me the son I want.'

She could have wept at the selfishness of him. Oh, yes, *he* was comfortable enough, doing what he wanted, going out drinking. Though why he kept harping on about having a son when he hardly seemed to notice his daughter, she couldn't understand. But so far, thank goodness, the little sponge had worked and she hadn't fallen for another baby.

When he'd gone out, she allowed herself a treat and pulled Renie's letters out of their hiding place to read about her sister's wonderful new life. He'd never once asked about Renie since their big argument after he'd burnt the first letter, and she'd never mentioned the letters, though she knew he hunted around every now and then, trying to make sure he knew what she was up to.

So far he hadn't looked in the coal cellar, where she kept the letters in a tin under a pile of coal. It seemed the safest place, because *he* never offered to fill the coal scuttle or carry it up for her.

This wouldn't go on for ever, she vowed yet again. She and Sarah would escape from him somehow. She'd scrimped to save money in her own bank account, though it wasn't much to build a new life on. She'd also started learning Pitman shorthand, using a book from the library.

She practised it regularly, using bits of scrap paper from her shopping.

Women typists were working in offices everywhere these days. According to the newspaper articles she'd read in the library, the machines were much easier for female fingers to deal with, and although the wages were higher than other working women's wages, at about a pound a week, they were too low for men to seek that sort of employment if they could find something that paid better.

She had no way of learning to type at proper classes, but Mrs Garrett was letting her use the heavy old machine in her husband's study.

She'd started helping with the washing again, earning a little extra money. She hadn't told Cliff, would just say she was helping to type notes for Mr Garrett if he asked why she went round to the minister's house so often. But so far, he hadn't, didn't seem to care what she did with herself during the day as long as his meal was ready each evening and his clothes were washed and ironed.

The minister's wife had looked at her very solemnly when she'd first asked her help, then had shaken her head sadly and said nothing more about *why* Nell wanted to ·learn to type. But she worried sometimes that Mrs Garrett might let something slip to Cliff.

She did a lot of worrying these days.

Nell was glad when the weather was cooler for her daughter's first birthday. She baked a special cake and bought a little candle to put on it, and made some fancy little meat pies with buttery mashed potatoes for tea.

Cliff stared at the festive table when he came home from work. 'What's this in aid of?'

'Sarah's birthday.'

He sniggered. 'What a waste! She's too little to understand. But I'll enjoy the cake.'

She watched as he ignored the child, gobbling his food down as if he hadn't eaten for days. She wouldn't let him cut the cake until she'd lit the candle and sung 'Happy Birthday' to Sarah, who loved it when anyone sang to her.

Cliff didn't join in. He ate a full half of the cake, then slouched across the room to read his library book, ignoring them both.

Her feelings for him were turning into hatred, not indifference. She was glad when he went out to the pub.

That same month, Renie wrote to ask if she could come to stay with Nell for her week's holiday the next month. Clutching the letter, Nell felt a rare surge of happiness. Oh, how wonderful it'd be to see her sister!

She broached the possibility with Cliff and he looked at her with a sneer on his face.

'Oh, she's bothered to write, has she? We're suddenly good enough for madam, are we? Well, I'm not having her here.'

She stared at him in silence, then went and got his plate of food and dumped it on the fire.

He bounced to his feet then. 'What the hell do you think you're doing!'

'Going on strike. If men can do it, so can I. You can cook your own food from now on and wash your own clothes and—'

His fist took her by surprise, knocking her flying so that her head hit the ground hard.

When she came to, she was lying on the rug and he was fanning her face with his newspaper.

'You fell and hit your head,' he muttered.

'You thumped me and knocked me over.'

'Let me help you up.'

She shoved his hand aside. 'Don't touch me. Don't ever touch me again.' She became aware that Sarah was crying, sitting wailing in a corner, looking terrified. 'Are you going to hit the baby next? You could really do some damage to someone so small.'

She pulled herself to her feet and looked into the mirror. 'I'll have a black eye tomorrow. Everyone will know you're a wife beater.'

He stared at her in shock. Clearly this aspect hadn't occurred to him.

'And if they ask me how I hurt myself, I'll tell them. I'll say you hit me because I wanted to have my sister to stay.'

'All right, damn you, you can have her to stay – as long as she pays her way and you don't say anything about that bruise.'

She shrugged. 'I won't say anything. And I'll have to ask Renie to help out, because there's nothing spare in what you give me each week.'

But she took secret satisfaction in the thought that everyone would know he'd hit her, whether she admitted it or not. Their neighbours knew everything in the court, yes, and so did the members of the chapel congregation.

No one said anything next time she went out, but they

looked at her. Oh, yes, they looked. She tilted her chin and stared back defiantly at the world.

Only Mrs Garrett dared to say anything. 'Did he hit you?'

'I promised him I'd not talk about it.'

'He did hit you.'

She shrugged.

Mrs Rayner surprised her by stopping her in the street the next day. Nell knew her husband's employer's wife by sight from chapel, but had never had much to do with her.

'I've told my Don to have a word with your Cliff about hitting you,' the older woman said bluntly.

Nell looked at her in dismay. 'Oh, no! He'll think I told you and he'll be even angrier.'

'You need to fight back, lass.'

'I am doing. I'd already told him if he hit me I'd hit him back when he's asleep. But this time,' tears came into her eyes, 'I got him to let me have my sister to stay with me. So it was worth it. If your husband speaks to him, he'll change his mind again and say she can't come.'

Mrs Rayner looked at her sympathetically. 'Your Cliff's good at his job, earns a decent living, but I hear he drinks.'

Nell sighed. 'All the men who live near us drink. He doesn't come home drunk, though, so he can't be drinking that much.'

'I'll make sure your sister still comes to stay.' Mrs Rayner turned and walked briskly away.

How could she make sure of that? Nell wondered as she walked slowly home, pushing Sarah and wishing the little pram worked better. It always tried to pull to the right.

She waited anxiously for Cliff to finish work and come back, sure he'd be in a bad mood. She had the rolling pin nearby to defend herself with.

Sure enough, he burst into the house and greeted her with, 'You broke your promise. You told people.'

'I didn't say a word.'

'I don't believe you.'

'They guessed. You can't hide a bruise like this.' She slammed her hand down on the Bible. He knew she wouldn't tell lies when she did that. 'I swear I didn't say anything.'

He was staring at her as if she was a total stranger and suddenly she couldn't bear it. 'Cliff, can't we start again, try to get on better? We used to talk, be friends.'

'A man doesn't talk to his wife. He talks to his mates at the pub.' He sighed and sat down at the table, surprising her by saying, 'I'm sorry I hit you, though. I am . . . really.'

She sat down opposite him, not knowing what to say.

He looked across the table at her. 'It's all gone wrong since we came here. I miss Swindon. I miss the railway works. I miss my family. We'd be going on the annual works trip if we'd stayed there. I always used to enjoy the employees' outing.'

'We could go on our own trip here. It's not expensive to go on an excursion to Blackpool.'

'It's not the same. Nothing's the same.' He looked across at the stove. 'Is that pan burning?'

'Oh, no!' She jumped to her feet and ran across to save her stew. When she turned round, Cliff was sitting reading the newspaper and he hardly said a word to her all evening.

She didn't know what to make of their conversation.

Did it mean he was willing to try a bit harder to get on? She'd guessed he was unhappy deep down, of course she had, but this was the first time he'd admitted it.

He was quieter for the next week or two, and didn't threaten any violence. He even said the stew was good one night. And he gave her back a shilling. He didn't say it was for the one he'd taken from the housekeeping, but why else would he have done that?

It wasn't enough to mend the distance between them, though. They were like two strangers living together, more polite maybe, but he still mostly ignored his daughter. That upset Nell a lot.

Just before Renie was due to arrive, Cliff asked, 'How long is she staying?'

'A week.'

'You'll enjoy that, at least.'

'Won't you enjoy hearing about London?'

'No. It's Swindon I want to hear about.' He looked sad when he said that.

'Then write to your family,' she urged.

'Not until I've something I can be proud of to tell them.'

'But—'

'My family are my business, just as your sister's yours.'

When he got that tight look on his face she gave up trying to talk to him because it was as if he'd closed his mind to the world.

Since the matron at the hotel understood the difficulties of Sunday travel, the staff's holiday weeks always began on a Saturday. Renie was to arrive in the afternoon.

Nell would have gone to meet her at the station in Rochdale, but she was ashamed of the shabby pram one of the ladies at church had lent her, on condition it was given back when no longer needed. Besides, it'd have cost money to take the train into Rochdale, money she didn't dare spend.

Still, she consoled herself with the thought that her sister knew her way here.

When she heard footsteps coming into the court, she rushed to the door and burst into tears, hugging Renie and holding her at arm's length, then hugging her again, till her sister laughed and tugged her inside.

'Look at us,' Renie said. 'Crying as if something bad has happened when we should be happy.'

Nell stared at her sister, envying the matching ankle-length skirt and longish tailor-made jacket over a pretty blouse. 'How smart you look! Is that the latest fashion in London?'

Renie looked down at herself and smiled. 'Yes. I bought this suit second hand, but it fits me well, doesn't it? Might have been made for me.' In turn, she studied her older sister and pulled a face. 'I remember that skirt. Doesn't he buy you any new clothes at all?'

Nell flushed in shame.

'There I go again!' Renie gave her another big hug. 'I'm never going to be famous for being tactful, am I?'

'How do you manage with the customers?'

She shrugged. 'I don't know. They're different, somehow. They seem to like me waiting on them, give me good tips.' She knelt down beside her niece, who was sitting on the rag rug playing with some wooden blocks. 'Isn't she bonny? I do wish you lived nearer so that I could watch her growing up.'

For a moment or two, Sarah studied her solemnly, then held her arms out to her young aunt to be picked up.

'She doesn't usually go to anyone else,' Nell said in surprise.

'Just you and Cliff.'

'Just me. He's not . . . um . . . interested in babies.'

Renie looked at her across the top of her niece's head. 'Things still not going well? You never talk about him in your letters.'

Nell shook her head, not trusting her voice. She listened to Renie talking to Sarah, then, when she was in control of her emotions, said as brightly as she could, 'How about a cup of tea?'

'I'm dying of thirst. Make us a big pot and I'll drink it dry.'

Cliff came home from work soon afterwards. Saturday was usually a short day but he sometimes worked overtime. Nell didn't know what he did with the extra money.

He, too, studied his sister-in-law's appearance. 'Fine clothes! You must have been spending all your wages on them.'

Renie blinked in shock at this ungracious greeting. 'A lot finer than the rags my sister is wearing, yes. Everyone will think you're short of money, sending your wife out dressed like that. But in case you're worried that I can't look after my money, I got these second hand.'

He breathed deeply, ignoring what she'd said and turning to his wife. 'Don't I get a cup of tea when I come home?'

'I never know whether you'll be going straight out to the pub or not. There's some in the pot.'

'I want fresh tea, not stewed.'

She knew then what it would be like this week, with him emphasising that he was the master of the house and making their evenings miserable. She could feel herself flushing with embarrassment again. To her relief, Renie said nothing, just gazed at Cliff, as if he was an exhibit in a travelling circus.

Nell had made an extra effort with the tea, making a cake, but she wished she hadn't when he commented on that as if they never had cakes at other times.

When he'd gone out to the pub, she looked at Renie. 'If you can ignore him, he'll grumble less. It's how I find it best to deal with him. Luckily he goes out to the pub most evenings.'

'He was never comfortable to live with, but he's downright spiteful now.' Renie reached for her handbag and pulled out a Fry's Chocolate Cream bar, waving it triumphantly. 'We'll not share this with him. We'll eat it all ourselves.'

Nell's mouth watered at the sight of the bar. She hadn't tasted chocolate since before she left home. 'You shouldn't have,' she protested half-heartedly.

'Yes, I should. And while we're at it, I'll give you some money for my food. Don't tell me you don't need it.'

'It'd be safest to give it me daily.'

By the time Cliff staggered home, more unsteady on his feet than usual, Nell had heard all about the hotel, the staff and Renie's friends. Such an interesting life her sister led – hard work, but then whose life wasn't hard work?

When Renie left the following Friday, Nell sat and wept in despair.

Cliff came home from work, looked at her red eyes and sighed. But for once he didn't make a spiteful comment. 'She paid her way?'

'Yes. Every day she gave me what I spent on her.'

'She should have given you extra, for the trouble.'

'I'd not have taken it. It's no trouble to me to look after my sister. It was as good as having a holiday myself. And Sarah loved her aunt. Renie bought her a lovely little dress.'

'Hmm. That's good, anyway – saves us money.'

She couldn't wait for him to go out. As soon as he had done, she took out her shorthand book and began to practise. She was going to learn accounts next. One day . . .

Renie couldn't get time off at Christmas, one of the busiest times of year for The Rathleigh. She sent presents for Nell and little Sarah, clothes which she said she'd picked up cheaply at the second-hand shop. They didn't look cheap to Nell, and she took the tailored suit meant for her out of the parcel, holding it up in delight.

Cliff looked on sourly. 'She didn't think to send anything for me.'

'The way you spoke to her when she was here, why should she?'

'Well, it'll save me buying you new clothes, I suppose.'

'It will if you want me to wear this suit to scrub the floor. It'd make more sense to save it for going to chapel. My other clothes are worn out, though, and I do need some new clothes.'

After another of those heavy silences, throbbing with unspoken anger, he slapped a pound down on the table. 'You might as well have this now as at Christmas. You can use it to buy some clothes for yourself.'

She put it away quickly, before he changed his mind. With so little money, it'd have to be second-hand clothes again, things she altered to fit herself. She could sew, but she didn't have a gift for making clothes look smart. 'What about Sarah? She's growing out of her things.'

'Do you think I'm made of money?'

'You're not short of a penny or two. But if you want your daughter to go out wrapped in layers of rags to keep warm, while everyone sees you going out drinking most nights, that's what she'll have to wear.'

'You always have a sharp answer, don't you?'

'You always make a nasty remark.'

Another pound note was slapped on the table. 'I want to know how you spend this. Every single penny to be accounted for.'

She gave him a scornful look and didn't answer. If he asked, she'd tell him she wasn't making him a list of what she spent.

Oh, the frustration of being tied to a man you didn't even like!

Chapter Six

Spring seemed very late that year, after the warm weather of the previous year. One cold rainy day followed another. But eventually the days grew a little warmer, and as April replaced March and summer beckoned, people began to shed their extra scarves and shawls.

Nell loved to take Sarah for walks in the shabby pram and teach her daughter new words. Such a clever pretty child! She only wished she could provide her with a better life than this.

One Saturday afternoon the gas cooker refused to light, something that had happened a couple of times recently.

Nell turned to Cliff, who had just come home from work. 'We need to get this gas cooker repaired. It's not working again.'

He gave an exaggerated sigh. 'There's always something to take my money, isn't there?'

'We have to eat and you've always got an excellent appetite. I can't make a stew for your tea if the cooker won't light. Maybe the meat will go bad if I can't cook it, then it'll be wasted.'

That thought made him come across to look at the cooker, but he had no more success than she'd had in lighting the burner. He scowled, jingling a few coins in his pocket, then said, 'Last time it happened, we left it for a few hours, then it started working again of its own accord. I expect some damp's got in.'

'I'm sure I can smell gas.'

He sniffed loudly and shrugged. 'There's always a bit of a smell with these things.'

'What if the cooker doesn't work tomorrow?'

'It will.' He saw her open her mouth to disagree and held up one hand, scowling at her. 'All right! If it doesn't, I'll find someone to repair it on Monday.'

'I'll need more money to go and buy something different for tea today, then. Some ham, maybe, and a jar of relish. We'll just have to hope the stewing meat I bought will keep till Monday.'

He hesitated, then fumbled through the coins in his pocket, handing over a shilling with obvious reluctance.

She set her hands on her hips. 'I can't get much food with that, Cliff Greenhill! We need to buy enough for tomorrow as well.'

'The cooker will be working tomorrow.'

'And if it isn't?'

'We'll make do with bread and jam.'

'Then I'll need the money for an extra loaf. There's not a farthing to spare in the housekeeping money you give me. I can barely manage now Sarah's getting bigger and eating more. It'd be cheaper in the long run to get the cooker repaired.'

He got that stubborn look on his face. 'We'll see.'

Once he'd handed over another sixpenny piece, she turned to tell Sarah they were going to the shop.

But when she saw their little daughter curled up fast asleep on the rug, she didn't like to disturb her. 'Cliff, will you keep an eye on Sarah while I nip along to the shop? I don't suppose she'll stir and I'll be much quicker on my own.'

'All right.' He sat down with a newspaper he'd brought home. 'I'll try the cooker again in a few minutes.'

There was always enough money for his newspapers, Nell thought as she whisked a shawl round her shoulders and hurried to the corner shop on the next street. Unfortunately, there was a queue and she had to wait ten minutes. She kept checking the wall clock and hoping Sarah wouldn't stir. Cliff wasn't used to looking after their daughter, but even he wouldn't let her go near the fire, which was the main worry, and there was a fireguard in place. It'd be silly to go home now that she was near the head of the—

There was a loud booming noise outside and the ground shook. Everyone in the shop exclaimed in shock and stopped speaking to listen.

'What was that?' one woman asked.

Before anyone could answer, there was another loud noise, the ground shook again. Then there was a rumbling sound.

'Them noises both sounded like explosions to me!' an older man said.

People all tried to talk at once.

'It can't be.'

'What's there to explode round here?'

'How do you know it's an explosion?'

'I fought in the Boer War, didn't I? I've heard enough explosions to recognise one.' He was moving towards the door as he spoke. 'I'm going to have a look.'

They all pushed out into the street after him. There was a terrible smell and the air was full of dust and floating bits. Smoke could be seen above the rooftops.

'It was in the next street,' a woman yelled, her voice shrill.

'Don't go down that way!' a man shouted. 'There might be more to come.'

'It's them filthy anarchists,' the grocer said. 'I've been reading about them in the newspapers.'

Nell suddenly realised that the smoke was coming from the end of the street near Willow Court. Fearing for her daughter's safety, she pushed through the group of women, ignoring their cries of annoyance, and began running towards her home. She heard footsteps behind her, saw people running ahead of her, but all she could think of was Sarah.

When she turned the corner into Cassia Street, she stopped dead in shock, looking down the row of thirty houses. The smoke and debris were coming from the entry to Willow Court. There was so much black smoke there that terror filled her and she couldn't move.

It took her a while to work out why the street looked wrong, then she saw that the windows of houses near Willow Court were broken and . . . after creeping forward a few steps and staring at the dark, smoky part of the street, she realised that the entrance to the court looked wrong . . . different . . . more open. Then she saw that the buildings on either side of it in Cassia Street had also been partly demolished.

Another few creeping steps brought a view of her house, or what had been her house. Her daughter! She had to get to Sarah.

She set off again, pushing through the crowd, evading a man who tried to stop her. But as she got close, other men grabbed her and held her back.

'You can't go in there, love. It's not safe,' said an old man who was leaning against the wall of a nearby house. He kept dabbing at some cuts on his face with a dirty handkerchief. 'Look at it! That blast broke all the windows nearby, and it blew me right through the air. I flew, I did. Lost my shoe too. Lucky to be alive.'

'There's gas escaping still,' another man chimed in. 'Can't you smell it, missus? It's ruptured the mains.' He raised his voice. 'Don't anyone light a cigarette. We don't want another explosion.'

Shock held Nell paralysed for a few moments and the men keeping her back relaxed their hold. She was close enough now to see that the front of her house no longer existed. Only the back wall and parts of the side walls were still standing. Where the front room had been was filled with knee-high debris, and the kitchen was filled to shoulder height with rubble and the occasional jagged bit of wood.

Not only were the houses on either side of the entrance to the court badly damaged, but so were others inside it. They all looked as if they were leaning against one another.

As fear for her daughter overcame the shock, Nell tried again to push her way through.

'That's Mrs Greenhill! She lives at number one,' a woman yelled. 'Don't let her go near it!'

As everyone turned to stare at her, two fellows in blue workmen's overalls stepped forward to bar her way.

'You mustn't go in there yet, love. It's not safe.'

She flailed her hands, trying to get past them, yelling, 'I have to get through! My child's in there!'

There was a murmur from the crowd.

The man's voice grew gentler. 'You'll have to wait, love. There's no sign of anyone, but we're going to dig it all out and see if we can find them, see if they're . . . all right.'

She shuddered, feeling sick with terror at what this might mean.

The other man added, 'We have to go slowly, you see. We don't want to make sparks and cause another explosion. So no one can go in yet.'

'They've sent to the gasworks,' another voice called. 'Someone's coming to turn off the gas where the pipe from this street meets the next one.'

'But my husband and my little daughter were in the kitchen . . .' Her voice trailed away before the look of intense pity on the face of the nearest man.

'We can only wait, love,' he said gently.

'You come into my house and have a cup of tea,' a woman offered. 'I can boil the kettle on the fire.'

Nell shook her head. 'I'm not stirring till we . . . find out . . .' She didn't dare say it, didn't even dare think it, pushed to the back of her mind the unthinkable horror of what might have happened. All she could do was wait.

Other people waited with her – in silence, mainly, though there were occasional whispers. Every now and then someone sneaked a glance at her and caught her eye. She didn't want their pity, so looked away. All she wanted was her daughter. In her arms. Even if Sarah was . . . badly hurt.

When two men wearing the gasworks uniform pushed through the crowd, there was the sound of feet shuffling backwards, but no one said anything.

One of the gasmen stared at the houses, shaking his head. 'Never seen one as bad as that.'

His companion let out a low whistle. 'What the hell happened? We'll have to turn off the gas to the whole of Cassia Street before we dare let anyone go inside there.'

They moved back through the crowd, taking their handcart of tools with them, and went to the far end of the street. Pulling off their coats, they began to dig.

Like everyone else, Nell had turned to watch them. It seemed to take ages for them to dig down far enough to reveal the gas pipes. She didn't know how much time passed, but when they came back down the street and said the gas was turned off, she again tried to push through towards her house.

'Let me through! They'll need every hand to clear the rubble,' she called.

But the two men standing next to her grabbed her arms again and hauled her back.

'Leave it to others, love. The men will be stronger than a little 'un like you.'

She looked at them in mute appeal and again the woman offered her a cup of tea.

'I don't want any tea. I want them to get my daughter

out. I left her in the kitchen with my husband while I nipped to the shop.'

The woman exchanged quick glances with the men and whispered, 'Keep her here. Don't let her through till it's . . . safe. Till we know . . . what it's like.'

They nodded.

Men formed a chain and began passing the bigger pieces of rubble out, piling them in Cassia Street. Some of the men were in overalls, one was in a suit.

Nell could only stand there, icy with fear, hugging her arms across her breast, watching.

As the heap of rubble grew smaller, the men began to move more slowly, taking care how they lifted the bigger pieces.

'I can see a leg!' one called. 'It's a man. He's not moving. There's blood.'

Nell tried to press forward but her two guardians prevented that.

'Let them do their work, love.'

One man suddenly stumbled away from the rubble and bent over to vomit. The others worked on in grim silence. Whatever they were uncovering was hidden from the street by debris, but their faces said it was bad.

The people watching became very still and no one said anything as another of the rescuers stood up and closed his eyes for a moment, swallowing hard. 'Anyone got a sheet or blanket?' he called when he opened his eyes.

That caused a buzz of talk and one woman went into her house, coming out with a ragged sheet, which was passed to the men.

They worked on and then stopped again, holding a

brief conversation in whispers. Then a man with a flat cap left his companions and came slithering down the rubble. 'Where's the wife?'

'Here!' People pointed.

'Don't let her through!' He came up to her.

Nell was beside herself with fear and anguish. 'What's happened?'

He hesitated.

'*Tell me!*'

'It's bad news, love.'

'I have to go to my child. If she's hurt, she'll want me to cuddle her.'

'You can't do any good, love.'

'What . . . do you mean?' She couldn't, wouldn't accept what his eyes were telling her.

'I'm sorry but they're both beyond help now.'

It took a while for the meaning of these gently spoken words to sink in, for her mind to accept it, then she screamed and sank to her knees, sobbing, as the words echoed in her mind.

'No! No! *Nooooo!*'

'Let me through,' a voice called.

The crowd parted to let someone through, but Nell didn't care who it was. The gently spoken words kept echoing through her mind. *Beyond help*. No, it couldn't be true. It just . . . couldn't. They'd made a mistake.

Someone knelt beside her and it took her a minute or two to realise it was Mr Garrett.

She couldn't find any words, could only look at him pleadingly.

He put his arms round her, holding her close to his chest.

'I'm sorry, my dear. You must be brave. They were both killed. It's a dreadful tragedy. I'm so very sorry.'

'No!' But her denial was weaker now. Her throat was full of tears and the words were choked off.

'If it's any consolation, they must both have died instantly. They'd have felt no pain.'

'Sarah,' she stammered. 'My little Sarah. She can't be dead. She *can't.*'

Mrs Garrett joined them, puffing, as if she'd been hurrying. Another person with that pitying look on her face. She said something but Nell couldn't make sense of the words until they were repeated.

'Bring her to our house, Septimus.'

They helped her to her feet and she let them move her as they wished, because she couldn't seem to control her own body. What did it matter anyway where she went? She stopped to stare one last time at the gaping hole where her house had been. She could see her wooden chest, standing at a drunken angle on the remains of the floor at the back of the bedroom. In the kitchen was what was left of her solid-oak dresser. Nearby someone had thrown the sheet across the ground near the mangled remains of the gas cooker.

At least they'd covered the bodies up. You had to do that.

'How can a whole house fall down?' she asked, her voice a scrape of sound only.

'It was a gas explosion,' a man said. 'Must have been a leak. Strike a match and it'd be like a bomb going off.'

They'd said that before, but now the words suddenly sank in and Nell resisted the tugging arms. 'A gas explosion?

The cooker wasn't working. That's why I was out at the shop.'

'You've had a lucky escape,' one woman said.

Lucky. Nell tested the word in her mind, then shook her head. She didn't feel lucky.

Then she thought of something else. 'I need to see my daughter's body.'

There was dead silence round her.

'Where have you put her?' she demanded. 'Have you laid her down gently? Is she decently covered?'

Mrs Garrett put an arm round her shoulders and she couldn't shake it off.

Beside her, Mr Garrett cleared his throat, then said, 'It was a bad explosion, Nell. There . . . isn't much left of them. You don't want to see them.'

A man next to him said, 'I covered the remains up, missus. It's all as decent as we can make it.'

'Show me my daughter.'

He shook his head.

'I'm not going till I've seen her, held her . . .'

He closed his eyes for a moment, then said huskily, 'There isn't enough of her left to recognise, missus. You shouldn't see it. You should remember her as she was.'

Only then did the full horror sink in.

Nell heard someone begin screaming, dreadful high-pitched wails. Her limbs wouldn't move. She closed her eyes, wanting only blackness, oblivion.

It was a long time before Nell opened her eyes again, and even before she'd remembered, she knew she didn't want to wake up. 'Where . . . ?'

'You're in our house,' Mrs Garrett said. 'You must stay here till we can think what to do.'

Nell stared round and realised she was lying on the sofa in the front parlour, a room where the minister saw people who were in trouble.

She was in trouble, couldn't have imagined worse. But he couldn't help her. No one could.

She looked at the two kindly people standing watching her, saw their mouths opening and shutting, and closed her eyes again. Refused to listen. Refused to think.

Wished she had been killed too.

Mrs Garrett looked at the doctor. 'She's not answering, but surely she's conscious?'

'Her mind is too upset by the horror of what's happened. I've seen it before. I'll give her something to make her sleep.'

'She'll still have to face it when she wakes.'

'The human mind is a wonderful thing. It can start to heal itself, even in sleep. And she'll be calmed a little by the sleeping draught. But you should watch her carefully. She might want to harm herself.'

When they'd tipped the liquid, a little at a time, down Nell's throat, Dora waited until her guest had fallen into an uneasy sleep, then went to seek help in looking after her own children. There was no lack of offers when members of the congregation understood what she was doing for the poor bereaved woman.

After that she went back to sit beside the sofa on which they'd laid Nell. The doctor's potion had done its work and the poor lass was breathing deeply. But her sleep was troubled, even so.

Dora clasped her hand and wept for her.

When her husband joined her, she said simply, 'I can't understand why a loving God would do this to her, to anyone.'

'It's beyond my understanding too. A severe test of our faith.'

'If it'd been *my* only child . . . and you as well . . . I don't know how I'd have faced it. We've had our losses, but not so terrible.' She mopped her eyes again. 'I'm not leaving Nell to wake up alone. Mrs Rayner's taking charge of our children. That nursery maid is too young to be left unsupervised. I'm staying right here beside poor Nell.'

'I'll bring a mattress down for you to sleep on, then.'

She nodded, then fell to her knees to pray for her young friend.

As she stood up again, she remembered suddenly that all Nell's thoughts had been for her child, not a word about her husband. That didn't surprise her. Cliff Greenhill had been a weak reed, and selfish with it. He hadn't cared greatly for his wife and child – not that Dora had seen, anyway – and she hadn't forgotten the bruises where he must have hit Nell.

But still, he had family back in Swindon and they should be informed of his death. She'd look into that tomorrow, ask Nell for their address.

She pushed the mattress closer to the sofa and lay down to sleep, but it was an uneasy slumber and she kept waking with a start to check her companion. She was relieved that Nell didn't regain full consciousness during the dark hours of the night. It was the hardest time to face bad news.

As dawn gilded the edges of the blinds, Nell stirred, lying staring up at the ceiling for a few minutes, so that Dora, who was watching her carefully, wasn't certain whether she really had regained consciousness.

When she spoke, all she said was, 'I thought it was a nightmare, but it isn't, is it?' Then she turned her head into the pillow and wept, heart-rending sobs that brought tears to her companion's eyes too.

Dora could only crouch beside her, patting her, trying to make her feel less alone. But she wasn't even sure Nell noticed.

They couldn't persuade her to eat anything, but she drank several cups of tea over the course of the morning.

Mostly she lay staring into space, her eyes blind with sorrow, an occasional tear leaking out.

Dora could think of no words of comfort – what comfort could you offer to a mother who had lost her only child in this dreadful way, who didn't even have a proper body to mourn over, couldn't press a final kiss on her child's cold brow as Dora had once done when she lost a little son to measles? All she could do was clasp Nell's hand from time to time and continue to pray for guidance and support from a higher power.

Later the next morning some men turned up at the minister's house. Mr Garrett opened the door to them.

'We've been salvaging what we could from the Greenhills' house,' one of them said. He indicated some dusty objects on a handcart. 'Where shall we take them?'

'Better leave them here with me. Is this all there is?'

'All that's worth keeping. The rest is in pieces. We've still got to check the cellar, but the way down is blocked at the moment. We're trying to make everything safe because that damned landlord won't spend a penny on doing it unless the insurance pays. We don't want our kids playing among the rubble and getting hurt.'

'Could you bring the things round to the back garden? They can stay in the shed till Mrs Greenhill's ready to go through them. Are any of her clothes left?'

'Only a few. They're dusty and some of them have been torn by flying debris. There are a couple of books which were in the trunk, and a tin box. You'll have to break that open, I should think, it's so battered I doubt the lock will work, even if she has the keys.'

'Well, you're doing a good job. If anything else turns up, save everything you can. Who knows what she'll want to keep?'

'How is she, sir?'

Mr Garrett shook his head. 'Still in shock, I'm afraid, lying staring into space, weeping sometimes.'

'It doesn't bear thinking of, does it? They're taking up a collection to help her with the funeral costs. Can we bring the money to you?'

'Yes, of course. I'll put in a guinea to start it off.' He wished he could offer more, but this was a poor living. 'Thank you for doing this.'

The man shook his head sadly. 'It was all we could think of to do for her.'

'What about the . . . bodies?'

He shuddered. 'They've taken what's left to the undertaker's. You'd not recognise them, sir. Best they be buried together, the undertaker said.'

Mr Garrett didn't hesitate, shook his head. 'I don't think she'd want that. Ask them if they can put the baby's remains in a separate coffin.' As the man opened his mouth to protest, he added hastily, 'She'll want the baby kept separate. I know the family. I'm sure that's what she'll want.'

'If you say so, sir.'

Septimus supervised the transfer of the box and other bits that had been retrieved, leaving them in the garden shed for the moment. As he watched the men walk away, he felt desperately sad. And helpless. His wife had told him how strained relations were between Nell and her husband, and he'd seen for himself how the fellow neglected his family. He'd also seen a bruise once, the mark of a man's rough handling. It could only have been Cliff. You couldn't help wondering if there had been other bruises in hidden places. Some men treated their wives so badly. No wonder Nell hadn't asked what had happened to him.

When he went back into the front room, he whispered to his wife, 'I've just thought. We should send for her sister Renie.'

That caught Nell's attention. She turned towards them and said, 'No!' in a firm flat voice.

'But you need your family with you at this sad time, dear.'

'I don't want anyone. I just want . . . to be left alone to bury my daughter.'

'And husband,' he added gently. 'You'll have to let his family know.'

She was silent for so long he wasn't sure she'd heard him,

then she said, 'Will you send them a telegram, please?'

'I'll need their address.'

Mr Garrett noted it down and sent the telegram within the hour, telling the Greenhills their son had been killed in an accident, offering his condolences and asking if they wanted to come to the funeral.

'We should wait to bury them till Cliff's family can be there.'

'We can wait to bury him, but I'm burying Sarah as arranged,' Nell said harshly. She'd prefer to do it like that, anyway, keep Sarah to herself. She needed to stay on good terms with the Greenhills, though, in case her sister Mattie tried to contact her through them. She wasn't even sure they'd come. They'd been very disapproving of her marriage and Mrs Greenhill had accused her of taking their Cliff away from them and ruining his life.

'Are you sure?' he asked.

'About my Sarah, yes. They can do what they want with Cliff's body. I shan't be weeping over him. It's all his fault. I begged him to have the gas cooker repaired, but he wouldn't spend money on anything but himself, if he could help it. *He's* the one who killed our daughter, killed her as surely as if he'd stabbed her in the heart.'

Septimus didn't argue with her. If what Nell had just said was true – and there was no reason to doubt it – he too felt sickened by the thought that this accident could have been prevented.

How much worse must that knowledge make it for her to bear her grief?

A brief telegram arrived from Cliff's mother the following day.

CAN'T COME. HUSBAND GRAVELY ILL. NEPHEW FRANK COMING INSTEAD. ADVISE ADDRESS AND WAIT FUNERAL FOR HIM.

Mr Garrett sent another telegram, then arranged lodgings for the nephew, whose name none of them knew, with one of his parishioners. He also contacted Cliff's cousin George.

Nell was still refusing to contact her sister, and since they didn't have an address for Renie, they could do nothing about that. But it was sad that she'd not have any family with her at the funeral.

When they buried Sarah two days later, Nell was supported by the Garretts, with former neighbours and members of the congregation standing behind her.

People from the nearby streets came to the funeral too, to pay their respects, but Nell didn't acknowledge them, seemed more like a sleepwalker that day.

'Did you see her eyes?' one woman whispered to her companion. 'No light in them at all.'

'Others have lost children,' her companion said. 'She'll have to pull herself together. Life goes on.'

'Others haven't lost their children in such a terrible way.'

'No. You're right there. I've cried a few times thinking about that poor child. I used to see her at the shops, always smiling, such a bonny little thing.'

Nell stood by the grave for so long that Mr Garrett signalled to the other people to leave, even his wife. He waited patiently for Nell to move, and when she did, offered her his arm.

As they walked slowly out of the chapel grounds, she said abruptly, 'I want a headstone for my Sarah. The best money can buy.'

'My dear, you haven't much money left and your neighbours have given as much as they can afford.'

'I'm not expecting them to pay for it. I shall save up for a headstone myself.'

He sighed. 'I'll speak to Portermans about how much it'd cost. They're the best monumental masons.'

'An angel in white marble to watch over her.'

Chapter Seven

That evening, there was a knock on the door and Mr Garrett went to answer it.

A young man stood there, looking so much like a larger, stronger version of Cliff that it gave the minister a nasty shock. He pulled himself together. 'You must be Cliff's cousin.'

He nodded. 'Frank Greenhill.'

'I'm Septimus Garrett. Please come in.' He led the way into the front room where he usually talked to parishioners in trouble. 'Do sit down.'

'Where is she?'

'Mrs Greenhill, do you mean?'

His voice was deep, with a harsh edge to it. 'Cliff's wife. We don't think of her as a Greenhill. She isn't one of us.'

'She was a good wife to him.'

'Well, she isn't his wife anymore and the less we have to do with her the better.'

'She's suffered a tragic loss and I hope you're not going to add to her grief.'

'If I see her grieving for my cousin, I'll be surprised. She only married him to get away from that father of hers.'

'Did you tell her father about the accident?'

He shrugged and said nothing.

'I'll go and fetch Nell, then after you've spoken to her, I'll take you to the lodgings I've arranged. Would you like a cup of tea? You must be tired.'

'Yes, please.'

Mr Garrett paused in the hall, worried about this young man, because although Frank had been polite enough, he seemed very hostile towards poor Nell, and she didn't deserve any more trouble. But still, he couldn't refuse to let the newcomer see her.

Nell looked up as Mr Garrett came into the room. She'd wanted to go to bed early but her kind hosts wouldn't let her. They insisted she needed to be with people.

'Who was it, dear?' Mrs Garrett asked.

'It's Frank Greenhill. He wants to see Nell.'

There was silence, then she got to her feet. 'I suppose I'll have to.'

'I'll stay with you while you talk, my dear, then I'll take him round to his lodgings.'

She shook her head. 'I can tell him about the funeral arrangements on my own. I'll call you when I've finished.' She was afraid of what Frank might say. She couldn't imagine the Greenhills being kind or supportive, because they hadn't approved of her marriage in the first place.

Feeling apprehensive but determined not to give way, she went into the front room.

When Frank stood up, she shivered. He was tall and

muscular, not scrawny, but still, he had such a look of Cliff. Of course, he hadn't gone into upholstery, was working in the carriage-making section of the Railway Works, where you had to be much stronger.

'Well, at least you've been crying for him,' he said. 'When are the funerals?'

That unkind comment shook her and for a moment she couldn't answer, then she pulled herself together. Frank would be gone soon and she need never see him again. 'I buried my daughter today. Cliff's funeral is tomorrow.'

He frowned. 'Why aren't you burying them together? They usually put a child in its parent's coffin when they die together.'

'She deserved her own coffin. Heaven knows he kept her short of everything while she was alive.' She knew it was a mistake to criticise Cliff the minute the words were out of her mouth, because Frank seemed to swell up with indignation.

'I didn't think you could be as bad as my aunt said, but you're worse. Did you care for our Cliff at all? Or were you just looking for a way to escape from your father?'

She didn't answer, couldn't seem to draw breath, felt suddenly nervous of him. Which was ridiculous. What could he do to her here, in the minister's house?

'Cliff's funeral is at two o'clock,' she said and turned to leave. 'Mr Garrett will tell you the details. We were waiting for you to come.'

'Wait a minute!' He strode across to block the doorway. 'His mother wants to know what you're doing with Cliff's things? She wants something to remember him by.'

'Most of our things were destroyed in the explosion,

which blew the whole house apart. There wouldn't have been an explosion at all if Cliff hadn't been too mean to get the cooker repaired. Make sure you tell his mother that as well.'

'You heartless bitch! As if I would.'

She thought for a moment he was going to thump her, but he let his bunched fist drop. Still, it was right for them to have some memento of Cliff. 'You can have his tools, if you want. They were at the place he worked. They're no use to me.'

'There's money too. He was a saving sort of fellow. I'll speak to you again after the funeral, when you know what he left you. They ought to have a share of that too, to help them in their old age, because he won't be able to do that now.'

She couldn't bear to go on speaking to him, so left the room and let Mr Garrett take him to his lodgings.

She shuddered as she got ready for bed. She'd hated being in the same room as Frank Greenhill, not because of his resemblance to Cliff but because of his size. He was a big man, with an expression on his face like her father's. The sort who would hit you as soon as look at you.

And what did he mean about Cliff's money? That was nothing to do with him. Any savings left were going towards an angel for Sarah's grave, not to the Greenhills.

Her husband's funeral was a quiet affair the following day. It was the cheapest money could buy. Nell couldn't escape going to it, not unless she wanted to create a scandal, especially not with Frank there. She stood stony-faced by the grave and couldn't shed any tears. As far as she was concerned, Cliff was a murderer.

Afterwards, Frank came up to her. 'When's the reading of the will?'

'He didn't leave one.'

'Have you looked?'

'Have you seen the remains of our house? No? Well, go and look yourself. There's nowhere to search.'

'There was nothing in his toolbox.'

She looked at him in shock. 'You've got it already?'

'Yes. I asked my landlady where he worked. It's only got his tools in it, though.'

'Then there's nowhere else to look.'

'You've not arranged anywhere for the mourners to meet for a drink?'

'No. I can't afford to. If you've got the toolbox, I'll say goodbye to you. You'll be wanting to get home to Swindon and your work.' She turned and left him, glad to see the back of him.

After breakfast the next day, Mrs Garrett sent the children upstairs with the young nursemaid, then looked expectantly at her husband.

He turned to Nell. 'Isn't it time you looked at the bits and pieces they retrieved from your house, my dear? You let my wife sort out the clothes that were still wearable, but you've refused to touch the metal box.'

'Because it's *his* box. I didn't want to touch it till he was buried. Anyway, I can't do it today. You said you'd come with me to the savings bank to ask about the joint account Cliff and I had. Perhaps there'll be enough money in that for a headstone for Sarah.' She still had her own savings book, because it'd been hidden in the lining of her shopping bag, as usual, but it seemed only right that *he* pay for the headstone.

As she and the minister were walking to the bank, Nell noticed the weather for the first time in days. It was sunny, a beautiful spring day. That seemed wrong. She'd rather it was raining.

When they were ushered into the manager's office, she explained about the joint account and the bank book being destroyed.

He looked down his nose at her. 'Do you have proof of who you are, young woman?'

'I can bear witness to her identity,' Mr Garrett said. 'Mrs Greenhill is a member of my congregation and has been for the past two years.'

The manager's expression softened a little. 'And you have a joint account with your husband. Now that he's dead, the money in that will revert to you, of course. Do you know how much was in it?'

'I can't remember. I haven't looked at it for a week or two.'

He consulted a big ledger. 'There's not much, only a few pounds. Your husband recently withdrew most of the money and deposited it in his own savings account.'

'*What?*' The anger flared so fiercely that for a moment Nell felt to be burning up with it. Cliff had even stolen her money, as well as killing her child. It wasn't till Mr Garrett laid one hand on hers that she got control of herself.

'The remaining money in his personal account must

surely belong to Mrs Greenhill now,' the minister said.

'Is there . . . um . . . did he leave a will?' the manager asked.

They both turned to Nell.

'Not that I know of. Even if there had been, it'd have been destroyed in the explosion.'

'Ah. Yes, of course. In that case, we shall have to ask a Justice of the Peace to approve payment to you. Are there any children?'

She couldn't answer that. Her throat closed up if she so much as thought of Sarah.

Mr Garrett said, 'No children. The little daughter died in the explosion as well.'

'Oh. I'm sorry. Then we can settle this very simply, without causing you any more pain than necessary,' the manager said.

There was silence and she realised they were waiting for her to respond, so she forced out a 'thank you' and that seemed to satisfy them.

The manager's office felt to be closing in on her, and once the paperwork had been dealt with, she stood up abruptly. 'Can you . . . bring me the money we agreed on, Mr Garrett? I'm not . . . myself. I need air.'

She stood up and fled, running down the street to the minister's house like a madwoman, heedless of how people stared at her.

Frank saw her running down the street and wondered what she was fleeing from. But no one followed her. He hefted his bag in his hand. He'd been going to catch a train back, but she'd come out of the bank and he wanted to know what she'd found there. It must have been something to do with Cliff's savings.

He didn't believe her about the will. Cliff would definitely have made one, and he wouldn't have left everything to *her*, either. He had too much sense.

Frank decided not to stay in the lodgings Garrett had found for him, but find some of his own. No need for them to know he was still here. He could afford to spend another day here.

He sent a telegram to his aunt and uncle asking them to notify the people at work that he was helping the poor widow. He paused as he thought of her. Even though she was grieving, it had still surprised him how pretty she'd grown. He hadn't expected to fancy her. Not that he'd do anything about that. But still . . .

He banished that thought. Before he went back to Swindon, he had to find someone who'd keep an eye on her and let him know what she was doing – especially if she seemed to have inherited any money.

That bitch wasn't going to profit from a Greenhill's hard work, not if Frank could help it.

When she got back, Nell entered the house via the kitchen and went up to the attic to think about what she'd found out. Cliff had taken most of the money out of their joint account and put it into his own account. Why? What had he been planning to do with it? And where was his bank book? Had that been destroyed in the explosion? Or was it in the tin box?

She became aware of footsteps coming up the stairs, slow footsteps, so it must be Mrs Garrett, who was rather stout and found two flights of stairs trying. Nell sat up and turned to face the door.

'Are you all right, my dear? Septimus said you ran out of the bank.'

'I couldn't bear to talk on and on about money when my Sarah lies dead.' Impatiently she brushed away another tear.

Mrs Garrett came across to sit beside her on the bed. 'It's early days yet. Your grief is still fresh and sharp, but believe me, it will ease.'

'I'll never forget Sarah.'

'Of course not. Any more than I've forgotten dear little Robert, who died when he was two. But it *will* ease.'

'I didn't know you'd lost a child. I'm sorry.'

'It's been several years now. Many women go through this. There is no choice but to carry on with your life.'

Nell couldn't argue, but now she understood why Mrs Garrett seemed to know what to say to her. 'You're very kind. I'm nothing but a burden.'

'You're not a burden and you're welcome to stay here as long as you wish. If you help me in the house, as you suggested, you'll be more than paying your way. I don't think you should do anything until you've . . . well, come to some form of acceptance and thought carefully about your future.'

'Thank you.'

'Now, there's something else that needs doing. You've not yet looked at the box they retrieved from your house. You really should go through it. I gather you told the bank manager there was no will, but you don't actually know that until you've checked the box, do you?'

'I can't face it today. I'll do it tomorrow.' She wished she could just hurl the box into the nearest reservoir and forget about it. 'Isn't that the front door?'

'Yes. But my husband will answer it. Come down and join us for a cup of tea when you've washed your face.'

The following day Nell decided to get the ordeal over. News had come of the sinking of the *Titanic*, a horrendous tale, with over fifteen hundred lives lost. She listened to people discussing it. They lowered their voices when she was nearby, as if that would make any difference.

One man had lost his wife and four children. Four! Nell couldn't imagine how he could survive that. Somehow the thought of him helped her to start coping with her own loss, though she didn't tell people that, or they might think her heartless.

It had stopped raining and was a beautifully sunny day. 'Would you mind if I opened the box outside?' she asked. 'It still smells bad.'

'Good idea,' Mr Garrett said at once. 'I'm a firm believer in the restorative power of sunshine.'

She sat on a wooden bench looking at the box for a long time. It still had a sort of burnt yet sour smell. Someone had wiped the top of the box clean. Of what? She shivered. Mr Garrett had taken an axe to it, which had left one side gaping. She knew he was worried that she might hurt herself if she tried to use the axe. Or even that she'd try to take her own life if left with free run of his tools, so he'd locked his shed.

He needn't have worried. If she died, there would be no one left to remember her child. That was the main thing that kept her going at the moment; someone had to remember Sarah.

At last Nell braced herself and emptied the contents of the box onto an old blanket spread on the garden path. She got down on her knees beside the papers, some of which had been slightly damaged at one corner by the axe.

Cliff had kept their birth certificates and marriage certificate in this box, she knew. Well, that was what he'd told her, anyway, though she'd never understood why he had to lock them away from her. She'd not seen any of them since the wedding.

She found other papers saying he'd completed his apprenticeship. She tossed those to one side, starting a pile for burning. What use were they to anyone now? After a moment's thought, she added his birth certificate to them. She kept her own, which was badly stained with water from their first rainy day in Lancashire, and of course, she kept Sarah's, which was clean and crisp still. The wedding certificate she hesitated over, then put it in the pile of papers to be kept.

Underneath these, she found a large sealed envelope, with 'WILL' scrawled on it. So there had been one. It was another thing he hadn't told her about. Why so much secrecy?

She opened it to find that he'd written it himself. No mistaking that spindly handwriting. The first sentence was full of long words and sounded very official. He must have bought a book to help him; there were self-help books for all sorts of things.

When she read the second paragraph, she gasped in shock and outrage and scanned the rest quickly. Then she took a deep breath and reread the whole thing more slowly. She couldn't believe what she'd found. He'd left everything he owned to his parents, to whom he'd also left the guardianship of any children he might have. He said he trusted his parents to look after the money, but feared his wife wasn't good with it.

Was he allowed to do such a thing? Cut her right out of the will? She didn't know.

And how dare he tell such lies? She was good with money, always made the housekeeping stretch, never got into debt.

She dashed away a tear that came as much from anger as from pain. She'd stopped loving Cliff even before Sarah had been born, and gradually started to dislike him for his mean penny-pinching ways, always at her expense, never at his own.

The dislike had turned to outright hatred after the explosion, because she believed *he* was responsible for their daughter's death. Now, this unfairness towards herself only added to the flaming bonfire of hatred he'd created in her.

She studied the will again. She didn't think it'd been drawn up by a solicitor, because apart from the beginning and ending, every word sounded just like Cliff speaking. Anyway, he was too tight-fisted to pay a lawyer if he could manage without.

She'd never thought she'd be grateful for that meanness, but she was. Because it meant no one else knew about it.

She studied the other signatures. It had been witnessed by two men whose names were printed beneath black squiggles. No one she recognised. Who were they? Whoever they were, just let them try to have this will found.

She admitted to herself then that she was going to burn it.

It was still a while before she could control her anger enough to continue looking through the papers.

She found a bank book and opened it, looking first at the final total. She felt literally sick when she found that he'd saved nearly three hundred pounds over the years since he'd finished his apprenticeship. She'd gone hungry sometimes so that her daughter would eat well. And there'd been no need. No need at all!

He had never gone hungry. Not once.

Picking up the book she looked at it again. He'd recently deposited twenty-five pounds – the money he'd stolen from their joint account. There was enough to *buy* a decent terraced house, let alone rent one. They needn't have continued to live in a slum like Willow Court.

Why did he want so much money? What had he been planning to do with it? Run away and leave them penniless?

A well-worn notebook with hard covers gave her the answer – and a further surprise. It must have been written at work because she'd never seen it before. Maybe he hadn't always been doing overtime for Mr Rayner, but working for himself in the peace of the cluttered workroom.

The book contained details of upholstery and furniture repair businesses for sale. Advertisements cut from the *Rochdale Observer*, the *Manchester Guardian* and the *Manchester Evening News* were pasted to its pages. There were lists of supplies needed to set up as an upholsterer, carefully costed, wages that would have to be paid to an apprentice or a qualified man. Then there were addresses of manufacturers of upholstery fabrics, webbing and other supplies, with comments on what they were like to deal with and the quality of their goods.

Cliff had been planning to open his own business, but he hadn't said a word to her about it. Not – one – word.

She realised something else. That was why he'd waited to contact his family. He wanted to present himself to them as a success, not a failure.

For a moment sadness swept through her, sadness for the dreams that would never now come true for him.

But why hadn't he let her help him? Why keep it such a close-guarded secret?

She didn't need to think about the answer to that for more than a few seconds. Because he blamed her for his 'fall' as he'd called it sometimes. Yet it was he who had forced her and got her pregnant, he who had caused their 'fall'. He'd never once admitted that, always set it at her door, saying she'd led him on.

She wrapped her arms round herself, feeling both angry and sad, then bent to her task again. What was she going to do with all this stuff? It seemed a shame to just throw the careful calculations away and—

'Are you all right, Nell?'

She looked up to see Mr Garrett standing near the back door, watching her. Something told her he mustn't see these papers till she'd decided what to do about them. 'Yes, thank you. It's a slow business and very upsetting, but it has to be done. I'm glad now that I've started it, though.'

His expression lightened a little. 'Do you need any help? You have only to ask.'

'No, thank you. I'll . . . um . . . come to you if there's

anything I don't understand. It's just letters and stuff so far. And his bank book. He had some money saved. Will that come to me now, do you think?'

'In the absence of a will, I'm fairly certain you'll get the money.'

But there *was* a will, she thought as she watched the kindly minister walk inside. Mr Garrett wouldn't have left his wife out of *his* will. Anyone could see how much he loved her and their children.

Once he'd gone into the house, she spread the will open and looked down at it again. Who'd have thought a piece of paper could hurt you so much?

She'd done it before she admitted to herself what she was going to do: stuffed the envelope and paper into her bodice. There was no will now, as far as she was concerned. She'd earned the right to inherit his money by her hard work and thrift, by bearing his child. Just let anyone say different!

Underneath the notebook was another envelope, the last item in the box. She didn't want to open it, wasn't sure she could cope with another nasty surprise.

It took her two readings to work out that this was a life insurance policy, one covering both Cliff's life and hers. And the sum payable to the survivor was . . . *a thousand pounds*!

She couldn't breathe at the thought of that huge sum, had to press one hand against her chest to hold her fluttering heart still. Then she looked at the insurance policy again. Perhaps it had run out.

No, it was valid until October.

Did that mean she would get the insurance money?

It was a huge sum, but she would give every penny of it to have her daughter back; yes, even put up with *him* again if she could only hold Sarah in her arms, tickle her, kiss her.

'I think you've done enough for now, dear,' Mrs Garrett called across the garden. 'You're looking very pale and strained.'

Nell looked down. There were no more papers. 'I've finished.'

'Was it . . . did you find any bad news?'

'Some would say it's good news. Cliff took out an insurance policy on his life. I'm not sure, but I think it'll bring me some money. I need to ask Mr Garrett about it. I don't know how to deal with it.'

Nell folded up the papers and put them back into the shattered box. On second thoughts she put the papers she'd intended to burn back with the others, in case they were needed, then got to her feet.

Mrs Garrett was waiting for her in the kitchen. 'I'm afraid my husband's gone out, but he'll be back in an hour or so. The children won't be back for a while yet and I've let Mary go and see her mother for an hour. Could you just keep an eye on things down here while I have a little rest? You know what to say if anyone comes to the door.'

'Yes, of course.' Nell knew Mrs Garrett was convinced that ten-minute rests were what kept her going. And she certainly looked refreshed whenever she managed to snatch even this small amount of time for herself.

Feeling guilty, but no less determined, Nell went to stand in the hall and listen, to make sure Mrs Garrett wasn't coming down again. She heard the bedroom door open and shut, then the bedsprings creak.

Now was the time to do it.

Slipping across to the old-fashioned kitchen stove, she pulled out Cliff's will, and without a moment's hesitation, thrust it into the heart of the fire. She watched as it was quickly consumed, then used the poker to disperse the blackened flakes of burnt paper.

Whoever the witnesses were, there was nothing now to show that the will had ever existed. But even if the witnesses came forward, she would feign ignorance, say she'd never even seen a will, that it hadn't been among his papers. Then it occurred to her that Cliff wouldn't have shown them what the will said anyway. As she'd found out to her cost after they married, he was the most secretive person she'd ever met.

She stayed kneeling on the rug in front of the fire, feeling a chill that came not from the wind that was rising outside or the grey clouds starting to cover the blue sky, but from the way her husband had behaved to her.

Shamefully. Cruelly. He hadn't cared for her at all, had only wanted to use her.

If she didn't need to keep in touch with his family in case her sister Mattie contacted them, she'd never speak to any of the Greenhills again.

She was glad Frank had gone back to Swindon. She didn't want him finding out about the insurance policy and she'd hated being with him. The way he'd looked at her, even though she was newly widowed, had shocked her to the core. It wasn't just the hostility, it was . . . lust. She shivered at the thought of him even touching her.

When Mr Garrett returned, Nell showed him the papers she'd found.

'Wasn't there a will?'

'There's no sign of one.' That was more or less the truth – now.

'Do you understand about the insurance policy, my dear?'

'I think so. Cliff's death means they'll have to pay me a thousand pounds.'

'Yes. You're very fortunate that he was so thoughtful.'

She didn't comment on that, didn't want to tell any more lies to this decent man. 'I don't know how to claim the money, though.'

'We can check that with the insurance agent who sold it to him. See, his name and address are here.'

'Oh, yes. If I do get the money, that means I can get a proper headstone made for Sarah. One with an angel on it, to watch over her.'

'Will that comfort you, my dear?'

She stared at him, then shook her head slowly. 'Nothing will really comfort me, but it seems right to mark where she lies. Um . . .'

'Is there something else?'

'There'll be a lot of money left. What shall I do with it?'

'You must put it in the bank, where it'll be safe until you need it and where it will earn you interest. Have you any idea what you're going to do with yourself once you've sorted out your daughter's headstone?'

She shook her head. 'Not really. I can't seem to think clearly.' She indicated the pile of papers. 'Will you help me deal with these, please?'

'I'd be happy to. And you'll stay with us for the time being?'

'Yes. I'm grateful for your help. Without you, I'd have been lost.'

'And Nell . . . don't you think it's time you told your sister what's happened?'

'I suppose so.' She wasn't looking forward to that.

She wrote a letter to Renie that night, keeping it short. The first tear took her by surprise, and others followed before she could move her head away, so that the ink ran together and words were blotted out. If Renie saw that, she'd quit her job and come running. That mustn't happen. She didn't want her own tragedy to spoil her sister's life.

Nell started again, taking more care with the second letter, ending by begging Renie not to come rushing up to see her.

I won't be staying here, anyway.

Until she wrote those words, she hadn't made up her mind about what to do. Now she knew she'd be moving on. She desperately wanted to get away from the pitying looks and hushed voices – and from the memories.

She received a long loving letter from Renie by return of post, and read it only once, because it hurt so sharply to dwell on what had happened.

She kept dreaming of Sarah, woke murmuring her child's name, wept into the privacy of her pillows every night.

The Garretts gradually resumed a more normal life. The two children not yet at school spent their days playing with their mother and the young nursemaid.

Mrs Garrett seemed to understand that Nell didn't

want to look after the little ones, so let her help with the housework, which the daily maid, a grim-faced widow of about forty, was grateful for.

In between undertaking various spring-cleaning tasks, Nell went with Mr Garrett to see the bank manager, talked to the local Justice of the Peace, and dealt with the insurance company. She learnt to speak crisply and not let Mr Garrett speak for her, or else the men she had to deal with treated her like a slow-witted child.

She kept busy enough to go to bed every night tired, so she got some sleep, but she couldn't get tired enough to ensure a full night's sleep. She'd lost weight, knew she looked strained, but pride made her keep herself neat in the new clothes she'd had to buy to replace those lost in the explosion.

But wherever she went, she took care not to pass the end of Cassia Street, making long detours if necessary to avoid it. She didn't want to see any sign of what had happened in Willow Court. Mr Garrett said the local council had ordered the rest of the buildings in the court to be pulled down, because they were unsafe. People weren't allowed to build such courts nowadays. They were not only old-fashioned, but unhygienic.

She nodded when he told her, because he seemed to regard it as good news, but what did she care about the news? It was too late to save her daughter.

By the end of June, the insurance money had been paid and Nell had over thirteen hundred pounds in her own savings bank account. As soon as the angel tombstone had been erected over her daughter's grave, she intended to leave the North and make a new life for herself.

But though she racked her brain, she still couldn't think what exactly to do. All she knew was that she felt much better out in the open air and that she wanted to go back to Wiltshire eventually and look for her older sister Mattie.

News of the money spread quickly through the little town, people marvelling that a young woman should have so much. A few even congratulated her on her good fortune, but she told them it wasn't good fortune to lose a child, and after that had happened a few times, no one else said anything.

Chapter Eight

Frank stared at the envelope his aunt had handed to him when he got home from work. His cousin's bad luck had been his good fortune because he'd gone to live with them to help out. His aunt certainly knew how to make you comfortable – and how to do it without spending extravagantly.

'Go on, lad! It's from Lancashire. Open it,' his uncle said.

He ripped off the side of the envelope to find a grubby piece of paper, with a badly spelt message printed on it.

Dear Mr Greenhill

Everyone's talking about it. It seems your cousin had took out insurrence on his life and his wife got the lot. £1,000.

She's still staying with the minnister.

I look foward to receeving payment for this information, as we agreed.

J. Styles

Frank glared at the piece of paper, unable to speak for anger. His hunch had been correct. He knew Cliff wouldn't have left his family unprovided for. Greenhills always looked after their own.

Only *she* wasn't their own.

He passed the piece of paper to his uncle, who read it and cursed. His aunt snatched it out of her husband's hand, read it and wailed aloud.

Then they both turned to him.

'You'll have to do something about it, Frank.'

'What can I do?'

'Go and see her. Tell her she owes us some of that money.'

'Why should she pay us?' Frank wouldn't, if it was him. But he did like the idea of getting hold of some of that money. 'I'll have to think about it. I can't keep taking time off work or I'll get the sack.'

'You'll think of something. You always were a clever lad. She's not going to get the better of us Greenhills.'

He couldn't stop thinking about it. She was rich now. If he didn't do something, another lucky fellow would get Cliff's money.

It was a talk at the Women's Afternoon Club at the chapel which gave Nell an idea about what to do next. She'd only gone to get away from Mrs Garrett's kind fussing, not even knowing what this month's talk was about.

It turned out to be about hiking, which was a popular summer activity with some people. It wasn't one Nell had ever considered taking up, and even if she had, no one she knew could afford to get away and walk for days on end.

Even though they had holidays from work, most people had families and children, which left little, if any, money to spare. No, as far as she was concerned, hiking was for richer people.

Lucky them!

Only . . . she was comfortably off now, some would say rich. She could do what she wanted. She began to listen more carefully.

The speakers were two vigorous-looking women from Manchester, a Mrs Petherby and a Miss Porter, who were neither young nor old. They produced slides of the places they'd been to see, showing the audience their special knapsacks and walking boots. They were full of suggestions about how even married women with children could occasionally escape into the countryside for a few hours to get some fresh air into their own and their families' lungs. Which just showed how little they knew of ordinary people's lives.

When the talk was over, Nell sat where she was for a moment or two, much struck by what they'd said. She wasn't poor now, so she could do what she wanted.

If she dared.

She went across to the speakers and waited patiently till they'd been supplied with cups of tea. She listened with interest as they answered other people's questions. There was no hurry. Time was something she had too much of.

When her turn came, she said, 'I might like to do some hiking, but I'm not sure exactly what I'd need or how to set about it.' After a moment's hesitation, she added, 'My husband was killed suddenly and I think time to myself in the open air might help me recover.'

The older of the two women, Mrs Petherby, at once took Nell aside. 'Let's talk about this more privately. Flora, love, keep folk away from us for a while.'

Her companion waved one hand and turned to deal with another lady who'd come up to ask something.

'Have you the money to do this?' Mrs Petherby asked bluntly.

'Yes. My husband had an insurance policy.'

'You look as if you need a restful time.'

Nell could only manage, 'I do.'

'Why don't you come to us in Manchester and stay a night or two? We'll take you shopping, help you set yourself up for hiking and show you how to plan a route.'

'You'd do that?'

The speaker gave one of her jolly laughs. 'I'm the founder member of our local Fresh Air Movement. I want to make the world a healthier place.' Her voice grew softer. 'And when life troubles me, I get out into the open air to work out what to do. It always helps. My husband died a few years ago, you see, after only a year of marriage, so I know how you feel. I still miss him. Thank goodness I had my sister Flora to turn to. Don't you have any family, dear?'

'None who could take me in.' Nell didn't tell her that she hadn't missed Cliff in the slightest, that it was a relief to be rid of him. She hadn't told anyone that, because she felt guilty, but she couldn't change how she felt. 'Are you sure it'd be all right?'

'Of course I am. We women must help one another in this modern world, because the men won't, will they?'

Nell had never thought of it that way. 'Then I'd love to come. When would suit you?'

'How about the day after tomorrow? That gives you time to prepare. Unless you have something else to do here still? Only it's best to take advantage of the summer if you want to go on a long hike.'

'I've attended to everything that was needed. I'm just . . . searching for something to do. All I know is, I don't want to stay here and I feel better in the open air.'

'That's a good start.' Mrs Petherby pulled out a business card and handed it to her. 'We'll see you the day after tomorrow, then. Come in the afternoon, it doesn't matter exactly when you arrive. I'd better go and speak to other people now, or someone's sure to take umbrage.'

She clapped Nell on the back and walked back to join her companion.

Nell looked down at the business card. She'd seen such things but no one had ever given her one before. It was usually men who dealt in business cards, not women. She looked across the room, envying the two smiling speakers their confidence and knowledge of the world.

And that last thought, more than anything, decided her to do it. If she went out into the world, she was bound to learn so much. Why, she'd only ever seen Swindon and this part of Lancashire. She knew little, even about her own country.

Anyway, what had she to lose?

By the time she got back to the Garretts' house, it was teatime.

After all the clearing up and getting the children to bed, it was late enough for her to excuse herself and go to bed as well. She needed to think good and hard.

She didn't mention what she was going to do – not yet.

In the morning the sun was shining and Nell stood by the open dormer window, breathing in the fresh air, admiring the oasis of greenery the garden offered.

To her surprise, she'd had the best night's sleep since . . . *it* had happened. And she felt even more certain of her decision. Going away would set her free. Strangers wouldn't know what had happened to her, would just treat her normally. And oh, how she longed for some quiet time in the fresh air!

Her kind hosts stared at her in shock when she announced her plan after breakfast.

'My dear, you can't possibly go off on your own!' Mrs Garrett said at once. 'I know this is 1912 and young women have a lot more freedom than I ever had, but it'd be *dangerous*. Oh dear, I wish I'd never suggested you went to those talks.'

Mr Garrett was more thoughtful once the first shock was over. 'If you had someone to go with you, it might be a good idea, but I really can't allow you to go on your own.'

She didn't say that she was twenty-three years old and he wasn't her guardian. She didn't want to get into an argument. Then the solution came to her.

'I'll still go over to stay with Mrs Petherby and her friend, though, to find out as much as I can,' she said. 'Even if nothing comes of it, going to visit them will be a change, won't it? I'm sure that'll be good for me.'

He nodded at once. 'Good idea. Then you can come back and we'll discuss it. If we can find a lady hikers' club nearby, you can join it and get in some practice.'

'Are there such clubs? I've never heard of anything like that.'

He hesitated, then said in an apologetic tone, 'There are quite a few clubs of various sorts, but these are usually for women of . . . um . . . better means than you had before. Now that you have some money, and with my wife and myself to sponsor you, there are quite a few clubs you might join. I'm fairly sure there's a lady hikers' club in Rochdale – or was it Oldham? Anyway, if you're going to visit Mrs Petherby, that'll give me time to make enquiries.'

She went up to her room, deciding to wash a few garments by hand before she went. The maid was happy to let her use the outer scullery and mangle, where a woman came once a week to do the family's laundry. Although the day was quite cloudy, there was a brisk wind and the clothes dried quickly, so Nell heated the flat iron and soon had them dealt with.

To her relief, two ladies called on Mrs Garrett in the later afternoon to discuss a charitable matter, so she could go up to her room and pack, safe in the knowledge that no one would be likely to come in and find out what she was doing. They'd expect her to take an overnight case, but not all her clothes. Indeed, Mrs Garrett had told her where to find one in the attic and to borrow it.

She also took the opportunity to sew a pocket into her handbag for the new bank book, which had a frighteningly large amount of money in it.

That made her wonder if she was wise to take that bank book with her. Maybe she should move some of the money into another savings account and send this bank book to the Garretts for safe keeping, or to her sister? No, not Renie. The Garretts would be safer, since they weren't likely to move away.

That reminded her that she had to tell Renie what she was doing, so she wrote a long letter about it. This time she didn't cry all over it . . . well, not much. She'd been in luck. The monumental masons had already had a beautiful white marble angel ready, except for the wording. So it now stood keeping watch over Sarah.

With everything settled, Nell felt calm and emotionless, divorced from everything. She wasn't sure whether that was good or not, but it was how she felt. Doing something was certainly easier than weeping all the time.

As the train pulled into Manchester's Victoria Station early the following afternoon, Nell felt suddenly nervous, for all the calm certainty she'd experienced during the past two days about what she was planning. Now that she was on her own in a strange city, she became all too aware of how vulnerable she was.

She stood still for a while, watching other people, working out what was going on. Eventually she made her way to the cab rank, where there were some horse cabs to one side and three modern motor cabs to the other side. She'd only once ridden in a motor vehicle, when she was running away with Cliff, and had no idea whether they'd be more expensive, but she had a sudden urge to try riding in one.

Approaching one of the drivers, she asked how much it would cost to go to the address Mrs Petherby had given her.

He looked at her clothes with a shrewd eye and said, 'It's not cheap, love. That street is quite a way out. Look, you're new to the city, aren't you? If you wait half an hour, I'll take you there for a special price of two shillings because it's on my way to pick up a gentleman I bring into town every week. You can get a cup of tea for twopence while you wait.'

His kindness made her feel much better. 'That's very good of you. Thank you. I'll do that.'

He pointed to the station clock. 'Keep an eye on the time and come back at half past two sharp. I can't afford to wait. I'm only taking short fares till then.'

She walked across to the refreshment room and followed his advice. There was nothing like a cup of tea to hearten you – even one as stewed as this. She'd be ashamed to offer this to anyone.

No one looked at her or bothered her in any way as she sat waiting, keeping one eye on the clock. They were all too busy getting on with their own lives. Just as she was getting on with hers. That was a relief after all the attention she'd received lately, however well meant.

The taxi driver waved to her cheerfully and helped her inside, then started the motor and chugged slowly out towards some streets that looked very crowded and busy. Nell clutched the leather loop beside her seat, surprised that with so many vehicles entering or leaving the station they didn't collide with one another. She felt tense for a while, but gradually relaxed and began to enjoy the feeling of being driven in luxury.

Mrs Petherby's house was a large villa in a street of similar dwellings, the sorts of houses where people had maids and gardeners. For a moment, the contrast between this place and Willow Court overwhelmed Nell, but she pushed that thought aside. She'd been invited to stay, hadn't she? So they must think she was good enough.

She paid the taxi driver and thanked him, then got out and walked briskly up the path to the front door.

Mrs Petherby opened the door before she could knock. 'Saw you coming from the front sitting room. Come in, my dear, come in!' She raised her voice and bellowed, 'She's here, Flora! Told you she would be. Tell Mary to put the kettle on.'

She turned to beam at Nell. 'I'll show you to your bedroom, then we'll have a nice cup of tea.'

Nell hid her amusement at how loud Mrs Petherby was, even in her own home. No wonder she'd had no trouble making herself heard in the church hall. But she was kind too, and made you feel very welcome.

The bedroom took Nell's breath away. It was far more luxurious than any she'd ever slept in before – fit for a duchess, with a shiny satin quilt. Just plain cream in colour, with satin stripes round the edges in the same colour. It'd show the dirt. 'What a beautiful room!'

'Call me Joanna.' She stared round. 'It is pretty, isn't it? My sister's the one who sorted out the house. Flora's good with that sort of thing. My husband had to put up with me, poor lamb, and unfortunately I've got no eye for decorating. It was a wonder he chose me and not Flora, but we got on so well, never stopped talking.' She paused to sigh regretfully, then raced on again.

'Pity Flora never married. Lucky for me, though. We rub along together very well, and we both enjoy hiking.'

She opened the top drawer so vigorously it nearly fell out. 'You can put some of your things in here and hang the rest in the wardrobe. No need to get your clothes creased before you start off. Come down soon and we'll have a tea tray waiting for you.'

She picked up the suitcase and dumped it carelessly on the beautiful quilt, which made Nell gasp in dismay.

'Good that your suitcase isn't too heavy. You can't take too much with you when you're hiking.'

It only took Nell a few minutes to unpack. She went to glance out of the window. The weather was closing in and clouds were chasing one another across the sky. It'd be raining soon, but even so, the garden looked pretty, with soft pinks and mauves, and so many flowers she didn't even try to work out their names.

She felt rather nervous of taking afternoon tea with the two ladies, but they were so friendly she found herself eating with a good appetite for the first time in ages. She didn't make a fool of herself because she'd been observing the Garretts' table manners for weeks and had learned to eat in the same way.

Once they'd finished, the tea tray was carried away by the maid and Joanna went across to take a piece of paper off the mantelpiece and wave it triumphantly. 'We've been doing some calculations and this is a list of what you'll need.'

Nell studied it in silence. A good tweed skirt and matching jacket, a knitted waistcoat, a mackintosh, two blouses, two Princess petticoats, three pairs of knickers with three sets of detachable stockinette linings for each, several pairs of good, black, wool stockings, stout boots, knitted slippers and a soft felt hat. Rags for her monthlies. The latter were going to be hard to deal with, even with the hints the ladies had given her. Knapsack, money belt, writing materials and a book.

Joanna cleared her throat and asked gruffly, 'Can you afford all that?'

'Oh, yes. My husband had taken out life insurance, so I have over a thousand pounds. But I think I need to change to two savings bank accounts. I don't want to take my main bank book travelling with me.'

'Good thinking. You're a sensible woman.'

Flora smiled at her from across the room. 'I'll take you shopping tomorrow for whatever you still need, especially a good pair of boots. Joanna doesn't have the patience to shop all day.'

'Can't abide crowds,' her sister said cheerfully, continuing to speak so loudly Nell was beginning to wonder if she was going deaf.

'I love shopping,' Flora said. 'Not that we can buy you the pretty things you deserve, not if we're to be practical. But you have a lovely face and figure, and you'd look charming if you took a bit more care. I know a better way of doing hair that would suit you and it's very practical for hiking. I'll show you tomorrow.'

Nell was surprised to be described as lovely. Cliff used to call her pretty once, when they were courting, though not once had he said it after they'd had to get married. She'd grown used to thinking of herself as past such vanities. But she was only twenty-three. That thought came as a shock. She wasn't old yet, even though she felt it sometimes. She stole a glance at herself in the huge mirror over the fireplace. She looked very different from the naive girl who'd run away from Swindon, but . . . not in a bad way.

'I'll help you plan your route after we've eaten,' Joanna said. 'We've plenty of maps. You'll need to buy a good one for yourself while you're out.'

They went on to show her some photos of their hiking holidays. They looked so happy and healthy. She wanted to be like that. Not to forget Sarah – as if she ever could – but to make a decent life for herself and to move forward with confidence.

The evening meal was served at the late hour of seven o'clock, which surprised Nell. She watched how the ladies dealt with the cutlery and water glasses, but even a more elaborate meal wasn't a problem, because she enjoyed eating daintily. A sudden memory of her father shovelling food into his mouth, burping and chewing noisily, made her shiver. What was he doing now? Had Mattie got away from him as well? Surely she must have done? Mattie was so clever, she'd not have been caught.

When Joanna had gone to find a map, Flora said quietly, 'My sister's enjoying helping you with this. It's what she wished she'd done when her husband died. It's over ten years now, but she still thinks of him, says she'll never remarry. But you're much younger than she was when she was widowed. I just wanted to assure you that time's a great healer.'

Nell couldn't pretend with these two. 'I didn't love my husband. It's my little daughter I'm grieving for. She died in the same accident.'

'Oh. I'm sorry. I didn't know.'

'My husband wasn't a kind man and it was his meanness that killed our daughter.' She hadn't meant to

163

go into any details and snapped her mouth shut before she made herself cry.

Flora leant forward to clasp her hand for a moment. 'I'm sorry. I'm sure spending some time in the fresh air will do you good.'

The wind howled suddenly round the house and she grimaced. 'As soon as the weather improves, of course. If it rains when you're hiking, as it will, find the nearest town and stay in a good hotel. Buy yourself a book or two and have a nice rest.

'You could write a diary, though it'd be better to buy a fountain pen for that. It'd give you something to do in the evenings. Dear Joanna always frets when we're hiking and it rains, but who can control the weather?'

Chapter Nine

Shopping with Flora was another revelation. They went first to the bank, where Nell drew out twenty pounds. She hesitated to take so much, but she didn't have to spend it all, did she?

She was thrilled by the huge department store, Kendal Milne. She'd never seen anywhere like it and could have spent a whole day just walking round, looking at displays of goods, some of which she hadn't known existed. The ladies' clothes were so elegant she kept stopping to sigh over something. Imagine living your life dressed in clothes like those.

The shop had a tunnel under Deansgate, so that you could walk to the annexe without getting wet or having to cross the street through the busy traffic. It was just another thing done for the customers' comfort.

The prices shocked her at first, but she hoped she'd hidden that.

She clearly hadn't, because after a while Flora looked at her thoughtfully. 'It's too expensive here for you, isn't it?

We always shop here because our mother and grandmother did, but we can go and look at Lewis's, if you like. I'm told their prices are cheaper, but their goods are still of excellent quality.'

'Yes, please.' No matter how much money she had, Nell didn't think she could spend two guineas on one pair of boots. She just couldn't.

She stopped dead in the street at the sight of Lewis's Department Store, which was even more imposing. It had a tower on the street corner, and rows of big windows along the two street frontages that met beneath the tower. Surely the goods sold here would be as expensive as those in Kendal Milne's?

But no, they weren't, and though she spent a lot of money, she knew the brown tweed suit she'd bought would wear well. The skirt was less full than she'd been used to, but that seemed to be the fashion for 'country garments'. It came barely to her ankle, with flat front and back panels, but side panels with gores so that you could stride out. The jacket came to just below her hips, and was double-breasted, with a belt and flat pockets on each side.

As for the boots, they felt instantly comfortable, something she hadn't found with the second-hand shoes she'd had to put up with in the past few years.

'Don't skimp on boots,' Flora whispered. 'You'll be doing a lot of walking. And you'll need another pair of lighter shoes for the evenings, don't forget.'

Nell hesitated over some practical golf shoes, then, as her companion pulled a face at them, she gave in to temptation and bought some black leather shoes, with a petersham bow trim across the front, pointed toes and one-inch Cuban heels. They were so pretty she couldn't resist them.

'They must sell everything on the face of the earth in this store,' she whispered to Flora.

'They like to think so. I must say, I think my mother was wrong and the things they sell are of just as good quality as in Kendal Milne's. I shall persuade Joanna to come here next time, for a change. Now, how about that tam-o'-shanter instead of a hat? No, better get a hat with a brim in case it rains. Felt's more practical than straw for the weather.'

Nell felt overwhelmed and had stopped keeping track of how much she'd spent.

'You need at least one pretty blouse for best,' her mentor said, 'and some much prettier underwear. Ribbon trimmings are very fashionable and Princess petticoats are practical as well as pretty.'

'But there's no one to see them! What does it matter if I buy the plainer ones?' Nell protested.

Flora stopped dead in the aisle of the shop. 'Are you "no one"? Don't *you* count? And you're twenty-three not fifty-three, so why choose dowdy clothes?'

Nell couldn't think what to say to that, but judging by the little nod of satisfaction Flora gave, her expression said it for her. She bought the pretty underwear and a charming nightdress too.

'What about a corset?' Flora asked in a whisper.

'I don't wear them,' Nell admitted. 'I'm so thin I don't need to control my figure. And anyway, I could never afford them . . . before.'

'I envy you. My sister and I are too big-built to go without. Though you're not flat-chested.' She moved on from the corsetry counter.

Nell was relieved. To preserve the decencies and save money, she and her sisters had always made themselves bust bodices from strips of material gathered down the centre front, with ribbon straps and a two-button fastening at the back. The boned bust bodice she'd seen on display in a corner would probably be uncomfortable for walking. Richer women might be happy to sacrifice comfort for elegance, but she wasn't.

When everything on the list had been covered, Flora said thoughtfully, 'You really ought to buy some sort of a timepiece. How about a pendant watch to pin inside your jacket?'

The idea was good, but Nell didn't want to spend a lot more money. 'Could we buy one second hand, do you think?'

Flora looked at her in shock, then gave a wry smile. 'You're right. You have to be careful. I know some jewellers sell good quality second-hand goods.'

'I'll look for one tomorrow, then. We've too many parcels to do it today.'

Before they left the store, they added one more parcel, because Flora insisted on buying her a copy of Arnold Bennett's *Clayhanger* as a present. 'I know it's a large book, but it'll last you longer and I'm sure you'll enjoy it.'

Nell clutched the package, thrilled by this. She'd never owned a brand-new book before.

Flora insisted on taking themselves and their parcels

home by cab, another extravagance for which she insisted on paying. But what was one more thing after a day's spending that made Nell feel breathless at the thought of how much money she'd gone through?

The following day Nell went with Joanna to the local branch of her savings bank and asked to withdraw a hundred and ten pounds.

The cashier frowned at her bank book, then looked at her and summoned the assistant manager to attend to them.

'My dear. young lady, that's a rather large amount of money. Are you sure you need it all? You drew twenty pounds out yesterday, after all. Does your husband know what you're doing?'

He'd spoken to her so patronisingly, she answered quite sharply, 'That's my own business, I think. And I'm a widow. But I've changed my mind about the money. I'll withdraw everything but a thousand pounds.'

He looked at her in outrage at this increased amount, then turned to Joanna, as if asking her to help him. She stared back at him without a change of expression.

Nell leant forward. 'And if you try to tell me what to do with my own money again, I shall move my whole account to another bank.'

'Very well, Mrs Greenhill. As you wish. I was only offering you guidance out of the best intentions.'

Outside Nell let out her breath in a whoosh. 'How dare he question what I wanted to do with my own money! And why?'

'Because of the way you're dressed, I'm afraid. I

suspect he thought you were my servant. You did right to stand your ground. Never let people like him boss you around. It's your money and you have every right to do what you want with it. After my husband died, people tried to tell me what to do, but I wasn't going to have that. And if you want to know, *I* think you're being very sensible about how you're making your arrangements.'

They walked to the nearest Post Office Savings Bank and Nell opened an account there, putting in the money she'd withdrawn. She felt easier in her mind not to be carrying several hundred pounds around with her and was careful to push her new bank book into the pocket in her handbag for safety. Even the couple of guineas she had left in her purse seemed a huge sum after the way she'd had to count every farthing for so many years.

Once that was done, they went to hunt for a jeweller's shop which sold second-hand goods, but on the way there, they passed a clockmaker and saw some watches in the window.

Nell found a pendant watch there at only a pound, rather battered but good enough for her purpose. It had a keyless winding system, in which the watch itself was rotated against the back.

'It's a good one, that, for all it's had a hard life,' the clockmaker told them. 'Don't know how it got so battered, but it hasn't affected the works. I checked that when it was brought in. I don't sell anything that isn't in good working order.'

When they got back, Nell and Joanna went over the route again. They'd decided she should start in Cheshire, perhaps in Cheadle, and move first towards Wilmslow and Knutsford, then across country to Chester, from where she would have a choice of routes.

'No use walking through miles of suburbs,' Joanna said. 'No sounds of nature or pretty views to gladden your heart there.'

Would they gladden her heart? Nell wondered. When she was alone with her thoughts, would trees and streams be enough to divert her from her sad memories? But already she was less lost in her grief, because she'd found something to do. It made her feel guilty sometimes, but people were right: life had to go on.

Being with the two ladies had helped her a lot as well, especially seeing the way Joanna had made a new life for herself after losing the husband she'd clearly loved at a young age.

Nell felt only relief to be away from Cliff, but oh, she still ached for Sarah, had never yet gone to bed without shedding a few tears for her daughter.

She wrote a letter to the Garretts, thanking them for their help and explaining that she'd decided to start hiking after all, and was leaving from Manchester. She enclosed her old bank book and asked them to look after it till she sent for it, because she didn't want to risk carrying it with her. It wasn't an easy letter to write, because she knew they'd be upset and worried about her.

She then had the even more difficult task of writing to Renie, trying to explain to her sister what she was doing and why, knowing Renie would be hurt. She ended with a promise to send postcards whenever she could, and on that thought, she went back to add the same promise as a PS to her letter to the Garretts.

'I shall leave tomorrow,' she announced when she went down for dinner.

But the weather prevented that. She woke in the night to hear rain pattering lightly against the windowpanes. The grey skies and low cloud that greeted her in the morning promised more rain to come.

'You'll have to stay another day or two,' said gruff Joanna. 'Plenty of books to read. No use fretting.'

'I'm being a nuisance.'

'Bless you, no! If we can help you . . . at this time . . .' She whisked out her handkerchief and blew her nose hard, then changed the subject.

She was very brave. That was the only time she'd become emotional, while Nell often had to fight against tears.

Nell was on edge for the whole time she waited for the weather to clear up. She wished now that she hadn't posted the letter to the Garretts. What if they came searching for her, tried to insist on her returning?

Frank Greenhill arrived in Milnrow in the evening, after a long day's travelling. How stupid it was to have to change trains whenever you moved from the territory of one railway company to another! On some stretches there were through carriages, which were unhooked and connected to another engine, which was better. But it still delayed you. There wasn't even one of those on this trip.

By the time he'd made a second change of train at Birmingham New Street, he was in a foul mood. Who cared whether the London & North Western Railway owned this stretch of track? All he wanted was to travel as quickly as possible to his destination, to stop that fool of a woman wasting his cousin's money.

Of course, he had to change trains again at Manchester, didn't he?

Luckily, he was in the same lodgings as last time. He'd go and see *her* first thing tomorrow morning and make it plain that if she wanted a peaceful life, she'd have to share her money with the family. It was only right. Cliff would have expected that.

And Frank had an idea about how he could get his hands on all the money.

Nell was woken at just before six by the sun shining through a gap in the curtains. She slipped out of bed and went to draw the curtains back, revealing sunny skies and a freshly washed world. The beauty of it all enticed her to stand by the window for several minutes. She seemed to crave the beauty of nature.

Excitement filled her. Time to be on her way.

She visited the bathroom, lingering for a moment to look at the wonderful fitments. She'd miss the luxury of having a water closet indoors and a bath where you just turned on the tap and hot water came out.

In her room she dressed in her new tweed skirt and jacket, and packed her rucksack, something she'd already practised doing. It was a bit heavy, but she needed everything she put in it, and she definitely wasn't leaving out her precious new book.

By the time she went down to the kitchen for breakfast, she was ready to leave, and it was still only half past seven.

Mary greeted her with a smile and said she'd bring a cup of tea through to the breakfast parlour.

'I need to have my breakfast early, if that's all right, so perhaps I should eat it in here. I'm leaving today, you see, as soon as I've eaten and said goodbye to your ladies.'

'They're both awake and I've taken their tea up. If you're in a hurry, you could knock on their bedroom doors to say goodbye, then have a quick breakfast in here. If you don't mind doing that, miss.'

Nell beamed at the maid. 'I'm happy to eat in here. I'll go and see them now.'

She knocked first on Joanna's door, then Flora's, but they both insisted on coming down in their dressing gowns to say goodbye properly, which delayed things.

She ate her breakfast to the accompaniment of more advice, mostly things being repeated. She'd have liked to push her plate away and simply leave, but they'd been so kind to her, she couldn't do that.

At last the meal was over and Mary presented her with some sandwiches wrapped in greaseproof paper plus a couple of apples and three wedges of heavy fruit cake, the latter being highly recommended by Joanna as one of the best foods for the road. She had to carry that in a little cloth bag Flora found for her, with long handles that fitted over her shoulder. She wondered if it was worth carrying this extra weight, because she had been planning to buy food en route. But once again, she didn't want to upset kind people who were trying to help her.

As she stepped across the threshold into the bright sunshine, Nell felt a sudden stab of nerves, then told herself not to be silly. This was what she wanted . . . needed . . . *had to do*, to prove she was worthy of being alive when others were dead. She couldn't explain it any better than that, even to herself.

She forced a smile as she submitted to sudden extra hugs, then set off at a smart pace down the road, not looking back.

Frank knocked on the front door of the minister's house at eight o'clock in the morning. He didn't intend to give *her* time to go out.

Mr Garrett opened the door and looked at him blankly.

'I'm Frank Greenhill. I came up for my cousin's funeral. Can I see Cliff's wife, please?'

'Oh yes, I remember. But don't you live in Swindon?'

'What's that to do with anything? I came to see Cliff's wife.'

'Nell's not here.'

'This early? Where's she gone? It's important I see her. Family business.'

Mr Garrett hesitated, then said, 'Come in. We had a letter from her yesterday. She's in Manchester. Or at least, she was in Manchester. I'm not sure if she's still there.'

By the time he'd explained what Nell was planning to do, Frank was feeling furious. He kept his anger hidden.

'Could you give me the address of these ladies, please? It's Cliff's parents, you see. They're in a right old state and they need to see her.'

Mr Garrett hesitated, then wrote down the address on a piece of paper.

Frank went straight to the railway station. He couldn't

believe that two women could be so stupid as to go off hiking like men. And then tell others to do the same. Women's place was in the home, looking after their husbands and children.

He'd make sure Nell gave up the idea. Hiking! Of all the stupid things!

It just went to prove that she wasn't fit to handle so much money.

Sticking to the plans Joanna had helped her make, Nell started her travels by taking a bus into the city centre, from which she had to get a train out to Cheadle.

To her horror, in the railway station she saw Frank Greenhill. At first she thought she was mistaken, but no, it was him. He had an angry look on his face. What was he doing back in Lancashire? She slipped behind a kiosk, but kept an eye on him.

He was obviously asking directions. He went to wait at the bus stop, and though it was risky to keep watching him, she had to see him leave. She was dismayed to see him get on a bus out to Joanna's area. He must be looking for her. Why?

And then she realised why. The insurance money. Somehow he'd found out about it. Well, the Greenhills weren't getting any of it. It was her security, her way of making a new life for herself.

She watched Frank get on a bus, and after it had pulled away, she went to find out about the next train to Cheadle. She kept an eye on the other passengers getting on to the train, and not until it pulled out of the station did she relax. She'd got away. He'd not find her now. She'd make sure of that.

When she got off the train, she stood in the entrance to the small station, trying to get her bearings. Two other passengers pushed past her, not caring who she was. But when a woman with two small children looked at her as if envying her freedom, it somehow gave Nell the courage to ask directions from her.

She followed these and was soon into the open countryside, not hurrying, taking time to stop and look round. She was pleased with the comfort of the boots, relieved to be on her way, terrified . . . all at the same time.

But surely there was no way Frank could follow her from now on? Especially if she didn't take a direct route. Or if she changed her destination.

At the next crossroads, she left the main road, turning down a lane. After walking for two hours, she sat by a little stream to eat her sandwiches. She hadn't enjoyed a meal so much for weeks, simple as this one was.

By mid afternoon she was tired and had decided to stop soon. When she came to a delightful little village, she went into the shop and asked if anyone let rooms to travellers. Joanna said that outside town, such enquiries often led you to decent places that took in visitors.

The woman behind the counter studied her for such a long time Nell began to wonder if something was wrong.

'Hiking, are you?'

'Yes.'

'On your own?'

'Yes. I'm a widow.' That sounded more respectable than a single woman, surely? 'My name's . . . Greenhill. My husband died recently and I needed to get away.'

The woman's gaze flicked down to her ring finger. Nell had taken off the wedding ring, but the mark it'd made was still there. 'Lost your ring?'

'No. I didn't want to be reminded of . . . anything.'

'Bad, was he?'

She was startled by that. 'How did you—?'

'You see a lot of things when you run a shop. People would be surprised sometimes at what I see.'

'Oh. Well . . . we weren't exactly happily married, I must admit.'

The woman's expression was now sympathetic. 'I have a spare bedroom and I do take in visitors. The room's free tonight, as it happens, but I'll need you out by nine o'clock so that I can change the bed. There's a commercial traveller comes every week. Four shillings a night I charge, and that includes a decent breakfast.'

Nell remembered Joanna's advice. 'May I see the room, Mrs—?'

'Cherley. And it's 'Miss'. I live here with my mother.' She lifted up the counter flap to let Nell through. 'It's downstairs, at the end of that corridor.'

The room was small and plainly furnished but clean, situated next to the scullery.

'We've not got a fancy bathroom but I'll bring you a jug of hot water at seven.'

Nell eased off her knapsack, which seemed to have grown heavier as the day progressed. 'The room is fine. Do you want me to pay now?'

'Morning will do. I'll just finish showing you round.' Miss Cherley led the way towards the back of the cottage and outside. 'The lavatory's over there. And you're welcome to sit in the summer house if you like. It's nice in there on a sunny day.'

There was a call from the shop.

'*Coming!* I'll have to leave you now, Mrs Greenhill. Make yourself comfortable. Tea's at six. My mother serves it, then takes over the shop to give me a rest. Unless we get busy.'

Nell was more tired than she'd expected. Back in the room she took off her boots and jacket, wriggling her toes and easing her shoulders, which still seemed to be carrying the knapsack. She donned her old pair of shoes, which she'd stuffed in at the last minute. Fancy owning three sets of footwear! She had the new shoes with her, but they were too good for walking round gardens. On that thought she took them out to admire them and stroke the shiny new leather. Like the walking boots, they fitted perfectly.

She didn't even bother to take her book but strolled outside, stopping to look at the ripe red strawberries and raspberries. The sight of them made her mouth water. She also recognised lettuces, spring onions, radishes, peas, beans, and surely those were carrot and beetroot tops? How wonderful to grow your own food, not to have to buy the cheap wilted ones from the market just before closing time!

In the summer house she found a wooden chair that was so comfortable she closed her eyes and leant back. She woke with a start to see an old lady smiling down at her.

'Tea's ready, Mrs Greenhill.'

'Oh, thank you. Sorry. I don't usually fall asleep in the daytime.'

'I've had many a good nap in here.' She patted Nell on

the shoulder. 'Healing, it is, a quiet place on a sunny day.'

Tea was delicious and did indeed offer her the produce of the garden. Cold meat, cheese and salad with crusty new bread, followed by strawberries and raspberries with cream. Nell couldn't resist the second helping she was offered of the latter. 'If you're sure you have enough?'

'Bless you,' said the old lady. 'We've plenty more where that came from at this time of year.'

'I've never tasted any fruit so delicious.'

Nell went to bed early, and for the first time since the explosion, fell asleep quickly.

She woke at six o'clock by her new watch, and lay listening to a wonderful chorus of birdsong until her hot water arrived at seven o'clock on the dot. She got ready in a leisurely way, studying her face in the mirror. You look thin and tired, Nell Greenhill, she thought, and your face is too pale. Well, time and an outdoor life would remedy that.

She enjoyed a delicious breakfast of porridge, followed by ham and eggs, with bread and butter and jam. She'd never eaten so heartily in her whole life.

Clearly, her hostess was itching to turn out the room ready for the next visitor, so Nell put the final things into her knapsack, consulted her map again and found a roundabout route to her next goal, Wilmslow. There was something about villages that made her feel better. They were not only pretty, but they weren't full of pushing, rushing people, as Swindon and Manchester had been.

She decided to avoid towns as much as possible, even if it took her longer to get to Chester. That thought made her stop. Why was she going to Chester, anyway? That had been Joanna's suggestion, but really Nell wanted to head south. She intended to be back in Wiltshire before winter set in, but she could take her time getting there.

In fact, she could do whatever she wanted. Oh, the joy of that!

She left immediately after breakfast, though it was still only half past eight. No need to walk briskly, she told herself. Hiking doesn't mean hurrying.

She stopped to rest after about an hour's steady walking, leaning on a fence to watch a mare suckle its foal in a field, stopping about a mile further on to sit for a while on a grassy bank in the dappled shade of some young trees.

Why people said the countryside was quiet, she didn't know, because there were plenty of noises: a chorus of the various bird songs and calls, not all of them pretty, insects buzzing, the occasional motor car or horse vehicle going past, a cow mooing in the distance, always something happening.

The air felt so clean she breathed deeply. Yes, spending time alone was the right thing to do, she was even more certain of that now.

Frank rapped on the door of the house, feeling a little wary because places like these belonged to the gentry.

A maid opened the door and looked down her nose at him. 'Tradesmen to the back door.'

'I'm not a tradesman. I've come to see Mrs Greenhill. I was told she was staying here.'

A lady came out of a room to one side. She nodded and the maid left. 'Can I help you?'

Frank breathed deeply. As if she hadn't overheard

him telling the maid what he wanted! 'I need to see Mrs Greenhill.'

She frowned as she looked at him. 'Why do you ask?'

'I'm her husband's cousin. I need to see her on important family business.'

Silence. Was she deaf?

'Nell's left. She's gone hiking. I couldn't say where she is now.'

'She must have said she was going somewhere!'

'No. That's the whole point. She's just enjoying the countryside, going where the whim takes her.' She reached out to shut the door but he held it open.

'Take your hand off that door or I'll call the police.'

He scowled and stepped back. The door shut in his face.

An hour later he returned, going along a little alley he found between the back gardens. They delivered coal and such this way, he'd guess. Well, he was going to deliver something else.

He waited to make sure no one was around, then hurled the stones at the greenhouse, smashing several windows. He didn't wait to see what happened, but ran off as fast as he could, smiling.

No one treated a Greenhill like that and got away with it.

But there was nothing to do then except go to the station and catch a train home. He thought about it as the train jolted along. It wasn't over yet. Nell would be bound to go back to Swindon in the end. It was where she and her family came from. He'd heard that one of her sisters was still living nearby in the country.

And he'd be waiting for Nell. He was going to get

hold of that money, whatever it took. He couldn't stop thinking about it, the unfairness of her getting it all.

Two days later Nell was south of Wilmslow. She hadn't gone far because she was enjoying visiting small country churches, stopping to read the inscriptions on the tombs or going inside and marvelling at the beautiful stained glass windows.

She hadn't known places like these existed. So many generations had come and gone in them and the continuity of that comforted her, told her not all children died. Many people had lived to a fine old age. It was comforting to find a seat in that softly coloured light from the windows and just sit quietly. So very comforting.

She was making for the village of Alderley Edge, hoping to spend the night there, then go up to the escarpment that Flora had told her about, south of the village. It apparently had beautiful views over the countryside. She couldn't get enough of beautiful views, had spent her whole life until now without knowing any.

That afternoon, however, the sky began to cloud over and the air became markedly cooler, with the damp feel of approaching rain. She decided not to get her umbrella and mackintosh out yet and trudged on.

A motor car approached from behind her and she stood to one side to let it pass. To her surprise, it stopped beside her. It was driven by a very modern young woman with such short hair Nell felt rather shocked by it. The woman had a small felt hat too, not like the huge ones ladies usually wore. Only she must be a lady to be able to afford a motor car.

'Would you like a ride? I don't think any more buses are due today.'

'Yes, please. I'm hoping to find somewhere to stay in Alderley Edge till the rain's passed.'

'Hop in, then. No need to get wet. I'm going there too and I bet we beat the rain.'

She talked non-stop while driving at a breakneck speed through the narrow lanes. Nell found she only needed to make appropriate noises or comments every now and then to keep the conversation going.

And indeed her good Samaritan did get them into Alderley Edge just as the first drops started to fall. 'You could ask for a room at the hotel,' she said as she stopped to let Nell out. 'Hope you enjoy your walking holiday.'

'I'm sure I shall. Thank you so much for giving me a lift.'

'My pleasure. Us modern women must help one other, don't you think?'

Modern women? Was she one of those? Nell wondered. She smiled. Perhaps she was now.

The hotel looked expensive, but the rain was getting heavy, so she hurried across to the shelter of its entrance. Still she hesitated. She didn't want to be extravagant with her money, just couldn't, and anyway, the couple who passed her and went inside looked so well off, she felt out of place, especially in her hiking gear.

Taking out her umbrella, she set off walking along the street. When she found a greengrocer's, she bought two apples and asked the motherly woman there about finding lodgings for a night, or perhaps two if the rain continued.

Once again, she was scrutinised, but today she'd put on

her wedding ring, hoping it would help convince people that she was respectable.

'On your own, love?'

'Yes. I'm a widow. I'm taking a walking holiday.'

Another searching look, then, 'The lady at the bookshop lets out a room sometimes. Mrs Brinkley. She's a widow too. You could go and ask her. She's very sharp-spoken, but that's just her way. She's got a good heart.'

'I'll do that. Thank you.'

It wasn't just a bookshop. Crammed into its tiny interior were notepaper, pens, pencils, envelopes, blotting paper, simple account books and many more items for writing.

Mrs Brinkley was indeed blunt, questioning Nell at length before she agreed to let her have the attic bedroom for a night or two, and to provide breakfast and evening meals.

'Nothing fancy, though.'

Nell was delighted to find that the room looked out over the street and spent a few minutes watching people scurry past. This place was much more her style than a fancy hotel.

Later that day she bought three picture postcards from her hostess and wrote to her sister and friends. The evening meal was plain but adequate and once again she slept well.

The following morning, in between showers, Nell went to find a postbox. It felt like a burden off her shoulders to have sent the postcards. Her friends and sister would know she was all right and she'd remain free to do what she wanted because she couldn't give them an address to write back to.

When she got back, she found the redoubtable Mrs Brinkley in tears, clutching a crumpled telegram. 'What's wrong? Can I help?'

'I got this a few minutes ago. My older brother's ill, not expected to recover. I have to go to him. Only he lives in Stockport and I've no one to mind the shop. I don't want to upset my customers by closing. You have to provide a service or they go elsewhere.'

The doorbell tinkled and a lady came in. 'Just looking at the books, Mrs B,' she called to the owner.

Nell lowered her voice. 'Shall I make you a cup of tea? And I can keep an eye on the shop while you decide what to do. I'm sure your customer won't mind if I serve her.'

'Mrs Rawson likes to find her own books, doesn't like to chat. Are you sure you don't mind?'

'I'm happy to help.'

Quarter of an hour later, Mrs Brinkley came back into the shop just as Nell was wrapping a book for an elderly gentleman, folding the brown paper carefully round it and tying the string into knots that gave it a little loop for carrying. She put the money in the till and turned to her hostess.

'Your lady bought a book as well. I didn't call you, because you've pencilled in the prices. Was that all right?'

'Yes, and thank you. I needed time to think. Look, I wonder . . .' She stared at Nell, took a deep breath and said, 'You have an honest face.'

'Um . . . thank you.' She looked at Mrs Brinkley in puzzlement.

'Are you in a hurry to leave Alderley Edge?'

'No. I'm not in a hurry to go anywhere.' She suddenly guessed what was coming.

'Then would you look after my shop for me for a day or two? We have a lot of wealthy folk in the town since they built the villas, and some of them come in every week to buy a book. They might take umbrage if the shop was shut. Some people complain about the incomers, but they've been a godsend to me. I'll pay you a wage and you can have the room free – though you'll have to look after yourself.'

Two hours later, after giving Nell some hasty lessons on shopkeeping and introducing her to a neighbouring shopkeeper who would come in each evening to cash up, Mrs Brinkley left for the railway station.

It was strange being on her own in the shop, but Nell had no time to worry because there was a steady trail of customers, not only for the books, but for the writing equipment. Each one had to find out what had happened to Mrs Brinkley, so the day passed in a flash.

She hadn't realised she might be able to find work on her travels. Or that she'd enjoy it so much.

When the postcard arrived, Joanna pounced on it with a cry of triumph. 'She hasn't forgotten us.'

Flora came to look at the card. 'She sounds to be . . . I don't know . . . healing. Don't you think?'

'Yes. I'm so glad she got away before that dreadful man turned up. If he'd smash our greenhouse for no reason, who knows what he was intending to do to her. The only problem is, we can't warn her to watch out for him.'

'She'll settle somewhere, then we can tell her. I wish the police had caught him.'

'They can't even be sure it was him. No one saw him do it.'

'Who else could it be? I'm quite sure it was him.'

Mrs Brinkley sent a letter to the neighbouring shopkeeper two days later to say her brother had passed away and to ask how things were going. He came in to share the news with Nell and ask if she could continue looking after the shop.

'I'd be happy to do that. I'm finding it very interesting.'

He nodded approval. 'And I'm hearing that you have a nice manner with customers and are very helpful.'

She beamed at him, delighted by this praise.

When Mrs Brinkley came back three days later, she was so pleased with how Nell had managed that she invited her to stay on for two more days. 'You can't miss seeing the Edge. It's beautiful. My Dan and I used to go up there when we were courting.'

So since the weather had turned sunny again, Nell spent a magical day wandering through the woods, stopping every now and then to enjoy a particularly fine vista over the plain below, which was patterned with farms and chequered fields stretching into a misty heat haze in the distance. She'd heard the legends, but there was no sign of the White Wizard today, only dappled sunlight . . . and peace.

It was a full week after her arrival that she left, and she took with her a letter from Mrs Brinkley saying how helpful and hard-working she'd been.

'You might want to work here and there, since you're determined to tramp all over the place. It won't hurt to have testimonials, and if they want, people can write to me to check up on you. I don't mind. You were a godsend to me.'

Nell surprised herself by giving Mrs Brinkley a sudden hug. 'Thank you. You've helped me more than you know by trusting me.'

'Get along with you. I can't be doing with all this fuss.'

But she was smiling – and so was Nell as she went on her way.

Chapter Ten

Feeling much more confident, Nell travelled on. A leisurely week's walking brought her to Sandbach, a pretty little town with more of the attractive black and white houses scattered here and there. She stood at one end of High Street and decided to stay a night or two in more luxury. Somehow she had to do her washing and she desperately wanted a proper bath. She'd grown to love them at Joanna's house.

The small commercial hotel she found down a side street provided her with a comfortable room and a proper bathroom at the end of the corridor – baths sixpence extra. She washed her underclothes while she was bathing and got the use of the mangle from the owner, plus the loan of a clothes horse to dry them on in her room. It only just fitted in, but she didn't mind.

All the staff were polite and helpful, but clearly didn't care who she was or why she was hiking, as long as she paid for the room and behaved herself. She liked the sense of privacy that gave her.

At six o'clock, an excellent three-course meal was served. All the other diners were men. After a polite nod, they carefully avoided her eyes. She'd met quite a few commercial travellers on her travels, chatting to them inside shops or while waiting for the local carrier or omnibus to take her on a mile or two.

These men spent much of their working lives on the move, going from one small shop to the next to take orders. She didn't think she'd like that. Once she'd finished her travels, once she felt *right* again, she wanted to settle down and make a home for herself, however humble. And where else would she do that but Wiltshire, which increasingly seemed to beckon to her?

But she wasn't ready to catch a train and go there yet, because it would also mean going into Swindon and asking Cliff's parents if they'd heard from Mattie. It would take all her courage to do that. She was terrified of running into Frank, but if she went during working hours, surely she'd be able to avoid him.

And what if she bumped into her father? If Bart found out about her money, he'd never leave her alone till he got hold of it. Money had been his god for as long as she could remember, the thing he loved most in the world. That and beer. His daughters were only useful to look after him. He'd never really cared about them. It had been her half-sister Mattie who loved them when their mother died, Mattie to whom she and Renie turned when they were in trouble, Mattie who must be somewhere near Swindon, surely?

After she'd eaten, Nell retired to her room to finish the book Flora had bought her. She'd post it off to the Garretts the next day, to keep safely for when she was settled again.

The following morning, it being a Thursday, there was a market in Sandbach, so she lingered to wander round the stalls. She found one selling second-hand books, among other oddments, and picked up a much-worn copy of *Ziska*. She remembered Mrs Brinkley at the bookshop turning up her nose at Marie Corelli's books, saying that writer was only fit for giddy housemaids and wrote rather naughty stories. When pressed, she'd lowered her voice and said the author talked about feelings which were best kept in the bedroom between husband and wife.

Nell couldn't resist opening the book to see how it started, to see if it seemed at all naughty.

Dark against the sky towered the Great Pyramid, and over its apex hung the moon.

The image that conjured up was so vivid and so far away from her own troubles that she continued to read the first page, then bought the book. She liked the thought of being transported to ancient Egypt, even if she didn't believe a story like that could ever happen in real life.

'They always sell quickly, Corellis do,' the stallkeeper told her as he gave her the change. 'I read in the paper once that she sells more books than Conan Doyle, Kipling and H.G. Wells put together. Imagine that. She must be rich, lucky thing.'

Nell chatted for a while, then asked directions. But as she was about to set off on her travels, she thought she saw Frank at the other side of the market. For a moment she froze. It couldn't be!

The seconds seemed to tick past very slowly as she watched the man chatting to someone.

'You all right, missus?' the stallkeeper asked.

'What? Oh, yes. Just thought I saw someone I knew.'

She moved on a few paces, still watching the man, her heart pounding. Then he turned round and she sagged against a wall in relief. It wasn't Frank. It was just a big man who looked a bit like him. She must stop being so stupid. Frank Greenhill would soon forget about her. She'd not be going back to Swindon for weeks. And when she did, she'd take care to stay out of his way.

She followed a narrow road which she'd been told would take her southwards, her mood lightening as she left the busy market behind. She was hardened now to tramping all day, loved the countryside and looked forward every day to new sights and experiences.

It wasn't wrong to feel better, was it? Life had to go on.

It was a good thing the weather stayed fine, because two nights later she arrived at a tiny hamlet where, to her dismay, no one took in guests. 'How far is it to the next village?'

'Four miles.'

'Oh dear, and is there no carrier or motor bus?'

'Not in these parts, nor we don't want them smelly things coming here, neither. You can't beat a horse, I say. You know where you are with a horse.'

'Do you have a loaf left? And some cheese?'

She set off again, cutting the end off the loaf with the one knife she carried, because she was too hungry to wait. She munched it as she walked, together with a piece broken off the white, crumbly local cheese, because she wanted to find somewhere to sleep before dusk.

Suddenly she cried out in shock as she felt her foot

turn on a stone and couldn't stop herself falling. Pain shot through her ankle and she lay on the ground for a minute or two, waiting for it to subside. When she tried to move her foot, she yelped as pain jabbed up her lower leg. There was no one to help her and her right ankle was swelling fast. What was she going to do? She couldn't lie here in the road all night.

She tried getting to her knees, but banged the ankle again and moaned.

'Ought to put it in some cold water,' a voice said behind her. 'Gran made me dangle my foot in a stream when I hurt it.'

She jerked in shock and twisted round to see a plump dark-haired lad standing looking down at her. He made no attempt to help her get up.

'Could you help me stand up, please?'

He edged backwards. 'Mustn't touch people.'

'Well, could you go and find someone else to help me?'

He considered this, frowning.

She looked at him in puzzlement. What sort of person didn't immediately go to the help of someone who'd had an accident?

'I'll go and ask Gran,' he said, and before she could say anything, he shambled off along the lane in the direction she'd been heading.

She could only pray that he'd tell someone and they'd come to help. She thought it was only a sprain, but it was badly swollen and looked bruised. With some difficulty she managed to crawl to the grass verge, but the pain of moving knocked her sick.

The boy had been right about one thing: the foot ought

to be immersed in cold water. She told herself she could do nothing but wait – and hope. It'd probably take a while for him to get to the next village. Surely he would fetch help, though?

To her surprise, however, she heard voices only a few minutes later and saw a group of four, two men, an older woman and the same lad, come striding along the lane towards her. From the looks of them, she suspected they were Gypsies. She'd never had anything to do with Gypsies but people didn't speak well of them. Would they help her? Would she be safe with them?

The woman was older and the others held back as she approached Nell. She knelt down and stared at her, such a piercing gaze that Nell felt as if her very soul was under scrutiny.

'I'm Vancy Rose, but most folk call me Gran.' She checked the ankle with fingers that were very gentle, then turned to the young man standing next to her, a big fellow with dark unruly hair. 'We can't leave her lying here. You and Saul better carry her back. She's only a little 'un.' With that she turned and strode away along the lane.

Nell stared up at the young man who'd been told to carry her.

He smiled. 'Don't look so frightened. We're not going to hurt you. I'm Lije, this is Saul and the boy's Rory. We'd better get that knapsack off you. Saul, you carry her things and I'll carry her.' As he was speaking he began to slip the knapsack straps off Nell's shoulders. As he handed it over, he said firmly, 'And no touching anything in it.'

Saul pulled a face at him, picking the knapsack up as

if it weighed nothing and slinging it carelessly over one shoulder.

The youth hopped from one foot to the other. 'I found her, didn't I, Lije? I found her.' Then he saw the bread and cheese she'd dropped and snatched it up off the road, cramming it in his mouth, heedless of the fact that it was covered in grit.

'Sorry about that,' Lije said. 'The poor lad is always hungry. But I don't suppose you'd have eaten it after it fell in the dirt.'

'No. He's welcome to it.' She'd realised by now that the youth was slow-witted, poor fellow.

'What's your name?'

'Nell Greenhill.'

He looked down at her left hand. 'Where's your husband?'

'Dead.'

'Don't you have friends or family to stay with? Even *our* women don't usually go travelling round the countryside on their own.'

He swung her up in his arms and she forgot to answer, because that made her feel helpless yet protected, which was such a relief, though it took her breath away to be so close to his big warm body. Cliff had been thin and wiry, not much taller than her, but Lije was even taller than her father, and he was muscular and tanned from an outdoor life. But he wasn't like Bart Fuller. Lije had a cheerful friendly face, and she didn't feel at all afraid of him.

'Take a fall, did you?' he asked as he began walking.

'Yes. My own fault. I wasn't watching where I was putting my feet. Are you taking me to the next village?'

'No. To our camp. It's much closer.'

She wasn't sure she liked the thought of that.

As if he'd read her mind, he said quietly, 'No need to be afraid, Mrs Greenhill. We've never murdered anyone yet. Gran'll look after you. She's a great one for waifs and strays, Gran is. She says if you're kind to others, the world'll be kind to you.'

'It's a nice thought.'

'But you don't believe it?'

'No.'

Another of those assessing looks. 'I think the world's been unkind to you.'

She couldn't bear to talk of that, so shook her head slightly and looked away. To her relief, he respected her silence.

It only took them a few minutes to walk down the lane and turn off it onto a narrow track. The other man hadn't said a word the whole time. He moved forward to open a gate to the left and checked that the lad shut it carefully after them.

'We camp here every year at this time,' Lije said. 'The farmer doesn't mind as long as we don't steal anything or make a mess. And we don't. We always give him a couple of our baskets in thanks. And pegs. People always want pegs.'

'Sick of the sight of the damn things, I am,' Saul muttered.

'Language! We have a lady here,' scolded Lije.

Saul shrugged and moved slightly ahead.

They turned into a field and there in the corner were several Gypsy caravans, colourful ones which looked well cared for, plus a couple of small carts. The vans were gathered in a sociable way round a central fire, with the horses standing together nearby, as if they too enjoyed company.

As Lije walked across to the most brightly painted van, Gran came to the door and called, 'Take her to the stream first. She needs to soak that foot. Give it a few minutes, then bring her back to me and I'll bandage it.'

He changed direction, walking past the caravans, ignoring the people who stared and the children who whispered to one another. There was a stream at the lower end of the small field and he set her down gently on one bank. 'Better get your stockings off, unless you want to soak them too.'

She blushed, wondering if she could manage to do that without showing her upper legs. With some difficulty she managed to get her suspenders undone and started to push the stockings down, but it hurt too much to finish the job and she couldn't help whimpering in pain.

Lije bent down to lift her feet gently in turn and pull off the black woollen stockings. He chuckled. 'No need to blush. I've seen women's legs before more than a few times.'

He was surprisingly gentle as he helped her place her right foot in the chilly water flowing past, then the left one. 'There. That'll help.'

He went to sit on a nearby tree stump and wait. He didn't try to make conversation, so she didn't either. Then she realised something.

'My knapsack!'

'Saul will leave it with Gran and it'll be safe there. She'll look through it at what you've got, but she won't steal anything. She might offer to buy something, though. They don't like us going into shops, you see. Don't trust us.'

'It's mostly got dirty clothes in it.'

'You're blushing again. I never saw such a lass for blushing. My sisters get their clothes dirty too. Do you think I'm too blind to see their underwear hanging out to dry? Don't you think they see my drawers whenever they wash 'em?'

'You're very blunt-spoken.'

He shrugged. 'I say as I see. And you're very closed to the world.' He laid one of his huge tanned hands on hers. 'It's a beautiful world mostly, you know, even if bad things happen. Listen to those birds getting ready to sleep. And look at the patterns in the water, or the way the setting sun's colouring the sky. I don't know how folk can bear to shut themselves away from it all.'

She followed his pointing finger from a row of birds in a tree, to the water, which was starting to reflect the red-gold of the sky, and then she looked up to the sky itself. 'It is beautiful.'

'And that beauty's free for all who bother to stop and look at it.' He closed his hand over hers and gave it a quick squeeze. 'It'll come better, lass. Whatever it was that hurt you, it'll come better.'

She didn't try to answer that, continuing to enjoy the sunset sky. After a few minutes the pain of the cold water on her ankle brought her attention back to her present problem and she eased one foot out of the water.

'Probably had enough for now. Let's get you back to Gran. Here, hold tight to your shoes and stockings.' He dumped them in her lap, scooped her up and carried her back to the caravans.

Gran was sitting outside hers and stood up as they approached. 'Bring her inside and I'll bandage that foot.'

When Nell was lying on a padded bench that ran along part of the inside of the van, Gran told Lije to leave them to it and came to sit beside her with a roll of clean rag. 'Lift your skirt and I'll bandage it nice and tightly. It'll be all right in a day or two, though you'll not be able to walk much for a while. You might as well stay with us. We're not going anywhere for a day or two.'

Nell stared at her in surprise and Gran gave her a smile so like her grandson's that she looked suddenly much younger.

'Do you have room for me, Mrs . . . er . . . Gran?'

'If you're not too proud to use that bench for a bed. It's Lije's but he can sleep outside. He does that half the time anyway. Hates to be indoors, that lad does.' She continued to bind the ankle slowly, making sure the bandage would support her, but wasn't too tight. 'Hiking, were you?'

'Yes.'

'You won't be able to walk away from your troubles for ever, you know.'

'How did you—?'

'Sorrow in your eyes. And young women don't usually walk round the country on their own, even widowed ones.' She finished binding the ankle and fastened the strip of clean rag with a safety pin.

Nell surprised herself by confiding, 'It helps to get out into the open air.'

'Yes, it'd help me too. But you're not a wanderer, not

really. You're a home body. I'll read your palm before you go.'

'You must let me pay you for helping me.'

Gran drew herself up. 'We didn't ask for payment.'

'But I usually pay for my night's lodging and food. That'd be only fair.'

'We'll see when you go. Up to you what you feel like giving us. If it's nothing, that's all right too.' She stood up. 'Now, I'm hungry, even if you aren't.'

'I am. There's some bread in my knapsack, and cheese. You could add them to the meal. No use wasting them.'

Gran nodded, as if in approval, and went to the knapsack. She seemed to know exactly where to find the food in it and Nell remembered Lije saying his grandmother would look through the things but not steal any of them.

Somehow she didn't mind that. Gran was like no one she'd ever met before but you couldn't help trusting her.

The next two days seemed unreal to Nell, more like a dream. The fine weather continued, so at first she sat on a blanket on the ground, propped against a wheel of the caravan. Everyone was busy, either doing the domestic tasks, caring for the animals, making baskets or carving things in wood, mainly clothes pegs.

She asked if she could help and they gave her peas to pod and carrots to scrape. Later, a woman brought a small baby across to her.

'Keep an eye on her, will you? Just for an hour. Don't want her to choke or cry herself silly, but I've got the washing to do.'

It took all Nell's courage to touch the baby when she

whimpered, then she picked her up and cuddled her, not caring if anyone saw the tears running down her cheeks. She saw Gran give her a sharp look, but no one came near her. And when the tears dried, she found herself enjoying the snuggly little baby.

Lije came back from the farm with a wheelbarrow full of big chunks of wood and a bucket with a lid. It was set carefully in the middle so that it couldn't fall over. 'Here's the milk, Gran.'

'Go and stand it in the stream, you fool, or it'll go sour.'

The old woman seemed to be directing all the activities. But even so, her fingers were always busy at other tasks. Today she was weaving a small dish out of long stalks of grass, a job that seemed very skilful.

By the third day Nell was able to limp round with the help of a walking stick Lije had made her from a fallen branch. When she stopped for a rest, Gran came to sit by her, bringing the little basket to work on as they talked.

'That's very pretty.'

'It's nearly finished. I made it for you.'

Nell was surprised. 'For me? Why?'

'To remember us by. We shan't meet again.'

'How can you be so sure of the future?'

Gran smiled very slightly. 'No one's sure of anything in this world, but I can sometimes see what's likely. When *I* read palms, I don't tell lies.'

'Oh.'

She reached out and picked up Nell's hand, staring at it for a while, then looking at her sympathetically. 'You've had a bad time, lost a child. That's why you were crying when you held Tiddy's baby.'

Nell swallowed hard, not wanting to talk about Sarah, and tried to pull her hand away. But Gran kept firm hold and turned back to the hand again.

'You'll find another child to love.'

'No one can replace my Sarah.'

Gran looked at her sadly. 'I know that. I've lost two children myself. But the child you meet will help fill the empty space inside your heart.' She ran her index finger lightly along the creases of skin on Nell's palm.

'Hope grows and hope fades, but things *will* get better. Watch out for three big trees on a hill. Elm trees. You'll have reached the end of this journey then. They'll shelter you for a time, those elm trees will.' She frowned. 'You have an enemy. Be careful of him.'

Nell looked at her in surprise. 'I can't think who would wish me ill.'

'Be careful,' Gran said again. She traced the creases. 'You'll never be rich, but you'll never be short of money, either. And you'll live a long life. Happy mostly, but sad sometimes, as all lives are. But there'll be enough happiness to keep you going steady-like. What more can any of us hope for? You'll find the person you're looking for, but the other person you love isn't where you expect.'

She let go of Nell's hand. 'Don't believe me, do you?'

'I . . . don't know. I've never had my palm read before.'

'Time will show if I speak true. Now, it's going to be raining tomorrow, but we'll be moving on anyway. We'll get you to a town and you can find a comfortable place to stay for a few days, till your ankle's better. Don't do too much walking, even then. Take things easy. You're not in a hurry, after all.'

'I still want to pay you and—'

Gran held up one hand in a gesture to stop her. 'Gifts are good between friends, but we'll not talk of payment. My granddaughter, Phenie, is getting married soon. She admired your pretty underclothes when she washed them. Would you miss one chemise?'

'No, of course not.' Nell limped across to her knapsack and took out one of her two spare chemises, not without a sigh. She hoped she could find another as pretty to buy. 'Give her this one.'

Gran shook her head. 'You should give it her, since it's your gift. I'll send her over.'

Phenie came to the caravan, looking rosy and happy.

'I heard you're getting married,' Nell said. 'I wanted to wish you well and give you a present.'

When she held out the chemise, Phenie's eyes widened incredulously. 'For me? Oh, it's lovely!' She held it against herself, beaming, gave Nell a quick hug, and under her grandmother's eyes, calmed down and said, 'I wish you happy travelling.'

When she'd gone to show the chemise to the others, Gran held out the little basket, which was now like a small flexible bowl. 'Won't weigh you down too much.'

Nell took it with delight. 'It's beautiful. How do you manage to make the tiny patterns so perfect in every detail? It's like lace round the edge.'

'I've been practising for longer than you've been alive. But people won't pay as much for these, because they're small. They want bigger things for their money. I still make my lucky grass bowls for family and friends, though.' She studied Nell, head on one side. 'I don't think you'll wake up crying for your child again. You will weep now and then when something reminds you – mothers do – but you'll sleep more soundly.'

'Thank you for everything you've done.'

'Only brutes walk past someone in trouble.'

Lije came to find Nell. He was driving a small trap with a piebald pony pulling it and took her to a bus stop, from where she could travel into Crewe. 'Take the time to get better before you set off again,' he said as he waited with her for the bus.

'Gran said that too, and I will. Thank you for your help, Lije.'

'My pleasure.' He fumbled in his pocket. 'Here. This is a present for the child you'll one day love.' He smiled at her surprise. 'Gran's not the only one who can sense the future. You'll see.'

The bus came just then and she only had time to cram his gift in her pocket and climb awkwardly on board. When she craned her neck to look behind them, she saw him driving off down the road, not looking back. She wished he'd stayed to wave her goodbye.

She pulled the small piece of carved wood out of her pocket and found it was a whistle with tiny flowers and insects carved in the surface. It was a delightful piece. Any child would love it.

But whatever Gran had said, she couldn't imagine loving a child again. It left you too open to hurt.

* * *

Crewe was big and grey, not at all to her taste now she'd grown used to the open countryside, though the people she asked directions from were friendly enough. The air tasted smoky, and when she ventured out of the lodging house she'd found in a quiet street, the smells weren't always pleasant.

The following day her ankle was feeling a lot better, so she walked slowly round Market Square and part-way along Victoria Street, looking at the shops. She came to a draper's which sold ladies' underwear, so bought another chemise to replace the pretty one she'd given to Phenie. This one wasn't nearly as pretty, so she couldn't resist buying some ribbon to trim it with, even though she told herself this was stupid because no one else was going to see it.

But she'd had so many plain and practical garments in her life, so many second-hand clothes, that something in her hungered for dainty things to wear. Flora had been right that she should buy pretty things for herself, for the sheer pleasure of it. Renie would approve of that too, she was sure.

She wondered how her younger sister was getting on, if she'd received all the postcards. And on that thought, she bought three more postcards to send to her friends and sister.

While Nell was at the boarding house, fretting at the limitations her ankle imposed, there was a minor crisis. The landlady's daughter, who helped her mother with the hard work of running it, scalded herself badly while her mother was out.

Nell heard the screams coming from the back of the house and hurried along from the dining room, which was also the day room, to see if she could help. She found Janie in the kitchen and made her hold the injured hand under the cold tap. While the girl did this, Nell picked up the ladle and some peas that had been knocked off the table, and calmed the child down.

By the time Mrs Ransome came back, Janie was cradling her scalded hand, wrapped in a clean tea towel, and Nell was shelling the rest of the peas.

After scolding her daughter for daydreaming again and getting into trouble, Mrs Ransome apologised to her guest. · 'It's not right that you should be doing that. But how I'm to get tea ready in time without Janie's help, I don't know. Those men are always hungry when they come back from work.'

'I'm happy to help with any chores that I can do sitting down,' Nell offered. 'I'm a little tired of sitting on my own, reading.'

Mrs Ransome hesitated. 'Well, if you're sure you don't mind.'

'I'm happy to help, truly.'

So Nell spent the rest of the afternoon in the cosy kitchen, chatting and working, peeling potatoes, chopping onions and beating some eggs for a pudding.

By the time she limped along to the dining room, the meal was almost ready.

At this place it was hard for the men to ignore her as they had in the hotel, since the six paying guests were all seated round the one table. Two of them lived there permanently, three were regulars who had rounds in the area. They were polite to Nell, but chatted mainly to one another about sales.

With a sigh, she prepared to go and sit in her room, knowing that if she sat with them after the meal finished, conversation would be limited.

She met Mrs Ransome in the corridor.

'Are you going to bed already? I'm sorry if I've tired you out, Mrs Greenhill.'

'It's not that. It's just that the men are more comfortable on their own. People are a bit suspicious about a woman travelling on her own.' Nell had been refused a room at the first two places where she'd enquired, and knew that was the reason. 'I'm grateful that you let me stay here.'

'I only usually take men, but I had a spare room and . . . well, you looked respectable enough to me.' She smiled. 'And it was for more than one night, which is a big help because I'm saving for a visit to my cousin. And you being a widow too, well, I know what it's like. Look . . . why don't you come and sit with me and Janie in the kitchen? If you don't mind, that is.'

'I'd be happy to.'

Mrs Ransome gave her a cup of cocoa when she took supper in to the men. After she came back, she sat down with a sigh to drink her own. 'I wonder . . . if you don't mind . . . and you must say if you do . . . Would you be willing to help me tomorrow? I can provide you with a midday meal and I'll charge you less for the room. But I do need a bit of help till Janie can put that hand in water again.'

'I'd be really happy to help you. I don't like sitting idle.'

Nell felt amused but relieved to think she looked respectable. The wedding ring helped, she was sure, but as soon as she no longer needed its protection, she was going to remove it. She didn't want to keep anything that reminded her of Cliff.

Frank ate his evening meal, sneaking a quick glance sideways at his aunt. She'd aged since Cliff died, looked ten years older. So had his uncle. He'd heard at work that his uncle wasn't up to it these days, and would soon be moved to light duties. They did that to you when you got old, the railway company did. Tossed you aside like a used rag.

His uncle wouldn't need to work at all if Cliff was still here. Frank's cousin would have looked after his parents. His uncle wouldn't need to work if he had a fair share of Cliff's money, either.

It was all *her* fault.

She'd come back one day. And Frank would be waiting. They'd been good to him after his parents died, his aunt and uncle had, and he'd look after them in return. Whatever it took.

Three days later Nell set off again, using a bus service to take her out of town and only walking slowly. Her ankle was much better now and Gran had been right. Nell hadn't woken up crying again. She still felt sad, but you couldn't undo the past, could you?

The sun was shining, warming her face when she stopped to turn it up to the sun, like some of the flowers did. Birds were singing and calling, and it lifted her spirits just to hear them and see them darting here and there about their business. When a skylark started singing somewhere above her, she stopped to listen to the beautiful sounds it made. She hadn't even known what a skylark sounded like when she started this journey.

Lije had been right. She wasn't in a hurry, should take time to enjoy the places she visited. Apart from anything else, it seemed she was learning a lot of lessons on her travels.

During the next few weeks, she wandered gradually southwards, stopping now and then to take on seasonal work. She picked strawberries, and later, plums, sleeping in a barn with the other workers and leaving her knapsack with the farmer's wife during the time she was working.

She helped out in a corner grocery shop for a few days, worked in a market for a morning, selling fruit and vegetables, and helped a farmer's wife spring-clean some attics. Two days that job took and they threw away a lot of things that might have been of sentimental value once, like a child's battered rocking horse, but were no use now.

Nothing lasted for ever, that said to her.

It seemed as if fate was tossing jobs her way, making sure she stayed in contact with people.

Some women were frankly envious of her freedom, others worried about how dangerous this hiking might be.

Once, when she was staying for a few days in a market town, acting as waitress and general dogsbody at a busy café, she debated telling her sister she could write care of the café. But in the end, she didn't do it. Renie might have come rushing to see her, and she wasn't quite ready for that yet. Anyway, the postcards would reassure her sister, stop her worrying too much.

She didn't tell Joanna or the Garretts exactly where she was, either. She felt as if she was living in a fragile soap bubble that softened the world around her, and didn't want anyone to disturb that.

Of course, as the weather grew colder, she'd have to think of settling somewhere in or near Swindon, but for the moment, this life suited her better than anything else she could think of.

Chapter Eleven

In September the leaves of some trees began yellowing and fluttering to the ground whenever a stronger breeze shook their branches. The weather became noticeably colder, especially the early mornings and evenings, though there were still some lovely days to enjoy. Nell bought a knitted scarf and a man's sweater with a high roll collar to wear during the cooler times of day – and sometimes in the unheated rooms in which she slept.

In the end, inevitably, she took the momentous decision to return to Wiltshire, but she still wasn't sure she wanted to live in Swindon again. She could have gone there in less than half a day by taking the train, but she wasn't quite ready for that yet, so simply turned south and didn't allow herself to be diverted from her chosen path from then on. Well, not very often.

One day she'd gone to see a small lake someone had told her about and spent an hour watching the calm water turn choppy and grey before moving on. She'd thought she was on the right track again, but the road turned into a country lane which began taking her towards the north-west, as far as she could work out from the rare glimpses of the sun.

When the land began to rise gently, she looked for a turning that led southwards again, but this new lane didn't meet any other roads, only the faint farm tracks.

Should she retrace her steps? No, not yet. She'd just find out where this led first.

Her thoughts turned to what she would say to Cliff's parents when she went to ask them if they'd heard from her sister Mattie. Somehow she could never find words that satisfied her, though she'd tried to rehearse what to say several times now.

Lost in thought, she stumbled and nearly fell, which brought her instantly out of her reverie. She didn't want another sprained ankle. A drop of water on her cheek was followed by others and she looked up in dismay. When had those heavy clouds piled up? How could she have missed the rain starting?

Thunder rumbled across the land. Oh, no! She didn't like thunderstorms at any time and was afraid of being caught outside in one. She stopped to get out her mackintosh and umbrella, then tramped doggedly on, doing her best to ignore the rain which the wind blew under her umbrella. She wouldn't melt, after all, and her knapsack was more or less waterproof, so she'd have some dry clothes to change into later.

Then she saw that her lane crossed another road – at last! – and this one was wider so must have more traffic. Thank goodness! She turned on to it, and as the wind grew stronger, she had to close her umbrella. Without its protection she quickly became a lot wetter and that made her feel the cold more.

About a mile further on she reached another junction. She hadn't dared follow any of the rough tracks that led off her road. They might lead to farms, but they might not.

This new road looked to be quite well used, and was wider than the one she'd been following. The problem was to work out which way to turn. There were no signposts, no houses where she could ask directions, only the sodden countryside and the road itself. Shrugging, she turned right and carried on. The road must lead somewhere, after all, whichever way she turned.

To her enormous relief, she came to a bus stop with a wooden shelter over it and a small bench inside. The shelter was rough and ready, as if someone had built it for their own convenience, so there must be a dwelling nearby, surely? It was afternoon now and sometimes in the country there was only one bus a day, or one carrier's cart that took passengers, but she could shelter and rest for a while.

She groaned in relief as she sat on the narrow bench, glad to take the weight off her aching feet for a few minutes. She'd walked a long way today. It was possible to put up her umbrella here if she held it close to her body, which gave her some shelter from the rain.

Why hadn't she taken more care about where she was going?

She felt so exhausted, she leant her head back against the rough wood and closed her eyes, trying to ignore the chill wind and the flurries of raindrops it tossed under her umbrella.

Once she'd had a rest, she'd start walking again.

Hugh Easton reined in his horse and trap, surprised to see a woman sitting at the bus stop. A stranger, slumped in a corner, with an open umbrella held sideways to protect herself. What on earth was she doing out here alone at this time of the afternoon?

When she didn't open her eyes or seem to notice his presence, conscience compelled him to call, 'Excuse me, but are you all right?'

As she opened her eyes, she shivered uncontrollably. 'What? Oh, I got lost, I'm afraid. Are any buses due, do you know?'

'There are no more today, I'm afraid.' He thought for a minute she was going to burst into tears, but then she straightened up and drew a deep breath as if pulling herself together. That brave gesture caught his sympathy.

'I'd better set off again, then. Could you please tell me which direction the nearest village is?'

Surely she wasn't intending to walk there? She looked chalk white and was shivering. He pointed to the right. 'It's three miles away in that direction.'

'Oh, dear. I need to find somewhere to stay for the night, then. Is there a farm or house anywhere nearer that takes in travellers?'

'Not that I know of. And the next village is tiny, more a hamlet, really. There's no inn there and only a handful of cottages, none of which have spare bedrooms. The farms round here are small too, and in any case, there aren't many of them near this road.' The horse fidgeted, but he held it back, not daring now to drive on and leave her. He didn't want to find her lying dead by the road the next day.

'Will there be someone in the village I can hire to drive me to the next town, then?'

'I doubt they'd do it today. There's been a funeral and they're all a bit upset.' Most of the men had gone to the pub for a drink and everyone was angry about the motor car that had knocked old Jud down and killed him. They weren't in the frame of mind to be kind to strangers, and had barely managed to be civil to Hugh, who was an incomer, even if he did have local connections.

'Look, I think you'd better come home with me for the night. It's another two or three miles beyond the village to somewhere you'd be likely to find lodgings and there's a storm brewing, a bad one by the looks of it.'

She looked at him suspiciously and he didn't blame her. She didn't know anything about him. But on the other hand, he couldn't leave her out here to die of exposure.

'Thank you, but I'm sure I'll manage. One of the farms may let me sleep in the barn. I've done that once or twice recently.'

'If you're short of money—'

The umbrella she was using to shield herself from sideways gusts flapped to and fro, nearly blowing inside out, and she had a struggle to hold on to it. 'I'm not short of money, but when you're hiking, you sometimes get caught away from hotels and lodging houses.' She gave up her unequal struggle and with some difficulty closed the umbrella.

'We don't get many hikers out here. Were you trying to find someone when you lost your way?'

'No. I was just . . . making my way gradually towards Swindon.'

'You've a good few miles to go yet.'

'Yes.'

Lightning speared down from a clump of black clouds and thunder boomed almost immediately afterwards. The horse tossed its head and struggled to set off for home.

'You really can't stay here,' he said again. 'The worst of the storm's just about to hit us. Look, my name's Hugh Easton. I live at Hilltop Farm, which is at the end of Elm Tree Road – that's what the next lane is called.' He smiled. 'It couldn't be called anything else with three huge elm trees at the end.'

She gaped at him. Three elms! The Gypsy's words echoed in her mind, as they had done every now and then since she left Gran and Lije. *Watch out for three big trees on a hill. Elm trees. You'll have reached the end of this journey then. They'll shelter you when you need it, those elm trees will.*

Lightning lit everything up in a brief eerie glow, followed by a long menacing growl of thunder. She was so cold she couldn't feel her fingers and toes, and he was right. If she didn't find shelter soon, she'd be in serious trouble.

Gran had predicted her coming here and hadn't

warned her of danger. Did she have any choice but to take his offer? But Gran had also warned her of an enemy. Nell studied his face carefully. His eyes were grey and very steady, the sort of eyes you trusted instinctively. No, this man couldn't be her enemy. She knew that instinctively.

'I'm not leaving you here alone,' he said again. 'I promise you'll be perfectly safe with us.'

He'd said 'us'. She supposed he was talking about his wife and family but was shivering too much to ask who exactly lived at the farm with him. 'Very well. Thank you.'

'Good. Can you toss your knapsack into the back of the trap without my help? Sandy here is a bit nervous of storms and I don't want to let go of the reins.'

'Yes, of course.' She put her umbrella and knapsack into the back, then looked at him, not sure whether he meant her to ride in the back too or to climb up next to him.

As if answering her unspoken question, he held out his hand to help her up. 'Be quick. We need to get you somewhere warm. You're as white as a sheet.'

She let him heave her up on to the bench seat next to him and pulled the neck of her mackintosh up as high as she could, dragging the sodden brim of her hat down to cover the gap. It was only after they'd been driving for a couple of minutes that she realised how closely she was pressed against him on the small seat. But his body felt warm next to hers and she couldn't bear to move away from that warmth. She couldn't ever remember being this cold.

They turned off the road onto a narrow track, and when

she looked ahead she saw them: three huge trees, spaced out along a V-shaped gully that was too small to be called a valley, but was deep enough to protect the trees and let them grow tall. Beyond the final tree there was a group of buildings, but she couldn't see them clearly because the rain was slashing down sideways.

Another shiver racked her.

'Soon be there,' he said quietly.

When they drew up at the rear of the house, an elderly dog came limping towards them, woofing hoarsely and wagging its tail. Her companion drove the trap towards an outbuilding with an open part attached, covered by a roof. The horse moved under its shelter and stopped, as if it had done this many times before. An old man came out from the interior of the barn, moving to the horse's head and beginning to gentle it.

'Thanks, Fred.' Mr Easton swung down with easy grace and hurried round to help Nell.

She was so stiff with cold she found it hard to move. It was a good job he kept hold of her for a moment or two, because she wasn't sure she could have stayed upright.

'All right now?'

'Yes. I was . . . stiff with cold.'

'Just a minute.' He reached into the back of the trap to get her knapsack, then took hold of her hand. 'Come on. Run!' He pulled her across the yard towards the shelter of a porch. She hadn't realised quite how tall he was, but she didn't feel at all afraid of his size as she had of Frank. Strange, that.

The door opened just as they got there, and a girl

who looked about ten years old stood back to let them inside.

'Don't let Blackie in!' the man said. 'He's soaked and must stay with Fred.'

She pushed the dog outside, murmuring something to it, and shut the door. The noise of the wind lessened.

'You're wet through, Uncle Hugh!' the girl said accusingly. 'I told you to take your mackintosh today.'

'I know. I forgot. This is—' He broke off to smile. 'Sorry. I didn't catch your name.'

'Nell Greenhill.'

His eyes went to her wedding ring. 'Is your husband expecting to meet you somewhere?'

She was so tired of answering this question. She was going to take that ring off as soon as she got to Swindon. 'I'm a widow.'

'I see. This is my niece, May.'

Nell nodded to the child. 'Is your wife not here, Mr Easton?'

'I'm not married. Fred's granddaughter, Pearl, comes in from the village Monday to Friday to look after May and me. The rest of the time we manage as best we can.' He grinned at the child. 'May's getting to be a dab hand at cooking, even though she's only ten, but I tend to burn things.'

'He can be very absent-minded sometimes.' The girl gave him a fond look.

He led the way along the corridor and into a big kitchen. Nell's worries about her safety receded still further. He seemed a decent chap and he'd saved her from a storm that was so bad it was now rattling every window in the house.

Even indoors, claps of thunder kept interrupting their conversation.

'May I go closer to the fire?' Without waiting for an answer, she moved across the room, stripping off her wet gloves and hat as she went. She heard him speaking to the child.

'Everything all right, May?'

'Yes. I don't like storms like this, though. I'm glad you're home safely. Pearl said it was going to be a bad storm, so she went home early. I've been stirring the stew she left and making sure it doesn't burn. Fred came in a couple of times to check I was all right, but I'm old enough to look after myself.'

A particularly loud boom of thunder made her stop speaking till it was over. 'Fred said this house has weathered far worse storms than this one, so I felt safe, but you were outside in it.'

'I got back before the worst. I had to post that parcel today and I wanted to pay my respects to Jud. The whole village was at the funeral.' He gave her a quick hug and they both turned round to face Nell. 'Mrs Greenhill got lost in the storm, so I brought her here to shelter with us tonight. I need to get her something warm to drink, and I'd like a cup of tea too.'

He pushed a kettle onto the hottest part of the kitchen range, threw another couple of pieces of wood onto the fire and left the front of the range open to let more heat out. When he'd done that, he pulled a chair closer to the fire. 'Here you are, Mrs Greenhill. Get that wet coat off and sit down. You look ready to collapse.'

'I'm stronger than I look, but it is a relief to get out of

the storm.' Nell took off her coat and then the sweater too, because it was sodden at the neck and cuffs. As she sat down on the hard wooden chair, she couldn't help shivering again.

May ran across the room to pull something off the coat hooks near the back door. 'You could wrap this round you, Mrs Greenhill. It's Pearl's, but she won't mind. She uses it sometimes in the winter when she has to go in and out a lot.'

'Thank you.' Nell wrapped the shawl round her shoulders, enjoying the softness of the much-washed old wool against her cold skin. 'This is a lovely warm room.'

Mr Easton went across to what must be the pantry, returning with a covered jug of milk. 'It's our favourite room in the house. May and I spend a lot of time here. Would you get the biscuits out, please, dear?'

Nell wondered where the child's parents were, but didn't like to ask.

He seemed to read her mind and said quickly in a low voice, 'My brother and his wife were killed last year in an accident, so I came here to look after my niece. I'm not really a farmer, so we've let the stock go. We're still deciding what to do with ourselves and this farm.'

Nell had seen the sadness on the girl's face at the mention of her parents and felt her heart go out to the child. She too had lost her mother when she was young. But she'd had Mattie, always Mattie, to turn to.

Well, May had Mr Easton and he seemed a caring sort of man.

'I'll make us a cup of tea as soon as the kettle boils,'

he said. 'It's getting dark early because of the storm, so I think I'll light a few lamps. The brightness will cheer us up. We don't have gas out here, unfortunately. I much prefer gaslight.' He did this and by that time the kettle had boiled, so he made a big pot of tea and set it at the edge of the kitchen range to brew.

As the child finished setting out the biscuits, he asked, 'Which bedroom shall we give to Mrs Greenhill, May?'

'The one next to mine would be best. We'll have to make up the bed, but it's warmer at that side of the house.'

'Yes, you're right.' He turned round. 'Are you still cold, Mrs Greenhill?'

She nodded. She couldn't seem to get warm, close as she was to the fire, and could sense that he was keeping an eye on her.

'Tea's ready. Do you take sugar?'

She hadn't taken it for a long time, to save money, but suddenly she wanted something sweet. 'Yes, please. Just one teaspoon.'

He brought across a big mug. 'Not elegant, but it holds more and keeps the warmth in better than a cup.'

She wrapped her hands round it and took a careful sip of the hot liquid. Warmth trickled through her and she took another sip, then cradled the mug against her cheek, sighing with pleasure.

'I'll just go and get some sheets out to air for your bed.'

'We could fill a hot-water bottle too,' May said. 'Shall I get one out?'

She seemed a very sensible capable child, Nell thought, as she let them fuss over her.

When Mr Easton insisted she eat something, she forced

down a few spoonfuls of the stew to please him, but all she really wanted was to lie down somewhere warm and go to sleep. It was only late afternoon, but she'd exhausted herself.

In the end she felt she couldn't sit upright any longer. 'I'm sorry. I'm too tired to eat any more. Would you mind if I went to bed now?'

'Of course not. I'll just fill the hot-water bottle, then May and I will make up the bed.'

It was an earthenware bottle, the sort her family had called a 'piggy', and for a moment she felt nostalgia flood through her at the sight of it. Mattie used to fill a bottle for them on cold nights, but they'd also had each other to cuddle up to, three sisters sharing a bed, with Renie in the middle. Ah, she missed them!

'Hold this for a moment.' He thrust the bottle into her arms, gathered up the sheets which had been airing in front of the fire while they ate and gave them to May. He came across to stand beside Nell as she got up.

'I won't fall over,' she said in surprise as he put out one hand to help her.

'You look as if you will. I'll carry that knapsack up for you. This way.'

She found to her surprise that she had to make a big effort to lift one foot after the other. It felt as if she was climbing a whole mountain of stairs, though it was only one flight. At the top, she followed him into a neat little bedroom with a sloping ceiling at one side.

Mr Easton and his niece made up her bed while she sat on a chair, cuddling the bottle and concentrating on staying awake.

When the bed was ready, he asked in his beautiful deep voice, 'Will you be all right?'

'Yes. And thank you for your help.'

'If there are any wet things inside your knapsack, give them to May and she'll bring them down. I'll hang them on the ceiling airer overnight with your sweater.'

'Thank you.'

'Don't be afraid if I look in to check that you're all right when I come up to bed.' He opened the top drawer. 'Yes, I thought we still had some.' He got out a nightlight and set it in a little glass dish, produced a box of matches from his pocket and lit the little cup of wax with a steady hand. 'If you wake in the night, you'll feel better if you can see where you are. I'll light a new one for you when I come up to bed.'

'Mmm.' She felt too tired to speak, but that seemed to satisfy him. She waited for them both to leave, aching to get into bed.

Once they'd gone, she put the bottle to warm her place in the narrow single bed. She was tempted to crawl in beside it fully dressed, but it'd look bad to sleep in her clothes, so she summoned up the last of her strength to open her knapsack and pull out her night things. They felt cold and damp, but not wet. It was a good knapsack, had been expensive.

She didn't remember blowing out the lamp or getting into bed, but she must have done.

When she woke a few hours later, it took her a minute or two to remember where she was. Then she saw the night light flickering in its glass dish on top of the chest of drawers and remembered.

With a happy sigh, she snuggled down in bed, glad of the thick quilt on top of the covers and the hot-water bottle at her feet. The wind was still howling round the house, but the bed was warm and she felt safe here.

If he had looked in to check on her, he'd done it very quietly. How kind of him to take in a stranger like this!

Chapter Twelve

When Nell woke again it was light, and though the wind seemed to have largely died down, rain was still pattering against the windowpanes, blurring the world outside.

She sat up and reached for the old shawl they'd lent her. She had to use the chamber pot because her need was urgent, but she'd make sure she was the one to empty it.

She had no dressing gown, so pulled a blanket off the bed and wrapped that round herself on top of the shawl before making her way downstairs.

She opened the door to see Mr Easton and his niece sitting chatting at the kitchen table. The room was so warm and cosy, she longed to have somewhere like that. And the warmth came from their love for one another as well as from the fire. They looked up when she hesitated in the doorway.

'Do come in and join us,' he said with one of his lovely smiles.

'I hope you don't mind me using this blanket. I don't

carry a dressing gown with me and you have my mackintosh down here.'

He pointed to the ceiling airer. 'It should be dry now, but your skirt is still a bit damp, your jacket and sweater too.' He turned to his niece. 'Do you think we could lend Mrs Greenhill your mother's dressing gown?'

The girl looked at him in such dismay, Nell hurried to say, 'Look, I don't want to give you any trouble. I'll get dressed and use this blanket for extra warmth till I can put my things on again. I do have a change of clothes with me. I just wanted some water to wash myself in first, if that's all right.'

He didn't mention the dressing gown again and the girl didn't go to find it. Nell saw his lips tighten as he glanced at his niece and he shook his head slightly, as if concerned by her attitude. 'Why don't you sit down and have some breakfast as you are, Mrs Greenhill? You're perfectly respectable in that blanket. I'll carry some hot water up for you afterwards.'

She felt a bit embarrassed but sat down anyway. She didn't feel respectable sitting in her nightdress, not in front of strangers, but she was ravenously hungry, and thirsty too. Perhaps May didn't want her dead mother's clothes being used by a stranger. That was understandable.

Once she was dressed, Nell hesitated in her room, wondering what to do with herself. It was pouring down outside and she could hardly carry on walking in that. But she couldn't take it for granted that Mr Easton would let her stay another night, so she might have to.

She went to find him, but he wasn't in the kitchen.

The old man came in from the yard, shaking the rain off a ragged horse blanket he'd covered himself with.

'Morning, missus. You look better today. Good thing Hugh found you, isn't it?' He went across to the big teapot and poured himself a tin mug of dark liquid, the tea well and truly stewed by now.

'Do you know where Mr Easton is? Um . . . I'm sorry, but I don't know your name, Mr . . .'

'Just call me Fred. Everybody does. Hugh and the lass don't go to church when the weather's bad, so I expect they'll be in his study. That lass spends hours there, reading. She's always got a book in her hand, that one. He brought a lot with him from London and more keep arriving. It's a wonder their brains aren't addled.' He pointed to a door. 'It's down there. Last door.'

She went along a short corridor and knocked on the door at the end.

'Come.'

She went in, staying near the door, surprised when the girl gave her a hostile look. 'Sorry to disturb you, Mr Easton, but given how bad the weather still is, I wondered if you'd mind me staying another night. Not if it's inconvenient, of course.'

He'd stood up when she appeared. Lovely manners he had.

'Do come in. Of course you can stay. I'd expected you to stay, but I suppose I should have said so. I can take you to the nearest railway station tomorrow, if you like. I have to go there anyway to pick up a parcel.'

'That's very kind of you. I'd appreciate that. Can I do anything to help while I'm here? I'm not a bad cook.' She could certainly do better than the previous night's watery stew.

His expression brightened. 'That'd be wonderful. I'll come and show you what we've got.'

'*I* was going to cook today,' May said.

He smiled at his niece. 'I know, but you and I are not the best of cooks, so we'll let Mrs Greenhill do it, shall we?'

'Unless you'd like to help me?' Nell suggested, not wanting to upset the girl.

The hostility seemed to lessen a little. 'Yes, please. Do you know how to make cakes?'

'Yes, I do.'

'Could you show me? I'm not very good at cakes. I was just starting to learn when—' She pressed one hand to her mouth and her eyes filled with tears.

Mr Easton put his arm round his niece's shoulders and kept it there. 'We both love eating cakes.' He studied Nell. 'Are you sure you're well enough to do this, Mrs Greenhill?'

She looked at him in surprise. 'I'm not ill, Mr Easton. I was exhausted and chilled yesterday, but a good night's sleep set me to rights again. I'm never ill.'

'I must say you look a lot better.' He stood up. 'I'll show you where the things are.'

'I don't want to disturb you, if you're working. I'm sure May will be able to tell me all I need to know. What were you intending to have for tea?'

'Leftover roast lamb and potatoes, with cabbage. Whatever you can find for the other meals. There are always plenty of eggs.'

'Fine. I'll see to the meals, then.'

She went back to the kitchen, with May trailing behind, looking wary. But the girl thawed out a little as she showed Nell where everything was and they were soon chatting away.

It felt blessedly normal to be in charge of a kitchen again. Hers had been humble, but she'd organised it well and produced as good food as possible for her family in the circumstances, given Cliff's meanness.

She hummed as she worked, or she chatted to May. As soon as she was settled somewhere, she'd write to tell Renie. She missed her sister's letters.

She decided to prepare a nice onion gravy later to make the cold roast lamb more tasty, because she'd found some Oxo cubes. She didn't need to make that yet, though. She'd bought penny cubes sometimes, to make soup tastier, but never a whole tin of them like this. The cubes were so much easier to use than in the old days, when Oxo had been a liquid.

She whipped together a jam tart to have with custard for afters, since May said they always had plenty of milk. Then she gave the girl a lesson on making scones, followed by a simple sponge cake. There were indeed plenty of eggs. It was lovely not to have to make one do the work of two.

She'd have worked like this with her own daughter as Sarah grew older. That thought made her stand still for a moment, clenching her whole body against the pain.

'Are you all right, Mrs Greenhill?'

'Oh, sorry. Just remembering something.'

'You looked so sad.'

'Yes. It was . . . something sad.' She didn't say what,

didn't want to discuss her problems with a child who'd also suffered a sad loss.

They had potato-and-onion omelette at midday, with the newly baked scones and honey for afters. There seemed to be plenty of jars of the latter – not bought honey with labels on fancy glass jars, but jars of cloudy but delicious honey in a variety of shapes and sizes.

'Pearl's aunt keeps bees,' May said. 'So we swap them a lamb for a dozen jars – or we used to do . . . before. I don't know what we'll do next year.'

After they'd done the cooking, Nell cleaned out the pantry, which was in a bit of a mess, making sure to discuss with May what should go on each shelf. After all, the girl was the one who'd be using it. Nell would have to leave tomorrow. She sighed at the thought, not wanting to go.

Fred took his meals out to the barn, where he had a room in the old stables, so she let May prepare the trays for that.

'He's got false teeth,' the child whispered with a giggle, 'and they're a bit loose, so he doesn't like to eat in front of people.'

When Mr Easton joined them at midday, they hadn't finished sorting out the pantry. He sniffed appreciatively. 'That smells delicious.'

'I hope you enjoy it.'

He looked at the piles of stores still to be put away. 'You've been very helpful but I'm not a slave-driver. You don't have to work non-stop. Do you enjoy reading?'

'I love it.'

'Why don't you find a book and settle down for an hour or two this afternoon? I've plenty of books in my study.'

'I'll just finish the pantry first, if you don't mind. May and I have been planning where things should go.'

She went along to choose a book after she'd finished, looking round enviously. 'I've never seen a room with so many books in it.'

'That's because of my job, as well as my love of books. I work for a publisher. I'm an editor.'

'I'm not sure what an editor does.'

He explained how he helped the authors get their works into better shape, and corrected their spelling and grammar.

She was standing near a bookcase and couldn't help reaching out to stroke the beautiful leather binding on some of the books.

'You look as if you love books, Mrs Greenhill.'

'Yes. I used to borrow them from the library and occasionally I'd buy one second hand from the market. I usually managed to find something to read. May I borrow this one?'

'Rudyard Kipling? Please do. *Kim* is a great story. I really enjoy his books.'

'Thank you.'

May, who was now lying in front of his study fire on a thick rug, went back to her reading. Nell went to sit in the kitchen, feeling left out and chiding herself for that. She was a stranger here, after all.

She made sure she didn't neglect the cooking but she enjoyed a quiet hour's reading. She'd get this book from a library once she settled down somewhere and finish reading it.

Mr Easton was again very complimentary about the

meal, and about the cake May had helped make and ice. 'The rest of the cake and scones will be very useful over the next few days. If this young lady doesn't eat them all up today. Thank you, Mrs Greenhill.'

'My pleasure. I enjoy cooking.'

It began to grow dark as they were finishing their meal. He looked outside and said, 'Well, at least we should have a more peaceful night. The wind seems to have died right down and it's not raining now.'

Hardly had he finished speaking than there was the sound of a horse outside. He got up and went to the kitchen door. 'Ronald! Is something wrong?'

'I'm afraid there is, Mr Easton. My Pearl's broken her leg, so she sent me to let you know she can't come and help you, not for a few weeks or longer, the doctor says. She's sorry, but she doesn't know anyone else to send, either.'

Nell couldn't help overhearing and saw her kind host's shoulders slump at this news.

'I'm sorry to hear of that. I hope Pearl gets better quickly. Tell her we'll manage, but we'll miss her. And thanks for coming so promptly to let me know. Do you want a cup of tea?'

'Thank you, but no. Have to get back. At least the weather's clearing up. Goodbye.' He waved one hand and let the horse pick its own way out of the yard.

As Mr Easton shut the door, May went across to link her arm in his. 'What shall we do now, Uncle Hugh? I could take tomorrow off school, but I can't stay home all the time.'

'We'll just have to manage as best we can till we find someone to help. I'll go into Swindon and call at an employment agency. I'm sure they'll be able to find someone.'

Nell hesitated, but the more she thought of it, the better her idea seemed. 'Um . . . I'm not doing anything for the next few weeks and I need somewhere to stay till I can find a proper home for myself. I could do the job for you temporarily, Mr Easton.'

He swung round to stare at her, mouth open in surprise. 'You mean . . . you'd stay on here as housekeeper?'

'Yes. I'd have to live in, though, so if you want to try to find someone else who lives locally and can come in daily, I'll understand.'

'No, no! You'd be perfect. We've already tested your cooking and that certainly passed muster.'

Even May was nodding approval.

She would be happy to work here, Nell realised, but she had to find her sister as well. 'I'd have to go into Swindon, though, sometime during this week. I'm looking for my eldest sister, Mattie. We've lost touch with one another.' Thank goodness she still knew where Renie was!

'I can take you to the railway station in Faringdon and you can get into Swindon quite easily by train. I'm supposed to pick up a parcel there tomorrow, but it can wait a day or two. You'll need to settle in here first and find out what we need, then we can do some shopping while we're there. I have a list of the grocery supplies Pearl wanted and you might like to add to it.'

'I don't want to put you out. Maybe I can go to Faringdon by bus and ask to have the shopping delivered.'

'They don't deliver out here. It's too far. Anyway, there's no need. When we can't get things at the village shop, I often bring them from Faringdon. I have to go there regularly to collect boxes of books and papers from work, or to send them back. It's a pretty drive when the weather's fine. May and I will enjoy a little outing to pick you up again after school.'

He cast what seemed to be an anxious glance at May. 'I'm thinking of buying a motor car. It'll get me round so much more quickly. If it doesn't break down, that is. And if I can learn to drive one.'

'You said you didn't like motor cars, Uncle Hugh!' she said accusingly.

'I don't. But it takes too long to go to and fro with a horse and trap. I have duties with my job and mustn't neglect them. We really will have to consider moving up to London soon, May.'

The child glared at him, yelled, 'No! I won't go!' at the top of her voice, then ran out of the room, slamming the door behind her.

Nell didn't know what to say, so waited for Mr Easton to speak.

He sighed and gave one of those little shakes of the head that said he was upset with his niece's reaction, then looked at Nell. 'Now that you're staying, you'd better know what caused that outburst. May's parents were killed in a motor car accident, so she hates cars. And she refuses even to consider moving with me to London, swears she'll run away if I force her. I've waited, hoping she'll change her mind, but as you can see, she flies into hysterics if I even mention the subject.'

'But she'll have to go eventually because of your job.'

'Yes, and because my home is there. As for cars, I've

never wanted to learn to drive one, and I didn't need to when I lived in London, but out here in the country it's different. Cars are so much quicker than horses when you're far away from everything. It might have suited my brother to live here quietly, but it doesn't suit me. There's a young fellow in the village who's mad about cars. I'm going to ask Harry to help me choose one and teach me to drive.'

He was looking at her in a way that said he'd finished what he had to say, so she nodded. 'Thank you for telling me. I'll try to tread carefully with May.'

'That's all anyone can do. Now, about your wage, I'll have to find out what it'd be fair to pay you.'

She'd been thinking about that. 'Ten shillings a week and my keep would be fine.'

He frowned. 'That doesn't sound enough. No, I'd better check out if it's fair.'

When she went to bed in what would be her bedroom from now on, it took Nell a while to fall asleep, because she was so excited about her new job.

As for the money, ten shillings a week would be more than she'd ever had for herself from her earnings before, and she'd be quite happy with that. She was surprised he'd even think of paying her more than she'd asked for, but then she was beginning to realise that Hugh Easton wasn't like anyone she'd ever met before.

He was a large man – not fat, just sturdily built – but he wasn't at all intimidating, as some large men were . . . her father, for instance . . . or that horrible Frank. She didn't know why she kept thinking of Cliff's cousin. She wished she didn't need to contact any of the Greenhills again and would make sure she went to their house at a time when

Frank and Cliff's father were working, just to be safe.

She couldn't imagine Mr Easton being aggressive or hitting someone, but she could imagine Frank doing it – and Cliff had hit her once or twice. Mr Easton's expression was usually open and quietly happy, and he spoke to everyone courteously, listening to old Fred's rambling tales with every appearance of interest.

He'd looked concerned a few times, though, when dealing with his niece, whose mood seemed to change in a flash. That he loved her was obvious. That she was unhappy seemed obvious too.

Gran's prophecy had been right. Nell had reached the end of her journey here, for a while, anyway. She doubted she could have found anything that suited her better than this job. It would give her more time to work out what to do with herself. Now she came to think of it, Gran had even foretold that this would be a temporary stopping place. *They'll shelter you when you need it, those elm trees will.*

She was close enough to Swindon to try to find her eldest sister. Oh, how she longed to see Mattie again! And then . . . Nell couldn't think what she'd do with her life after that. There must be some job that was satisfying and useful. She certainly didn't want to lead an idle life.

The money she'd inherited from her husband gave her security to a degree she'd never experienced before, but it also took away the possibility of going back to her old life at the laundry. Well, she didn't want to. Who'd work in a steamy place like that if they didn't have to? Not her. It was not only hard work but boring too.

She'd considered all sorts of possibilities during her travels. She could open a corner shop. But that life didn't really appeal to her, and anyway, you needed a husband to run a shop properly. Even with two people working together, those who owned small shops worked long hours and most looked tired. As well as the selling, they had to worry about whether to extend credit to customers, and if they did, there was the ongoing problem of whether those customers would pay what they owed. No, not a corner shop.

But she wasn't well educated, even though she'd always read a lot. Her father had made each of them leave school and start work as soon as it was allowed. He'd found her a job before she'd even turned fourteen. No choice. Just, 'You're starting at the laundry on Monday.' She wondered what sorts of jobs there were for educated women, what sort of choices they had.

The only ones she could think of were teaching or working in an office as a lady typist, but you had to train for both those jobs and she only knew a little shorthand. Anyway, she didn't speak like ladies did, so would probably stick out like a sore thumb if she tried. She might have enjoyed being a teacher, but she hadn't got the education for that. And actually, after her days of freedom and an open-air life, she didn't want to be shut up indoors all day.

In fact, at the moment she felt to be neither fish nor fowl.

The job as housekeeper at Elm Tree Farm wouldn't last. Not only did Hugh Easton have to go back to London, he was well educated, attractive and wasn't short of money. She tried to imagine his life in London. He wouldn't need a full-time housekeeper if he had a wife, though people like him would probably have a woman in to do the rough work and maybe one to do the laundry too, like Mrs Garrett.

Actually, Nell couldn't think why a lovely man like him wasn't married already. She was quite sure *he* wouldn't keep his wife and child short of money, as Cliff had, and he wouldn't be so rough in bed, either. And he was kind, so very kind . . . not to mention being quite good-looking.

She told herself not to be so stupid. She shouldn't even be thinking about her employer in that way.

But she dreamt about him that night and blushed when she woke to think of those dreams.

In the morning, all was rush to get a sulky May ready for school. The child had to walk down to the end of the track to catch the morning bus into the village and it didn't seem to Nell that she wanted to go.

'Is May always so unhappy about going to school?' she asked as Mr Easton shut the door on his niece and came back for yet another cup of tea. That man loved his tea.

'She is since her parents died. She doesn't want to go out of the house if she can stay indoors, preferably in my study.'

'Poor child! Children that age should be playing out with friends while they still can. I lost my mother when I was young too. It's hard on a girl.' She caught herself on that. She shouldn't be offering him confidences about her life. Let alone, he was her employer, she didn't want to be the object of anyone's pity. She'd had more than enough of that.

'I lost my fiancée a few years ago, so I do understand what it's like to lose someone you love.'

His eyes took on a distant look and she didn't interrupt

242

for a moment. He must have loved his fiancée to look like that a few years later. Would reminders about Sarah always upset her? She couldn't imagine them not doing.

She didn't speak till he seemed to be paying attention again. 'Well, if you can manage without me doing the washing today, I'll carry on sorting things out and getting used to the house.'

'Oh. Mrs Compton comes in on Mondays to do the washing.'

'You keep a washing woman as well?' she asked in surprise.

'Sorry. I should have told you that yesterday, shouldn't I? But I was editing a rather interesting book and it was so good to have you here to take over the cooking and leave me free to work, I forgot about everything else.'

'That's all right. What time does she come?'

'She usually gets here half an hour or so after May leaves. She walks across the fields from the village – she lives at this side and it's a much shorter way if you don't mind a bit of mud. Call me when she arrives and I'll introduce you.'

Mrs Compton turned out to be a stocky woman with red hands and sparse greying hair. Nell introduced herself and explained why she was there. The other woman knew all about Pearl breaking her leg and would have settled in to gossip, but Nell didn't feel it was right to stand and chat when so much needed doing.

'Is Mr Easton busy today?'

'Yes. He said to tell him when you arrived, but I think he only wanted to introduce me, and now we've met, perhaps we can manage without disturbing him?'

'Oh, he doesn't notice anything once he starts work,

that man doesn't. "Absent-minded professor", I call him. But he's a good employer, all the same, very thoughtful and kind. That poor lass is lucky to have an uncle like him.'

The two women worked together getting the clothes ready, then Mrs Compton attacked the washing as if dirt was her personal enemy, thrusting some garments into one tub to soak and grating up some hard soap before tossing some of it into the copper and boiling up the whites.

There was everything a woman could need to do the family's laundry, Nell thought enviously, watching her companion open and shut cupboards. She'd never had a special room for washing like this. How much easier it made things.

'Don't you have anything to wash?' Mrs Compton asked, once she'd sorted everything.

'I didn't think I should put mine in.'

'Bless you, why not? A few more bits and pieces don't make any difference to me. You just keep the cups of tea coming – and I eat hearty at midday. They always give me a decent meal.'

The day passed quickly. Nell left Mrs Compton to her work and continued to investigate and tidy the various drawers and cupboards in the kitchen. Someone had once put together the household goods lovingly, she could tell that, with hand-embroidered tablecloths and matching crockery. But other items had been allowed to pile up on top of the neater things, as if they'd just been shoved anyhow into the nearest drawer. Was that Pearl's doing?

She wondered what May's mother had been like. There had been photos in Mr Easton's study, but she'd not felt it her place to stare at them yesterday and he was working in there now.

When she went up to make May's bed, some of her questions were answered. Standing beside the bed was a photo of a man and woman, with a much younger May between them. This Mr Easton looked very much like his brother – big and friendly were the words that came to mind. Mrs Easton was plump and smiling, her hair soft and dark, and May looked perfectly happy with them. The child had a shadowed look to her now, as if unhappiness lay beneath her smiles and chatter.

Nell made the child's bed. No one had changed the sheets on this one, but her employer's bed had been stripped, so they must do the beds in turns. She couldn't see any clean sheets around for his bed, so went to ask Mrs Compton where they were kept.

By the time the washerwoman left, having done some of the ironing as well, May had come home from school. Nell was feeling tired and the house was full of washing drying gently on ceiling racks, with the ironed garments taking a final airing on a huge wooden clothes horse that unfolded like three sides of a box. You needed a lot of space just to fit in equipment like that.

She'd hardly seen Mr Easton during the day, except when she took him his meals. Mrs Compton said he always ate in his study. He'd been in an absent-minded mood then; polite, but with his mind on other things.

However, he came out of his study as soon as he heard May's voice and joined them in the kitchen for a cup of tea.

'Have a nice day, did you?' he asked his niece.

May shrugged.

'What lessons did you do?'

'Writing, ciphering, history.' She sighed.

'Don't you enjoy school?' Nell ventured.

May shook her head, scowling.

'Why not?'

'The work's too easy and I get bored. But if you don't pay attention and sit quietly, she hits you with her ruler.'

Nell saw Mr Easton look angry at that and shook her head at him. You couldn't protect children from their teachers, and anyway, the occasional reprimand didn't hurt anyone. But she could see how easy it'd be for an intelligent child to get bored, because she'd often been bored at school herself. And she, too, had been afraid of her teacher. It was a lesson you soon learnt in life unless you were very spoilt: sometimes you just had to put up with things you didn't like.

When May had changed into her old clothes and gone out to play with the dog and talk to Fred, Mr Easton said, 'I'm a bit worried about that school. She's a clever girl and needs a better education than a village school can provide. But there's no other school within reach and I don't want to send her away to boarding school. She'll be all right when we get to London. There's a private day school nearby, and it has a good reputation.'

He went to stare out of the window, drumming his fingers on the sill for a moment or two. Just as Nell thought he'd finished talking, he said suddenly, 'I'd like to sell this place, because I'm not at all interested in farming and never could be. It's not a family farm. My brother bought it because he liked living in the country. But as you've seen, May gets upset if I even suggest moving to London. I suppose I can wait a while longer.'

'You're very good to her.'

'I do my best, but sometimes she needs a woman. I'm hoping she'll get on with you. You're very easy to talk to and you've got a lot of common sense.'

Nell was surprised by that compliment, but pleased.

'I've got a small share in the publishing house. I'm not just employed by it, I'm a junior partner. That's why I'm able to work from here for the time being, but there's so much more I could do if I were in London, so much more I *want* to do. Perhaps now you're living here, I'll be able to go up there more often, even stay overnight now and then.'

'I'll do anything I can to help. You only have to say. But we'd better not suggest it till May's more used to me – and till you are as well. You might not like having me as a housekeeper.'

He grinned. 'Don't tell me you're a criminal in disguise.'

She smiled back and clasped one hand to her bosom in an affected way. 'Oh dear. My dark secret is out.'

He threw back his head and laughed. 'Shall I call the police?'

She was surprised how easy it was to joke with Mr Easton. She'd never had a man tease her like he did before. Her father was a bully and Cliff . . . well, the less she thought about him now, the better. She wasn't at all sorry to be without him in her life. Or his horrible family.

Mr Easton looked at her thoughtfully. 'I think you should call me Hugh, and I'll call you Nell, if you don't mind. It's how I think of you already, actually. Mrs Greenhill doesn't seem like you, I don't know why.'

'Well, it was my husband's name. It doesn't feel like mine to me either, but what can I do?'

'You could change your name legally, or take your maiden name again. There are no children to confuse the issue.'

'Could I really? I think I'd like that. But it wouldn't be right for me to use your first name.'

He let out a scornful snort. 'Who says so? This is 1912 not 1812! And we're living together, I hope on friendly terms, so why not treat one another like family?'

She looked at him warily. What exactly did he mean by that?

He smiled. 'I didn't mean anything disrespectful to you by that . . . *Nell*.' He waited, and when she still didn't say anything, added, 'I got used to calling people by their given names when I was mixing with literary folk in London. But I won't do it, if it upsets you.'

Relieved that she hadn't misread the situation, she tried it out. 'It doesn't upset me . . . *Hugh*.'

He beamed. 'Thank you, Nell. I'm so glad we found you.'

She could feel her face growing warm with pleasure at that compliment. He didn't mean anything by such talk or using first names. He'd said himself he was used to mixing with artistic types and she'd heard that they were very different from ordinary folk. If it had been anyone from her old life, it'd have felt as if he was flirting with her. What a fool she was even to think of that!

Except in dreams. You couldn't help dreaming of

what life might have been like if you'd had a kind, loving husband. She'd seen it with the Garretts, had envied Mrs Garrett.

And Mr Easton – Hugh! – was good-looking as well as nice. She was still young enough to dream of a man so kind he made you feel like a lady, yet made you laugh too. It was lovely to laugh with someone. She hadn't done that since Renie went to work in London.

Chapter Thirteen

It was decided that Nell should go to look for her sister on Thursday and Hugh would take her to the nearest railway station, which was at Faringdon.

They set off quite early in the trap, dropping May at school on their way. It was a very small village and a tiny school, with only two classes – one for little children, one for older children. Nell could see that May was much better dressed than the others and watched over her shoulder as the child went to stand on her own in a corner of the yard, shoulders hunched, looking unhappy. Didn't May have any friends? Nell didn't ask Hugh because she wanted to talk to the girl first.

In Faringdon, they left the horse and trap at a livery stable and went to enquire about trains.

As there was half an hour to wait for the next one, which connected with a main-line train to Swindon, Nell bought the ticket and then they went on to the grocer's. Hugh introduced her to the owner and explained that she'd be buying food for his household from now on and it should be put on his account. He passed over a list.

She waved goodbye to him, feeling a bit nervous of travelling on her own. She'd not yet told Hugh about her husband and Sarah, but she might. When the time was right. People who lived together needed to understand one another and he'd been very open with her.

As the second train rattled along towards Swindon, she felt excited as well as nervous. She was longing to see Mattie or at least hear how she was and find a way to get in touch with her. Surely her sister would have written to the Greenhills by now, as they'd planned when they all ran away? Frank hadn't said anything about a letter, but it was well over two years now. That's what they'd agreed: wait two years.

Her father would be at the railway works, so she didn't need to worry about bumping into him, thank goodness. But she was worrying about how she'd be received by her mother-in-law.

When she arrived in Swindon, Nell stood at the entrance to the railway station, looking down the street. The town hadn't changed much, as far as she could see.

She took a roundabout way to the Greenhills' house, walking slowly and familiarising herself with the shops again. Not that she and her sisters had shopped in the town centre very often. They'd gone mainly to the corner shop, and to second-hand clothes dealers for their clothes – or to the market to buy fresh food and occasionally material to make their simple skirts and blouses. But they'd gone to look in the windows occasionally, as a treat.

She looked down at her tweed suit and smiled. She'd had nothing as grand as this to wear before.

When she got to the end of the street, she hesitated, still worried about how they'd be with her. Only one way to find out. Taking a deep breath, she told herself not to be so silly and walked briskly along the street.

Their house had always greeted you with sparkling windows, ornaments set out on the window sill, the pavement swept clean outside the front door and the step holystoned. Today it looked sad and weary . . . if you could say that about a house. The windows were dull, the brass knocker needed a good polish and the doorstep hadn't been mopped for a while.

She knocked and waited. Just as she was about to knock again, she heard footsteps shuffling along the hall and the door opened.

For a moment she and Mrs Greenhill stared at one another. It would have been hard to say who was the more shocked.

'What are *you* doing here?' the older woman asked, her voice sharp.

'I've come back to live in the area, so I thought I'd call on you and . . . say hello.'

'I wonder you've got the cheek to show your face here. You tricked my Cliff into marriage and now he's dead and it's all your fault.' Her voice was shrill and getting shriller.

'Don't say that. It was an accident, a dreadful accident.'

'He'd not have been there at all if it hadn't been for you. He'd have been at home where he belonged. I lost my only son because of you and I don't want you coming here again.' She took a step forward, arms rising as if to shove Nell away.

Nell took a hasty step backwards, shocked at the virulent hatred in the woman's voice and face. 'Please, Mrs Greenhill, don't be like that.'

'How should I be? Do you think a nephew can replace a son? You've got your blood money out of my Cliff. Didn't think to share that with us, did you?'

Nell was startled. How did they know about the insurance policy? Frank had left Milnrow straight after the funeral – hadn't he?

The neighbour on the right-hand side came out of her house and hurried across to put her arm round Mrs Greenhill's thin shoulders. 'Shh now. Shh.' She too gave Nell a hostile look. 'Leave her alone. Haven't you done enough?'

'I haven't done anything. It was her son who got me in the family way. But I'll go away as soon as I've asked her something.'

'What?'

Nell looked at Mrs Greenhill who was leaning against her neighbour, tears tracking down her cheeks. 'Have you heard from my sister, Mattie? She ran away at the same time and Cliff arranged that she'd contact us through you, but not till a year or two had passed. I don't know where she is and you're the only way I can hope to find her.'

Cliff's mother stared at her, then a gloating smile slowly creased her face. 'There is some justice in the world, then.'

'What do you mean?'

'I won't tell you anything. Serve you right if you never see your sister again. I'll never see my Cliff, will I?'

'You can't mean that!'

'Oh, can't I? If she sends a letter, I'll burn it. If she calls at the house, I'll tell her you're dead – like my Cliff. I do mean it. I do.' She started sobbing loudly again and the neighbour guided her into the house. She stopped in the doorway to look over her shoulder and yell, 'Don't come back here or I'll take a knife to you, I swear it.' The door closed with a bang behind them both.

Nell stared at the house, aghast. She couldn't believe anyone would be so cruel.

She heard a voice and turned to see an old woman standing on the doorstep of the house on the other side of the Greenhills'. She looked as if she'd said something and was waiting for an answer. 'Sorry. I didn't catch what you said.'

'I said, she'll not change her mind. Spiteful, the Greenhills are when they feel they've been slighted.'

'But I didn't do anything. It was her son who got me in the family way. He *forced* me.'

'She'll never believe that. You'd think her Cliff was a saint to hear her talk. You'll have to find your sister some other way.'

'There isn't any other way.'

The woman shrugged and went inside.

Nell felt chilled to the core and was far beyond tears. She'd been so hopeful as she made her way here, sure that Mattie would have got in touch by now.

Turning, she began walking slowly towards the station, not noticing anything around her this time, not caring either.

She got on to a train and somehow made her way back to Faringdon, only to realise she was back early. So she set off walking along the road to the farm, not wanting to sit around waiting for Hugh.

What if she never saw Mattie again?

When Frank came home from work there was no meal ready. Instead, his uncle was sitting in the front room with his arm round his wife, who was sobbing against him. 'What's happened?'

'*She* turned up today, asking if we'd heard from her sister.'

'Cliff's wife?'

'Who else?'

'Good. We can get some of that money out of her. Where is she staying?'

He had to repeat his question before his aunt would stop weeping and answer him.

'How should I know where she's staying? I never want to see her again. She looked well fed, was wearing an expensive tweed suit, while my Cliff is mouldering in his grave – a grave I can't even go and visit.'

Frank prayed for patience. 'I'll take you one day, I promise. We said we'd get our share of Cliff's money. We can't do that if we don't know where she's living.'

'Well, I didn't ask her, and I don't care about the money.'

'You ought to. What'll you do when my uncle can't work anymore? He's on light duties already. Shall you go into the poorhouse?' He was pleased to see that get her attention.

'I didn't think,' she mumbled.

'Did you tell her about the letter?'

'No. I don't want to make her happy, do I?'

He thumped one fist into the palm of his other hand. He was having trouble staying patient, but he mustn't upset them. They owned this house, and now Cliff had died, it'd be his once they died. They'd promised. But he wanted more, much more. He wanted the money.

He'd find out where she was. There had to be a way.

In the middle of the night he had a sudden thought. He hadn't told her about her father. Would she go looking for him next? He'd go round to her former house the very next day and find out, and pay one of the neighbours to tell him if she turned up, and if possible, find out where she was living.

When Hugh saw Nell walking along the road towards him outside the town, he reined in the mare, surprised when she almost walked past the horse and trap. 'You're back early. Is something wrong, Nell?'

She stopped and stood staring up at them as if she had trouble remembering who they were.

He turned to his niece. 'Get into the back, May.'

'No need to disturb yourself.' Nell clambered into the back of the vehicle before his niece could move. She sat on an old blanket and stared into space as the trap jolted its way back to the farm, not saying a word.

'We'll have to go back and get the groceries, I'm afraid.'

'Oh. I forgot. Sorry.'

Once this was accomplished they drove back to the farm.

When they got there, she clambered out without his help. 'I'll go and start tea.'

He said something quietly to his niece, who nodded. When they went inside, May vanished upstairs and Hugh went into the kitchen.

'Tell me what's upset you, Nell,' he said without preamble. 'Is it bad news about your sister?'

'I didn't find her. And there's nothing to be done about it, no way of getting in touch with her. I'll . . . be all right. I just have to . . . get used to it.'

He took the big kettle out of her hand and dumped it on the edge of the stove. 'You're upset and you've no one else to talk to about it, so talk to me.' When she didn't move, he took her hand and pulled her to the table. 'Sit down. I'll make a pot of tea.'

He kept an eye on her as he worked, listening. She spoke haltingly at first, but he asked questions and gradually the whole story of the past few years came flooding out.

What she told him horrified him, and when she started sobbing, he went to sit beside her and put his arms round her. How could you leave someone in so much pain to sob alone?

Especially when that someone was Nell Greenhill.

Only when Nell had finished her tale did she realise she was in his arms and he was stroking her hair. She tried to pull away, shocked that she'd given way to her emotions like this, but he kept a firm hold.

'Shh, now. It'll be all right.'

After a moment of futile tugging, she sagged against him again, needing someone to hold her. If he hadn't been there, she might have fallen to pieces.

His voice was deep yet soft beside her ear. 'You've had a lot of sad things to face. And on your own too. Poor Nell.'

'I don't usually . . . give in to it.'

'No. But we all have our low moments. I cried a few times after my brother was killed, though not when May could hear me. We'd always been close, Harold and I. I cried for Edith too. I was very fond of her.'

'It hurts to lose someone, doesn't it? I still miss Sarah so very much; miss cuddling her, miss listening to her, watching her play. But I don't miss Cliff at all. I feel guilty about that.'

'I'm not surprised. You said he was very unkind to you. Did he beat you?'

'Only a couple of times. All he wanted was a housekeeper and a woman in his bed. He was so mean with money I went hungry sometimes. If he hadn't been so mean, Sarah would still be alive.'

'His mother shouldn't have blamed you. Do you want me to go and speak to her, tell her the details?'

'You'd do that?'

'Yes, of course.'

For a moment she let herself believe it'd help, then sighed. 'It'd not change anything. They're a spiteful bunch, the Greenhills. You should have seen how his cousin looked at me after the funeral, as if I'd killed Cliff myself.'

She sniffed and fumbled for her handkerchief. 'Cliff was like that too, if someone upset him, always tried to get his own back. I don't know why I ever went out with him. I think I was dazzled by having a man who was doing so well at the works say he loved me, so I didn't see what he was really like. But he only said it to get his way with me. He never said it once after we were married, not once. He didn't even love his own daughter, because he'd wanted a son.'

She sighed and stayed where she was for a few moments, then pulled away. This time he let her.

'Thank you, Hugh. For being kind to me, I mean.'

'I didn't do much.'

'It seemed a lot to me to have someone to comfort me.'

He picked up her hand and patted it. 'I'm glad it helped. I'll tell May the bare details, if you don't mind, so that she'll understand if you get sad.'

'If you think it right.'

He didn't get up to leave but sat on, frowning now. 'There must be some other way to find out if your sister's been back.'

'Not that I know of. We didn't have any relatives nearby and my father would never talk about his family, said he hadn't any.'

'What about contacting him? Surely he'd have heard something if she'd returned?'

'I don't want to see him again. Not ever. Anyway, he'd probably thump me the minute he saw me.'

'Not if I was with you, he wouldn't.'

She shuddered at the thought of seeing Bart Fuller again, ducking his fists, hearing him yell. 'I'll have to think about it. Anyway, I doubt she'd get in touch with him.'

'Even if she hasn't, he might have heard something. And you should write to your other sister. Renie, didn't you say she was called?'

'Yes. I suppose I should do that now I'm settled. I've got out of the habit, I think.'

He stood up, smiling gently. 'You'd better put my handkerchief in the washing when you've finished with it.'

She stared down at the crumpled square of damp white cotton in her hand. 'Thank you. For everything.'

'I'm happy to help you in any way I can.' A hint of puzzlement crept into his face. 'It's strange. I feel I know you well, though it's less than a week since we met. It happens sometimes, doesn't it? People get on well, right from the start.'

She nodded. She felt that way about him too.

'So you've got a friend now, not just an employer. Which means you're not completely on your own.'

That touched her and more tears rose in her eyes. 'Thank you.'

'I'd better go and see May now.'

'I'll get on with making our tea.' But before she did she looked down at the sodden handkerchief and touched the drier edge with her fingertip. It was an expensive one. Which was a lesson to her. He might say he was her friend, but he was a gentleman and she was his servant. He was only being kind to her and she shouldn't read any more into it than that. He was the sort of person who was kind to everyone, such a lovely man.

When May came down, she looked at Nell as if she'd never seen her before and stayed there, helping with the tea.

Just once she said in a quiet voice, 'I didn't realise. That's why you understand how I feel, isn't it?'

Nell nodded, not trusting her own voice. She did care

about this poor child, but didn't dare get too deeply attached to her, because one day she'd have to leave, whether the child's uncle was her friend or not. She had to remember that.

The following morning Nell finished her main housework, then wrote a letter to her sister, Renie, telling her what had happened lately. When the postman rode his bicycle up to the farm, she had the letter and money for postage ready for him to take back to the post office. Hugh said postmen in the country often posted letters for you.

She watched the postman cycle away with a lump in her throat. Renie would be upset too when she got that letter and found out how cruel Cliff's mother was being towards them.

'Why don't you come for a walk?'

She jumped in shock because she hadn't heard Hugh come into the kitchen.

'Sorry. Didn't mean to startle you. Did you get your letter off to your sister?'

'Yes.'

'That's what's upsetting you?'

She nodded.

'Time to get you out into the sunshine. I'm a big believer in sunshine and fresh air when one's feeling down.'

'You mean, leave the housework and just . . . go out?'

'Yes. I'll show you one of my favourite spots.'

'You're coming too?'

He smiled. 'Don't you want me to?'

She felt flustered. 'Of course I do. It's always better going for a walk with a friend.'

'And yet you walked for months on your own. How did you cope with the loneliness?'

'I needed to be on my own for a while, to get used to . . . not being part of a family anymore, not having Sarah. I don't think I'd have recovered if I'd had to stay in Milnrow and see the ruins of my house, or watch them finish knocking down Willow Court. And visiting her grave upset me. I left a stone angel to watch over her.'

'I can understand that. I visited my fiancée's grave at first. But it did no good.'

'How did she die?'

'Pneumonia. She was twenty-three, an only child too. So sad.'

'Do you still think of her?'

'Sort of. But she's been dead for a few years, and it grows easier, more distant. Life goes on, Nell, and you can't change that. You have to go on too.'

'Yes. I've found that out.'

'Right, then. Get your coat and walking boots, and we'll be off.'

He took her along the upper edge of a grassy field and crossed another one full of cows. She hung back, feeling nervous of the animals, which seemed much bigger when you were close to them.

He took hold of her hand, laughing. 'They won't hurt you. They're gentle creatures. Look at their eyes, how pretty they are.'

She'd never thought of cows as pretty and still didn't really share his enthusiasm for them. Anyway, she couldn't concentrate on anything with him holding her hand. It made her heart beat faster, made her feel breathless. How did it make him feel? Why had he done it? Friends didn't hold hands. That was for sweethearts.

She tried to pull her hand away without seeming to make a fuss, but he kept a tight hold of it. When he gave her one of his lovely smiles, she couldn't think straight.

They got to a gate and he climbed to the top, helping her over, then jumping her down as if she weighed nothing. They stood there for a moment or two, facing one another, bodies close together, saying nothing.

He reached out and touched her cheek gently. 'You have beautiful skin, Nell. So fresh and rosy.' Then he held out his hand in an invitation to her to hold it again.

She ought not to have taken it again, but she couldn't resist. It was a relief when he didn't comment, just started walking again.

It made her wonder . . . He couldn't be attracted to her . . . could he? No, things like that didn't happen to ordinary women like her. He was just . . . a big friendly man, unconventional because of associating with writers. He felt sorry for her, that was all it could be.

But oh, she wished it was more. And that surprised her. If she'd met a man like him first, she'd never have looked twice at Cliff.

'Here we are!'

She blinked, then stared round. She'd been so lost in her thoughts she hadn't noticed where they were going or that they'd stopped moving.

They were standing under one of the elm trees, the one highest up the hill. The countryside was spread out below them like a chequered quilt: fields and hedges of all shapes and sizes, trees and roads, a man riding a horse, a few sheep in one field, a few cows in another. There was a row of pretty stone cottages in the distance, which must have had gardens in front of them because there was a frill of colour along the front. It was too far away to guess what flowers were still blooming. Something red, she thought.

'Coming up here puts things into perspective, shows how small we humans are, how big the world is, even this tiny part of it,' he said quietly.

'It's beautiful.'

'I normally sit down and feast my eyes on it, but it's too muddy at the moment to sit on the ground. If I were staying at the farm I'd build a bench here, so that anyone could sit and enjoy the view.'

'But from what you've told me, you want to move back to London.'

'Oh, yes. Definitely. That doesn't stop me enjoying the countryside, though. Besides, there are parks and gardens in London too, and it's easy enough to get out of the city at weekends. But I love the people there and my work too. I miss things like going to the theatre or to museums very much.'

'I've never been to the theatre or a museum.'

'Haven't you? I'd love to take you for the first time. Would you come to the theatre with me, Nell, if we were in London? Or go dancing? Do you like dancing?'

She could feel herself blushing. 'You shouldn't say things like that to me.'

'Why not?'

'Because . . . you're my employer. And I'm not a loose woman.'

He grunted as if annoyed by this remark. 'My dear

girl, no one would ever think you immoral. And I'd never treat you that way. But I'm a man as well as an employer and I have feelings. Just as you're a woman as well as a housekeeper. I'd like to get to know you better and I hope you'd like to get to know me too.'

She could only gape at him.

'I mean it.'

'Oh!'

'If the idea of that is unpleasant to you . . .'

She didn't lie well at the best of times, and couldn't offer him anything but the truth now. 'It's not unpleasant, not at all. It's just . . . a surprise.'

'There you are, then. We'll just start by getting to know one another and see where it leads.'

He didn't speak much for the rest of their walk, but he smiled quite often.

And so did she.

Nell had expected to receive a letter from Renie by return of post, but when nothing arrived on the Monday or the Tuesday, she began to worry.

'Your sister will write,' Hugh said when he saw her looking anxiously at the post which had just been delivered. 'She may have been busy.'

'It's not like her to wait. Renie usually rushes headlong into things. She'd at least have sent a postcard with a scribbled note.'

'If she doesn't write back this week, we'll go up to London next week and visit the hotel where she works.'

We? She looked at him warily.

'I need to go up to town on business. We can do both,

and in one day, if you don't mind setting off early. I'll ask Pearl to let May stay at her house after school till we get back.'

The thought of going up to London – and just for a day – took Nell's breath away. It might seem nothing special to him, but visiting the capital was something she'd never expected to do, let alone nipping up there for a quick visit.

The following day did bring her a letter. It wasn't Renie's handwriting but it had the name of the hotel embossed on the back of the envelope.

'Something's happened to her!' Nell held the envelope out for him to look at, her hand shaking.

'Sit down before you open it. I'll stay with you, shall I?'

She nodded, tried to steady her hand and slit the envelope with the nearest knife. There was one sheet of paper inside with the hotel's address printed at the top.

Dear Mrs Greenhill

I hope you'll forgive the liberty I took in opening the letter addressed to your sister, but since I've been receiving the postcards you sent her for a while now, I felt you ought to know that she's no longer working here.

Irene left the hotel earlier this year without giving notice, taking only some of her possessions with her. We have a box in store with the things she left, and we'd be grateful if you'd let us know where to send it.

Yours sincerely
Eunice Tolson
Housekeeper, The Rathleigh Hotel, London

The room seemed to whirl round and Nell felt as if she was about to faint. But Hugh was there, kneeling by her chair, putting his arms round her.

'Steady on. Just breathe deeply for a minute or two.'

She clutched him gratefully and did as he ordered.

He moved his upper body backwards a little to study her, but didn't take his arms away. 'That's my girl. You're looking a bit better now. Can you tell me what's wrong?'

Her voice came out sounding croaky. 'The letter. Read it.'

He bent to pick it up, sitting down next to her at the table and reading quickly.

She heard the sudden intake of air as he took in what it said.

'Where can she be?' Nell asked. 'I can't believe Renie would just go away without leaving a message for me. And why would she leave some of her things behind? She didn't have enough clothes to do that.'

'Who else might know?'

Nell's brain didn't seem to be working well, but eventually she managed, 'She might have written to Mrs Garrett, perhaps? No, they'd have told me if she had.'

'What about your father?'

She shuddered. 'I doubt it. Only as the very last resort. Anyway, he'd be more likely to throw her letter on the fire.'

'We'll go up to London on Friday. Write a quick reply telling the housekeeper at the hotel we'll be there mid morning and I'll take it into the village to post. I'll cut across the fields. I could do with a brisk walk.'

She wondered if she dared ask to go with him. She didn't want to sit here worrying. But first she had to write the letter.

When she handed it to him, he studied her and said in his usual quiet way, 'Never mind the housework. I'm not leaving you on your own to fret. Get your walking boots on and come with me.'

'Thank you.'

He took her hand again when they were walking. He kept hold of it when they got to the village and she tried to pull hers away. When she looked at him pleadingly, he said, 'You need the comfort and I like holding your hand. I don't care who sees us.'

'Oh.'

They called in at Pearl's once Nell had posted the letter. Hugh arranged for her to keep an eye on May on Friday after school.

Pearl, who was sitting with her feet up on the sofa, looked at Nell with undisguised curiosity. 'I'm happy to do that, sir. I'm so sorry to have let you down.'

He laughed. 'I'm sure you didn't break your leg on purpose, and luckily Mrs Greenhill was there to take over.'

Frank went to Bart Fuller's house and was pleased to see that he knew one of the neighbours slightly.

He explained that he was looking for Bart's stepdaughter, the one who'd married his cousin, and offered five shillings for any information about where Nell was living now.

'Why do you want to know that?'

'Family business. Nothing to do with anyone else. Do you want the job or shall I find someone else?'

'I'll do it. Or rather, my wife will. She gets on well with everyone round here. If anything happens, she's sure to find out.'

That afternoon, when they told May what was happening, she stared at them in shock, then cried, 'No! No, you can't go so far away! Don't leave me, Uncle Hugh.'

'It's important,' Hugh told her. 'I have to help Mrs Greenhill find her sister. And I'm not leaving you, just going away for the day. You'll be quite safe at Pearl's after school, and we'll probably be back before dark.'

She began to cry and wouldn't stop.

In the end, Nell decided that this couldn't go on and gave her a quick shake. Sometimes kindness wasn't the best way to treat an upset child. 'Stop that at once! You're being silly.'

May hiccupped to a halt and stared at her resentfully. 'It's not fair to leave me alone.'

'Life isn't fair, as we've both found out.' She realised her voice was a bit sharp and tried to speak more calmly. 'May, dear, I have to try to find out what's happened to my sister, and I've never been to London, so your uncle is helping me. I have two sisters and now I don't know where either of them is. How do you think I feel?' Her voice wobbled on the last words.

May looked at the floor, then up at her. 'Why can't I come with you, then?'

Hugh stepped in to answer that. 'Because you have to go to school. Our visit to London is only for one day.

If it was for longer, we'd take you, I promise.'

'It's still not fair.'

Nell found herself the target of May's scowls from then on. She tried not to let that bother her, but it did.

Chapter Fourteen

Paddington Station seemed so enormous to Nell that she stopped walking to stare round in amazement. It was much bigger than the station in Manchester had been, and the high curved roof was like a giant's greenhouse, supported on enormous wrought iron columns. The place was full of people, not only travellers, but workmen and railway porters and other people in uniform.

'They're enlarging the station,' Hugh whispered. 'It's taking years.'

'Why are all those people going down the stairs?'

'On the level below there's a station on the underground railway system. It's very easy to get around in London that way.' He gazed round the station fondly. 'I'd forgotten how much I love it here in the capital – the bustle, the sense of life.'

'Yet you gave that up for May.'

His smile was rueful. 'Only temporarily. And I hadn't expected it to take this long.'

'Maybe you'll have to put your foot down about moving.

Children don't know enough about the world to make the big decisions in life.'

He looked at her as if she'd said something startling. 'But she's grieving.'

'So am I. But I changed my life so that things wouldn't remind me of . . . what I'd lost. It's been a year now, hasn't it? It's up to you to change her life so that she can start to be happy again, somewhere away from all the memories.'

'You're very wise.'

'I don't feel wise.'

'As well as pretty.'

She could feel herself blushing. No one had ever made her blush as often as he did. And she loved his soft chuckles of amusement at that.

As they set off walking again, Nell was glad to take his arm and let him guide her through the crowds, something he seemed to do quite easily, while on her own, she'd have kept bumping into people, she was sure. In spite of her present anxiety, she had to smile at the thought of what a country mouse she must seem to Hugh. Until this year, her life had been very narrow and limited.

'Shall we go straight to the hotel where your sister worked and get that over with?' he asked. 'Or would you like to stop somewhere for a cup of tea first?'

Her amusement vanished as if a tap had been turned off. 'Let's go straight there. I'd rather get it over with.'

The hotel was one of a terrace of buildings near Kensington High Street. These weren't small houses like those in the terraces she knew, but large ones, built for rich people, she was sure. They were all four storeys high and all exactly the same.

'It's Georgian architecture at its best,' Hugh explained, seeing her stare. 'No fuss or frills, just simple, elegant lines.'

The hotel took up one end of the row and looked quietly elegant, as if it knew and was proud of its place in the world.

The door was opened for the group ahead of them by a uniformed commissionaire, who inclined his head. The two ladies were extremely fashionable, one wearing a hobble skirt, draped to emphasise its narrowness around the ankles. They were laughing with their male escorts, full of confidence, from their huge hats decorated with plumes and flowers, to their shiny pointed shoes.

Nell felt as if she shouldn't even be here, and she would never have dared enter the hotel on her own. Hugh was perfectly at home, just like the other group of people. He stopped to chat to the commissionaire for a moment or two, then drew her inside.

At the reception desk she let him explain why they'd come, then sat beside him on a hard overstuffed sofa to wait for Mrs Tolson.

A young woman crossed the huge foyer, stopped at the reception desk, then came towards them. 'Mrs Greenhill? The housekeeper sent me to fetch you. Please come this way.'

Hugh stood up. 'I'll accompany my friend, if you don't mind. She's rather distressed by all this.'

Her sympathetic glance said she was aware of the reason for their visit.

They went up in a lift, the first time Nell had ever been in one. Normally she'd have enjoyed the new experience, but today she was so desperate to find a clue as to what had happened to her sister that she stood unmoving as the young woman closed an expanding iron door, shutting them into a sort of cage. The lift trundled upwards, clanging and rattling. What if it suddenly broke down and they plummeted down to the basement? She shivered at the thought.

On the third floor they followed a very long corridor with a thick soft carpet to the far end, where there was a door marked *Private*. The area beyond wasn't nearly as luxurious. A page boy with a jacket full of shining brass buttons and a little cap on his head hurried along in front of them, and a young woman with a pencil stuck in her hair and a thick pile of papers in her hand hurried out of one door and into another.

The office they were ushered into was large and severely tidy. The woman behind the desk matched it. Her steel-grey hair was dragged back into an unfashionable bun and spectacles magnified her eyes, giving her a watchful, owl-like appearance.

'I'm Mrs Tolson. Please sit down, Mrs Greenhill.'

'This is Mr Easton, who's come with me today.'

'I'm a friend of the family,' he put in smoothly.

'I'm glad Mrs Greenhill has some support at this difficult time. Now, I have all the postcards you sent to your sister.' She passed across a big envelope. 'I don't think Renie received any of them. Could you please check that they're all there?'

Nell looked at the top postcard. 'This was the first one I sent.' She sifted quickly through the pile. 'They all seem to be here, though I'd have to check my diary too, but there's

no sign of the letter I sent to tell her about the accident.'
She hesitated, then added, 'My husband and child were
killed in a gas explosion.'

'I'm sorry to hear about your loss and to bring back the
grief.' Mrs Tolson waited a few seconds, then resumed her
gentle questioning. 'Are you sure your sister didn't give you
any clue that she was thinking of leaving? No, of course she
didn't, or you'd not have kept sending the postcards. What
am I thinking of?'

That remark made her seem more human and Nell
relaxed a little.

'I've been worrying that your sister might be in trouble,
you see. We'd have helped her if she had been, I promise
you, though it would have surprised me. She was a hard
worker and not the flighty sort. It does happen sometimes,
however, that young women are dazzled by London and
act foolishly, but she seemed quite . . . sensible, if a little
impetuous and outspoken.'

'Very impetuous. She sometimes rushed into things.
And she often spoke too frankly. I can't think of any
reason why she'd leave suddenly.'

'Perhaps you'd go through her remaining things and see
if that gives you any clues.' She went across to a cardboard
box sitting on a chair to one side. 'I put everything in
here.'

Nell joined her and went through the items, finding
mainly worn-out clothes and a couple of tattered books.
Nothing really personal, nothing to give her any sort of
hint as to why Renie would vanish. There were none of
her letters or the one photo Nell had had taken of Sarah
by Mrs Garrett. And of course, Renie wasn't the sort to

keep a diary. 'If someone had kidnapped her, she'd not have been able to take the rest of her things,' she said as she stepped back. 'So she must have gone willingly. I'm baffled too.'

Mrs Tolson sighed. 'Then there's nothing else I can do. Would you like to take these things away with you? I can provide you with an old suitcase.'

'I suppose I might as well. Just in case Renie comes back. You have my address at the farm?' Nell glanced at Hugh and saw him nod approval of that.

'Yes. I can contact you there if I hear anything.'

The two of them were quiet as they took the lift down to the foyer.

'Let's get a cup of tea and something to eat,' Hugh said.

'Not here. It'll cost a fortune,' she said automatically.

He laughed. 'Not quite a fortune. I'm ravenous. Aren't you?'

'Not very.'

But when the waitress brought them a selection of dainty sandwiches, he managed to persuade Nell to eat a few, and then to sample the pretty little cakes.

Afterwards they walked slowly to the entrance of the hotel. 'I don't think you're in the mood for sightseeing.'

'No. I'd rather go straight home, if you don't mind. Oh no, you wanted to call in at your office, didn't you?'

'It doesn't matter.'

'Of course it does. It'd be foolish not to go when we're so close.' She saw him frown. 'It'll make no difference to how I feel.'

She was almost as awed by the building Hugh took her

to as she'd been by the hotel. This one had a marble-floored hall from which footsteps echoed up a flight of stairs that went up for four floors. She could see right up the staircase from the hall because it twisted round the walls.

Gold lettering on the door to the right said 'Cates & Dover Enquiries' but Hugh went past that, along a corridor with white marble busts at intervals on pedestals. Nell didn't recognise who they were, except for one, which she thought might be Charles Dickens.

Hugh opened a door on the right at the end of the corridor. 'This is my office. I'll leave you in here while I go and see Mr Dover, the senior partner.'

The room was huge, rather chilly because there was no fire in the hearth, but the fire was laid and needed only a match to set it alight. Every surface had been carefully dusted, but the clutter of books on them reminded her of his study in Wiltshire.

When he didn't return, she went across to the glass-fronted bookcase to read the titles and authors on their spines.

The door opened and someone said, 'Excuse me, madam.'

She swung round to see a lad in a grey suit standing there. 'I've come to light the fire, Mrs Greenhill,' he said cheerfully, 'and to ask if you'd like a cup of tea and a biscuit.'

'Just a cup of tea, please.'

'Mr Easton will be another half hour at least, so I'm to give you this.' He held out a book. 'He thought you'd like something to read and this is the latest by one of his authors. It's a very exciting story!'

'Thank you.'

He went across to the fire, struck a match and lit it, waiting a minute to make sure it caught properly. As he went out, he nodded and said politely, 'Won't be long.'

She was soon seated comfortably in front of the fire with the book and a tea tray, but couldn't settle to reading because she was too worried about Renie. Where on earth could her sister be? Why hadn't she left word?

She heard footsteps and looked up as the door opened.

'Ah, here she is,' Hugh said heartily.

Behind the older man's back, he was looking at her strangely, as if pleading for her to understand. She braced herself for some new shock. But what he said was so unexpected, it took her breath away.

'Mr Dover, this is my fiancée, Nell Greenhill. Nell, this is the senior partner, Mr Dover.'

Still standing out of sight of his companion, he mouthed *Please help me*, so she took a deep breath and smiled, hoping she'd hidden her astonishment.

'My dear Miss Greenhill, I'm delighted to meet you.'

'Mrs Greenhill,' she corrected automatically, saw him gape and added, 'I'm a widow.'

'Oh, I see. Very sad. And so young too. But I'm very happy that this young fellow's found someone at last. We'd all given up hope of getting him married off. Have you two named a day yet?'

'Er . . . no.'

'We've only just got engaged,' Hugh said, coming across to put his arm round her.

That was true, she thought, and couldn't help smiling.

Mr Dover looked at her hand, then at Hugh.

'One of the reasons we're up in London, sir, is to find her a ring.'

'Good, good. I hope you won't wait too long to marry and settle down again. We need you back here, my boy. How is your poor little niece?'

'Improving slowly. But she still clings to the farm and weeps if I suggest moving to London.'

'Very sad. But you'll have to be firm with her now. She's had enough time to get over the worst and you can't let a child's wishes run your career. Shall we say another month?'

'I'll do my best.' Hugh took out his pocket watch. 'Now, I'm afraid we must leave if we're to buy that ring.'

'Jolly good, jolly good.'

When they went outside, Hugh looked at her ruefully. 'Old Dover and his wife have been trying to marry me off to one or other of their nieces for years. There seem to be dozens of nieces, and very plain girls they are too. He jumped to the conclusion that you were my fiancée and . . . well, it seemed best to let him believe it, or he'd have been pressing me to go to tea again.'

'I don't suppose it matters. Once you go back to work in London, you can tell him we've changed our minds.'

'Mmm. But we might not change our minds.'

She gaped at him.

He smiled, then shook his head as if clearing away some stray thoughts and picked up the suitcase again. 'We'll take a taxi to Paddington Station.'

All the way home she alternated between shock at what he'd said and worry about her sister.

What would he do next?

And what would she agree to next? He had a way of making you do what he wanted, in the gentlest possible way, whether it was going for a walk or pretending to get engaged.

He surely couldn't have meant what he'd said about changing their minds? No, she must have mistaken it. This so-called engagement was just a way of helping him, a convenience. It wasn't real.

It was nine o'clock before they got a still-sulky May to bed, and Nell wasn't sure whether to rejoin Hugh in the kitchen or go to bed herself. But she felt restless, so she went back down to make them a cup of cocoa, as she did most nights, but she took care to sit opposite him at the table.

'What are you going to do about your sisters now?' Hugh asked as he stirred his cocoa.

She didn't pretend to misunderstand him. 'I don't know.'

'You need to write to those friends of yours, the minister and his wife. They might have a letter from Renie for you.'

'Yes, of course. Why didn't I think of that? I'll do it tomorrow.'

'And there's still your father.'

'Only as a final resort, and I'm not sure I can face him, even then.'

She had the letter to the Garretts ready to give to the postman by the time he came the following day, and then could only wait to find out if they had heard anything from Renie.

In the meantime, she kept herself busy. There was a lot to do to bring the farmhouse up to scratch.

It was strange how comfortable she continued to feel when she was alone with Hugh. She didn't let herself hope for the impossible, but concentrated on enjoying his company and getting to know him better.

He seemed to be doing the same.

Though he did hold her hand a lot and smile at her and . . . She really should stop daydreaming.

The following weekend Nell agreed to keep an eye on May so that Hugh could get on with some urgent editing work which had arrived that week. She insisted the girl tidy her room and help with the cleaning. 'Your room is in a dreadful mess.'

May looked at her in outrage. 'Pearl was supposed to do that sort of thing, so it's your job now.'

Nell felt annoyed at this cheeky answer. She didn't believe in spoiling children, even ones whose families were in comfortable circumstances, and she wasn't going to put up with May speaking to her like that. 'Pearl didn't have time to do everything in such a big house and I shan't have, either. Besides, no one should be expected to pick up dirty clothes after a big girl like you. We'll make a fresh start from now on, and I'll check every day to make sure your room stays tidy.'

'It's *your* job to do the tidying up,' May said at once. 'And anyway, I always sit in my uncle's office and read at weekends. He *likes* me to be with him.'

'Of course he does. But he'll also like you to grow up knowing how to run a house. That's a woman's main job.'

Hugh came in just then and May fled to him, sobbing out her protest. But when he heard her complaint, he sat her down at the table and said firmly, 'Mrs Greenhill is right, May. You can't just sit around reading all the time and expect other people to pick up after you. That's lazy. I have work to do, and at your age, you should definitely be clearing up your own room. What's more, if Mrs Greenhill asks you to do something, I expect you to obey her as you would me.'

This made the girl sob even more wildly.

Nell beckoned to Hugh and moved over to the door, saying quietly, 'Leave her to me now. The more attention you give her, the more she'll protest.'

'Are you sure?'

'Oh, yes.'

'Don't let her be cheeky.'

'I won't stand any nonsense.' She went back to her work, and the minute the door closed behind Hugh, the sobbing lessened. She didn't even look at the girl.

'You're mean,' May announced after a few moments of silence.

'I'm doing what all mothers do, since you don't have one of your own now. I'm teaching you to do the housework, just as my sister taught me after my mother died.'

'*My* uncle is rich enough to pay other people to do the housework.'

'And he's sensible enough to want you to learn how it's done, and not grow up lazy and ignorant.'

'Well, I'm not doing it.'

'Are you really going to disobey me?' She waited and added, 'And him?'

There was dead silence, and when she looked again she saw a sulky scowling face. She put away the last dish. 'Right, let's go and do the bedrooms now. Yours is in great need of a complete turn-out. You can bring the polish and the dusting things. I'll take the broom.'

In the bedroom, she looked at the candlestick beside the bed, which was covered in melted wax. 'You'd better take this downstairs. We'll clean it properly later when we do the lamps.'

May snatched up the candlestick. 'In London, my uncle has electric lighting in his house, even in the bedrooms and servants' rooms, so there aren't any lamps or candlesticks to clean. And the Vacuum Cleaner Company come to the house every week to clean the carpets and floors.'

'Then why are you refusing to go and live there? I'd love to have such modern aids. I've never even seen a vacuum cleaning machine, though I've read about them. I don't enjoy cleaning lamps and candlesticks, either, but if I want to read in the evenings, I have to do it.'

May stamped her way down the stairs.

When she came back they worked in silence, with Nell occasionally giving a quiet instruction to do something, and May huffing and sighing, but doing it.

When they'd finished, Nell stood by the door with her hands on her hips. 'There. Your room looks so much better. And it smells better too.'

There was a sob beside her and she found May in tears, couldn't help taking the child into her arms and met with no resistance this time.

'What's the matter, dear?'

'Mummy used to stand there and say that. I miss her so much.'

Nell moved across to the bed and let the girl cry against her, tears rising in her own eyes.

When there had been quiet for a moment or two, she looked at May.

'You've been crying too,' the girl said in surprise.

'Yes. You reminded me of how I felt when my mother died. And how I felt when my daughter died a few months ago.' She felt tears run down her cheeks. 'Sorry. I shouldn't be troubling you with my sorrows, only I miss my daughter very much.'

A hand crept into hers. 'Uncle Hugh told me. I'm sorry you lost her.'

They sat for a while, but this time in a more companionable silence, then Nell stood up. 'Come on. Time to prepare lunch.'

She hoped they'd made progress today in getting on together, wanted very much to help this sad confused child.

A reply arrived from the Garretts on the Tuesday. Once the postman had left, Nell held the letter in her hand for a moment or two, afraid to open it, then told herself not to be stupid and tore the envelope, pulling out the single piece of paper it contained.

My dear Nell

We were delighted to hear from you and to know that your summer of walking has made you feel better. We have appreciated your postcards, but as

286

you say, it's time to stop wandering and make a new life for yourself.

Your job sounds very suitable and I'm sure Mr Easton will be satisfied with your hard work.

I'm afraid we haven't heard from Renie at all. I went to the post office to ask what had happened to the mail for Willow Court. They said there wasn't any as the people who lived there hadn't been the sort to receive letters, except for you.

I'm so sorry that we're unable to help you find Renie.

Please keep in touch and let us know how you get on. My dear wife and all your friends from chapel send their very best regards.

Septimus Garrett

PS Your husband's cousin Frank came back, but he'd just missed you. He said it was urgent family business, so perhaps you ought to go and see him.

Nell stared at the last sentence in shock.

'Bad news?'

'It's from the Garretts to say they haven't heard from Renie. And . . . look at the PS.' She passed the letter to him.

'Why would he go all the way up to Lancashire again? Did Cliff's mother say anything when you went to see her?'

'No. And I'm not going to see them again. I don't like Frank.'

'Let's sit down and plan what to do next, then.'

'It won't do any good to go and see my father.' But

she did sit down and let Hugh fuss over her, needed that comfort.

'We'll both go to see your father,' he said after a while. 'That's the only avenue left to explore now for your older sister.'

'I know Mattie won't have gone back to him, or even got in touch with him. He's not her father, after all. She and I just share a mother. You don't understand what he's like, Hugh. He's a horrible man, a real bully. All he cares about is money.'

'Nonetheless . . .'

She argued with Hugh, but though he remained as gentle as ever, somehow, an hour later, she found herself agreeing to go into Swindon with him on the Saturday afternoon to ask her father if he'd heard from Mattie.

'We should take May with us,' she said. 'It's not good for her to be left out. And anyway, we need to get her away from here regularly, if you're to take her back to London next month.'

'You seem quite set on getting me back to London.'

She blushed. 'I'm sorry. Perhaps it isn't my business when you go, or even whether you go.'

'Of course it's your business, especially if you're to stay with us, which I hope you will. My former housekeeper in London moved to another position a few months ago and my house is all dust covers and chilly silence at the moment.'

'You should take May to see it and ask her to decide which room she wants for a bedroom.'

'She and her parents have visited me there a few times. She knows the house and has always slept in the same bedroom.'

Nell sighed. 'I don't think May's sure of anything at the moment. Take her to London, Hugh. Visit the house, discuss the move and ask for her opinion about something there, anything.'

He sat frowning slightly for a moment or two, then he looked at her. 'I'm only going back to London if you come too . . . Nell?' he prompted when she didn't immediately answer.

'Are you sure you want me to stay on as housekeeper there? I've no experience of London ways.'

'As housekeeper for the time being. Perhaps more, later.'

She looked at him warily. Surely he wouldn't want her to continue pretending to be his fiancée?

'We're good friends now, aren't we, Nell?'

She nodded, still wary.

He picked up her hand. 'I think we could move on to become more than friends. In fact I want to do that. Don't you?'

She jerked her hand back in outrage. 'I'm *not* going to sleep with you!' She'd fallen into that trap once, wasn't going to do it again.

'*What?*' He looked at her with a puzzled expression, then anger replaced it. 'I wasn't asking you to become my mistress. I was trying to court you, in my own clumsy way. What have I ever said to make you think I would treat you like that? If you've changed your mind and don't want to get to know me better, you have only to say so.'

'Surely things don't need to change? You can tell Mr Dover that we're not getting married and—'

He stood up, shoving his chair back. 'But I do want

things to change between us. Think about it, Nell. Decide whether you want to find happiness, or whether you want to live alone inside that fence you erect round yourself every time I mention my feelings and ask about yours. And let me know when you've decided.'

He walked out of the room, his body stiff with indignation.

She sat there shocked rigid. Was that how he saw her? Sitting behind a fence? Not letting anyone get close to her, especially him? He was so wrong.

She bent her head and stared down at her clasped hands as she admitted to herself that she wanted him to court her. Oh, yes. She wanted it very much.

But she was terrified of it too. He was so much above her, she didn't understand how he could possibly care for her in that way. She'd made a bad mistake once, with Cliff, and had paid dearly for that. Hugh ought to be marrying a proper lady, someone of his own class, not an ordinary working woman like her.

And apart from her own feelings, she didn't want to ruin his life, cared about him too much for that. She pressed one hand to her mouth as she admitted to herself how very much she loved him.

Was it possible for them to be together? Should she let him court her?

It took her a full hour to gather her courage together and knock on the door of his study.

'Come.'

She took a deep breath and opened the door. 'Hugh . . .' Her voice faltered, but she moved into the room and went across to where he was standing by the window, determined to apologise. She stood beside him, not touching him, staring at her clasped hands as she began to say her piece. 'I'm sorry. I've been a coward, afraid to . . . even try.'

She sneaked a quick glance at him and saw his expression lighten. But he didn't say anything, just looked down at her and waited for her to continue.

'I'd like us to get to know each other better. Could we try?'

His smile was glorious. He pulled her into his arms, and before she realised what he intended, he began kissing her.

Before she could think about what she was doing, she was kissing him back. And oh, this was nothing like Cliff's hasty kisses. There was no fumbling, no hurting her breasts, nothing but the tenderest and yet most exciting of kisses. When that ended, he brushed her cheek with his fingers and then pulled her again into the cradle of his arms.

'Ah, Nell. I can't say how happy you've made me.' He drew back and smiled down at her. 'You look as if you've never been kissed before.'

'I've never been kissed like that before.'

A small frown creased his forehead. 'Wasn't it . . . good between you and your husband?'

She shook her head, blushing hotly. 'No. I didn't enjoy that side of things at all. You may as well know it. He said I was . . . unnatural, cold.'

'If everything goes as I intend, you will enjoy it with me. I'm quite sure you're not cold. But we'll take things slowly, make sure you grow used to kissing and caressing before we move too quickly to other delights.'

'Yes, please. Only Hugh . . .'

'What?'

'I still can't think what you see in me.' The caring in his face made her feel weak, it was so wonderful.

'I see a woman with an indomitable spirit, who walks through thunderstorms on her own and recovers from a tragedy that would have destroyed a lesser person. I see a caring and loving woman, who's kind to a grieving child who can sometimes be very rude. Someone who loves learning – and yes, I know you've not been formally educated, but you're nonetheless very widely read, and can discuss what you've read intelligently. I'm afraid I could never be fond of a stupid woman, however kind and pretty she was.'

'Oh.' Warmth flooded through her, relief that he didn't consider her stupid, and happiness too – such a warm fragile emotion.

'I also see someone who blushes delightfully when I give her a compliment, who's pretty and soft, and whom I want to kiss each time I see her, or even when I think about her.'

'Oh, Hugh.' She could feel her cheeks growing hot.

'Oh, Nell,' he teased, mimicking her. Then his smile faded and he spoke straight from the heart. 'I'm so glad I found you that day. I was beginning to think I'd never fall in love again.'

'Did you love her very much?'

'Of course I did. But she's not here and you are. You're different from her and I love you for your own self, I promise you.'

Chapter Fifteen

On the following Saturday, Nell, Hugh and May went into Swindon, something the child seemed to regard as a treat, but which Nell had been dreading. Even with Hugh beside her, she felt sick with apprehension today.

The trains were on time and they got there far too quickly for her peace of mind. Her family had lived in one of the railway houses. It could have been a nice little home if her stingy father had let them spend money on anything but his own comforts. She felt shuddery inside at the thought of seeing her father.

'Do you want to take a taxi?' Hugh asked.

'I'd rather walk, if you don't mind. It's not far. You will be careful when we get there. Don't let him goad you to fight.'

'You've said that several times already. I promise you, I'm not the sort to get into fights.'

He might not be, but her father was, and Bart was a dirty fighter who'd maimed for life a young man who'd tried to court her sister Mattie. She couldn't bear it if he hurt Hugh.

At the end of the street, she stopped and looked at May. 'My father can be very rough. If he starts fighting, you're to stand right back.'

May looked puzzled. 'You already said that.'

'It's worth repeating.'

'Stop worrying, Nell. We'll be all right,' Hugh said. 'I'm big enough to look after myself.'

As they turned into the street, she saw their reflections in the window of the corner shop and was surprised how much they looked like a family group. Maybe one day they would be. May needed a mother and Nell would like to have a daughter to love.

When they got to the house, Nell moved forward to knock on the front door. There was the sound of someone approaching it inside, the door swung slowly open and she braced herself.

But the person who opened the door was a complete stranger, a fresh-faced man, not much older than herself. And he looked very much at home. For a moment she couldn't find her voice, she was so surprised.

He looked from Nell to Hugh. 'Can I help you?'

'I was . . . I came to see Bart Fuller,' she faltered. 'My father. Doesn't he live here anymore?'

A voice from the back room called, 'Who is it, Jim?'

'Someone to see the last tenant, Alice.'

More footsteps brought a woman to join them. She was expecting a child and had another little one clinging to her skirt. She and the man exchanged worried glances.

'Did you know Bart well?' she asked.

'I'm his daughter.'

'Oh. Then you'd better come in and . . . I'll tell you what happened to him.'

This seemed a strange answer. Nell followed the woman into the front room, which was chilly, with its furniture stiffly arranged, clearly not used much. She frowned. That looked like her mother's china cabinet, and the sofa – it had a different cover, but it felt just the same as their old one. No, it couldn't be. She was imagining things.

The woman took charge. 'Please sit down.' She waited until they were all seated. 'I'm sorry to be the one to tell you that your father died a few months ago. The neighbours said he dropped dead in the back room.'

Nell gasped and the room seemed to waver around her as she tried to take this in. 'He's dead? My father's dead?'

'It must be a terrible shock to you. Would you like a cup of tea?'

'No, thank you.' She turned to Hugh. 'All this time . . . we didn't even know. Cliff could have come back to Swindon. I'm sure he'd have got his old job back, because he was good at his trade. But he wouldn't even write to his own family, he was so afraid of my father finding out where we were.'

Everyone except May was looking at her, two of them politely, Hugh with compassion. Suddenly all Nell wanted was to get out of the room, out of the house and into the fresh air. She couldn't weep for her father, was conscious of relief more than anything else, felt guilty about that.

Then it occurred to her that Bart had had possessions,

savings. It might sound mercenary, but her sisters might be glad of that money.

'Do you . . . um . . . know what happened to my father's things?'

'We have some of the furniture. His friend sold it to us. He was clearing out the house when we came to look round.'

'Which friend? Do you know his name?'

'Stan Telfor. Everyone knows him. He buys and sells things. He's done very well for himself. I have his address.' She got up and fumbled in a vase, muttering in annoyance and tipping its contents out before she found the scrap of paper she was looking for. 'There. Good thing I kept it, eh?' She held it out to Nell.

Hugh had to take it because she felt as frozen as a stone statue. He handed her his card. 'And if you hear anything of Mr Fuller's other daughters, please get in touch with me. Mrs Greenhill's been recently widowed and is now my housekeeper. She looks after my daughter and myself. I'll make it worth your while.'

He helped Nell up and they went outside.

After the door had shut, she turned to look at the house and let out her breath in a long groaning sigh. 'Sarah might still be alive if we'd known my father was dead,' she said. 'Cliff was a coward – and I let him be.'

'It's easy to be wise afterwards. Don't berate yourself.'

But she continued to look sadly at the house.

'What do you want to do now? Go and see this Telfor fellow . . . Nell?'

'Oh. Sorry. I was just thinking. I suppose we'll have to go and see Stan. I'd better warn you, though. He's like my father: a big man who gets into fights.'

But there was no answer at Stan's house. A neighbour from across the street opened the door and yelled, 'He's gone to see his parents, taken his family with him, and they won't be back till late.'

'We'll leave him a note,' Hugh said. He patted his pockets. 'Drat! I've left my notebook at home, and you can't leave enough information on a business card, though I'll leave him one of those as well. We'll have to buy some paper and an envelope.'

The neighbour came in to borrow a cup of sugar, though Alice knew it was really to find out who her posh visitors had been. She didn't mind. Joan was a good neighbour, if nosy.

'It was one of Bart's daughters,' she said. 'She didn't know her father was dead.'

'Fancy that!' She lowered her voice. 'They ran away, you know. All the daughters. One rainy day they just upped and left, and they've never been seen again. He was in a rage for weeks about that. Nasty old bugger, he was.'

'And now she's come back.'

'Yes. Did she say where she was living?'

Alice reached up to the mantelpiece and picked up the business card. 'She's working as housekeeper for this gentleman. He said to get in touch with her at this address if I heard anything about her sisters.'

'Fancy that.' She studied the card. 'He doesn't live in Swindon, does he? Do you suppose she's, you know, living with him?'

'He said she was his housekeeper, and she doesn't look

the sort to be anything else to me. Scrawny little thing, she is. They had his daughter with them too. No, I'm sure it's nothing else.'

The three of them walked towards the town centre and called at the Commercial Road Market, a modern place, built only a decade or so ago.

'It doesn't smell very nice here,' May whispered.

'It never does,' Nell said.

Hugh looked up at the ceiling disapprovingly. 'It must be freezing cold in winter with that high ceiling. I edited a book about commercial architecture once. The author wouldn't have approved of this place.'

Nell was getting used to the way he suddenly revealed pockets of knowledge, acquired in his work. 'Look, they sell stationery on that stall.'

They bought what they needed, though Hugh pulled a face at the quality of the notepaper. She sat down at one of the small tables next to a refreshment stall intending to write a quick letter.

Hugh didn't sit. 'You both look cold. I'll buy us a pot of tea and maybe this young lady would like to get some sweets from that stall over there?' He held out a threepenny bit.

May squealed in delight and took the small silver coin from him.

'Don't drop it and don't go out of my sight!' He turned back to Nell. 'We're taking a taxi out to Mr Telfor's house. You're looking tired now.'

He was right. She felt exhausted, shocked that her father could have been dead all this time. It seemed as if she ought to have known it. He was her father, after all.

She was glad to get home to the farm, and moved slowly through the evening, doing necessary chores mechanically, glad that Hugh left her to get on with them in peace.

That night, however, after May had gone to bed, he said, 'Let's sit in more comfort than these wooden chairs.' As she moved from the table to the small sofa, Hugh pulled her into his arms. She didn't resist, wanting the comfort, wanting him.

Though she'd half-convinced herself that she'd only imagined how wonderful his embraces were, he proved her wrong. When he kissed her, she couldn't even think straight, was only aware of him in the whole world. He made her feel loved and happy and warm. How could one man do all that to you with just a touch of the lips? Cliff never had.

He laughed softly as they sat down on the small sofa. 'I love kissing you, Nell, and unless you're the best actress in the world, you enjoy it too.'

She didn't lie, couldn't. 'I do love it.'

'We'll find your sisters, my little darling. We'll set your world to rights, then we'll build our own world together.'

She sighed and nestled against him, sure that if anyone could help her find Mattie and Renie, it was him.

Only . . . how could their love have a happy ending? She still couldn't believe in that, somehow.

She wouldn't know how to behave in his London life. She'd felt out of place just sitting in the elegant office, where even the office boy spoke better English than she did. And Hugh loved London.

He kissed her on the temple. 'Are you all right? You gave such a heavy sigh just then.'

She couldn't face any more sad thoughts today so told him the simple truth. 'I'm tired out. I think I should go to bed. It's been a difficult day, hasn't it?'

'Things will get better, my love.'

That was another difference between them. He truly believed the future would be brighter. She didn't trust fate at all. It could deal you a blow that nearly tore you apart, and without even a hint of a warning.

Joan's husband went round to see Frank Greenhill. She'd memorised the address on the card and written it down as soon as she got home. It was all very satisfactory and he pocketed the five shillings, thinking it an easy way to earn money. This money would go towards their annual holiday, which had to be saved up for carefully.

When he'd gone, Frank went to tell his aunt and uncle. 'She's living near Faringdon, not in Swindon. That's why we couldn't find her. She's acting as housekeeper to some fancy gentleman.'

'She'll be warming his bed too, if I know her,' his aunt said at once.

'They didn't think so. His daughter was with them and they seemed very respectable people.'

'She's landed on her feet, then – doesn't deserve it.'

'I'll go and check the place out tomorrow. Maybe it'll be worth paying my pal to take me in his motor car.'

'You'd not get me to ride in one of those things,' his aunt said at once.

She was turning into a proper old misery. He looked

round. But it was worth putting up with her because this house would be his one day – and some of that money too.

And Nell had better not cross him about this.

The following morning Nell, Hugh and May were walking back from the village, about to turn off onto the path across the fields, when they heard the sound of a motor car. They moved to the side of the road and it slowed down as it came near.

Nell stared at it in shock. Could that be . . . It *was*! Frank Greenhill. She reached out blindly for Hugh's hand and he looked at her in puzzlement.

The car came to a halt and the passenger stared at them. 'Nell,' he said. 'Fancy meeting you here!'

She couldn't speak for a moment, then said quietly, 'I'm visiting friends.' Tugging Hugh's hand, she moved on quickly, but she didn't hear the car start up again. As they turned off the main road, she glanced back and saw Frank still staring at her.

'Who is he?' Hugh asked quietly.

'My husband's cousin Frank. I can't think what he's doing out here. They aren't the sort to go out driving. The Greenhills usually only do things for money.'

The car started up again.

'Well, he's gone now. You'll probably never see him again.'

But Nell couldn't get the thought of Frank out of her mind, or the memory of the fierce way he'd looked at her. She couldn't believe their meeting was just a coincidence, either. He must have found out where she lived. But why was he bothering to pursue her? Cliff's mother had made it plain they wanted nothing more to do with her.

Was he still after the money?

She tried to shake off her worries and get on with her day, but although Hugh went to work in his study in the afternoon and May went out to play with the dog, Nell still couldn't concentrate on her book.

In the afternoon Nell heard the sound of a motor car approaching the farm and her first thought was that Frank was pursuing her. As it came up the lane to the farm and stopped outside, she looked out of the window. Thank goodness! It wasn't him.

Thinking it was someone who'd got lost, she went to open the door, but took an involuntary step backwards at the sight of Stan Telfor, looking as big and boisterous as ever. Common sense took over. They'd left their address for Stan, so he was here by their invitation. She was letting her nerves get the better of her.

He beamed at her as if they were old friends as he came towards the house. 'Living posh now, are you, Nell girl?'

'Shh, Stan. This is my employer's house and—'

'If this is Mr Telfor, you'd better invite him in,' said a voice behind them.

She glanced at Hugh, grateful that he was there. 'Come in, Stan.'

She took him into the kitchen, which felt like her domain now and gave her a bit of much needed confidence. At least this man wasn't scowling at her. In fact, he looked happier than she'd ever seen him before.

'This is my employer, Mr Easton.'

Stan stuck out his big hand and the two men shook. 'Pleased to meet you, sir.'

'Sit down and I'll put the kettle on.' It was a universal thing, a cup of tea – softened arguments, comforted you with its warmth. She'd never met anyone who didn't enjoy a cup.

When Hugh joined them at the table, Stan's smile faded. 'If you don't mind, sir, this is private business.'

'I'm a good friend of Nell's and I think she'd prefer me to stay.'

Stan looked across at her and shrugged as she nodded agreement. 'Sorry about your dad, Nell. Poor old Bart went to pieces after you lot left. He wasn't good at looking after himself and he'd been worrying about his health for a while.'

'He never said anything.'

'He wouldn't talk about something like that. Too frightened of losing his job if they found out he got pains in his chest whenever he did the heavy work.'

'Oh, I see. I've only recently come back to Swindon. I went to the house to see him and the new people told me he'd died. They said you'd cleared the house out, so we came to see you.'

'Yes. Nice young couple they are, saved me a lot of trouble by buying half his stuff.'

'It was very kind of you to do that, Stan.'

He shrugged. 'He was a good drinking mate of mine, old Bart was, for all he could get a bit grumpy at times. I heard your Cliff had died too, but no one knows how. You know how tight-lipped them Greenhills are. Never tell anyone what's going on unless it pays them to. How did he die?'

'The gas cooker blew up. He was standing right next to it.'

Stan let out a long slow whistle. 'Nasty, that. You're all right, though. You didn't get hurt?'

'No, I was out at the shop. But our little daughter was killed too.' She had to swallow hard to contain her grief. She could control it now, but it was always there.

He patted her arm awkwardly. 'Aw, no. Hard to lose a kid. I don't know where I'd be without my two stepsons. The eldest has started work now. I got him into a trade.' He leant back and smiled. 'So that's two of you sisters still living near Swindon now, eh?'

Nell was so surprised by what he said that she splashed herself with the boiling water she'd been pouring into the teapot and cried out in pain.

Hugh jumped up and held her reddened hand under the cold tap. Stan went across to finish dealing with the teapot.

'Which of my sisters have you seen?' she asked from across by the sink, trying to pull her hand away from Hugh and failing.

'Your Mattie. She's living out at Shallerton Bassett now.'

'Where's that?'

'Over to the west. Just a small village. Me and Bart went out to see her once.'

Nell burst into tears of joy and couldn't speak coherently for a few moments, she was so glad to hear that Mattie was all right.

Hugh wrapped her hand in a damp tea towel and guided her to a chair.

Stan shoved a cup of tea in front of her.

'I'm sorry,' she said. 'It's just . . . I wasn't sure I'd ever see either of them again.'

Stan looked at her in surprise. 'Has your Renie gone missing too?'

'Yes. She was working in London and she just . . . vanished one day. No one knows why or where she is.'

'She'll be all right. That girl was born to land on her feet like a cat. Cheeky little madam, she is, but you couldn't help liking her.' He drained his cup and went to pour himself another one without asking.

By now Nell was clutching Hugh's hand and happiness was tingling through her. 'Do you have Mattie's address, Stan?'

'Not her actual address.'

She looked at him in sudden fear.

'But I can tell you exactly where the house is. Big house it is too. Talk about landing on her feet. Some old lady left it to her. Oh, and she's got herself married as well. He walks with a limp, but he's a big strong fellow all the same. Bart tried to thump him. Stupid sod. Should have wished her well and stayed in her good books, like I did. She and I parted on good terms.'

'Why did *you* go to see her?'

'I had my reasons. Personal. I wanted to know something.'

'Have you heard anything from her since?'

'I sent word to her when Bart died, but it was her husband who came and sorted things out. I said I'd clear out the house and he told me to keep the money I got for the furniture. She didn't want anything of his. I sent them his bank book, though. I didn't realise how much he'd got tucked away, the old devil.'

'And you've not seen them since?'

'No reason to. I go out along the Bath road sometimes, but I don't think she'd welcome a visit from me, even though we smoothed things over that day.' He looked at her and added, 'I didn't know Bart was trying to force her to marry me, you know. I thought she wanted to.'

'He wasn't kind to any of us, just used us for his own purposes.' Then she turned to beam at Hugh. 'I can't believe Mattie's married! Oh, I do hope she's happy!'

'She looked at the fellow fondly enough,' Stan offered. 'I've got wed, as well. Good lass, she is. Best cook I ever met, my Betsy. Got two sons. Great little chaps, they are. I never thought I'd enjoy being a father so much.'

'Did you come all this way to tell me about Mattie? That was very kind of you.'

He shrugged. 'I like to take my motor car out for a run now and then. Betsy usually comes with me, but she's in the family way and she's feeling a bit tired today.'

'Congratulations.'

He smiled, a proud smile, without the old sharpness in it.

'You must stay for lunch, Mr Telfor,' Hugh said.

'I won't, if you don't mind, Mr Easton, though I'd not mind another cup of tea if you can squeeze one out of that pot. I told Betsy I'd not stay out all day. I'll just tell you first how to find your Mattie. You'd better write it down.' He explained and Hugh made notes.

Nell didn't need to make notes. She'd remember every word he said because she was longing to see her sister. 'You look as if you're doing well for yourself, Stan,' Nell said as she handed him a third cup of tea. 'You must be, if you can afford a car.'

He tapped the side of his nose. 'Ah. Not doing badly at all. Your Mattie's not the only one to have had a bit of luck. I've been dealing in this and that for a while now, on the side, like, but I'm dealing for a living now. We clear houses out when someone dies, and we buy and sell old things. Not like pawnbroking. I never could fancy that. But antiques and second-hand furniture are different.'

He leant back, obviously happy to talk about his success. 'You'd be surprised at how much some daft folk will pay for old dressers and such, even when they're scarred and scratched. My partner knows a lot about antiques and he's teaching me. I was no good at school, but I've picked this up quick, because it's *real* stuff. My partner runs our auctions and does the valuations, but I do the house clearances and keep an eye on things at auctions to make sure no one stirs up trouble. It's all done fair and proper, though.'

'That's wonderful.'

'Never a dull moment. Beats slaving at the railway works. They don't always treat you well when you get older and lose your strength. That'd been worrying your father for years. In my new trade I can work as long as I can stand upright, and I can get younger men to hump the heavy stuff around later on.'

When Stan had left, she went to sit down in the kitchen.

'Happy?' Hugh asked, with a smile of his own.

'Very. I can't believe how Stan's changed. Wasn't he talkative? I'm so glad for him. Um . . . can I have the day off tomorrow, please, to go and find Mattie? It'll take me all day, I'm afraid.'

'No, certainly not.'

She looked at him in shock, this was so unlike him.

He chuckled as he took her hand. 'I'm coming with you, and what's more, we're getting young Harry from the village to drive us in his motor car. Otherwise we'd spend half the day changing trains and we'd be stuck for transport out to the village once we got to Wootton Bassett.'

She relaxed again. 'You're so kind to me.'

'It's my pleasure.'

He was leaning forward, kissing her cheek when May came running into the kitchen from outside.

She stopped dead by the door, looking at them accusingly. 'No!' she cried and ran out again.

'Nothing's easy with May, is it?' he said ruefully. 'I'd better go after her, then I'll nip into the village to see Harry.'

Nell let him go, wanting time on her own to take in the news that Mattie was well and living only twenty miles or so away.

But whatever Hugh had said to his niece didn't reconcile her to finding the two of them kissing. May was sulky for the rest of the afternoon and hardly said a word to either of them all evening, while the looks she threw at Nell were angry and resentful.

Instead of her usual protests at any disturbance of her routine, May only shrugged when told to go to Pearl's after school the following day and stay there until her uncle came to pick her up.

When it was time for May to go to bed, Nell stood up to go with her as usual.

'I can get myself to bed, thank you!'

'I'll fill your hot-water bottle, then.'

'I don't want one.' May stamped off up the stairs.

Hugh turned to Nell. 'She'll come round. It was just the shock of seeing us together.' He frowned at the sounds of banging doors and things being thrown about that came from upstairs.

'It seems to have really upset her.'

'The world doesn't revolve round her and she'll have to learn that. I'm not letting anything come between us, Nell. And I'm not letting her be rude to you, either. You don't deserve it.'

Children could be rude without saying a word, Nell thought sadly. The way May had behaved upset her, most of all because it reinforced what she'd been telling herself. There was such a big gap between Hugh and herself. Would things ever work out for them? Was that possible?

She woke in the night and it took her a while to get to sleep. And it wasn't May or Stan she was thinking of, but Frank. He'd looked at her with such anger. Whatever Hugh said, she was sure it was no accident that he'd been passing.

Only how had he found her? She hadn't given Mrs Greenhill her new address.

Chapter Sixteen

The following morning Harry picked them up early in his motor car, which he told Nell proudly was a Vauxhall A-Type. It was shining with polish, just as his face was shining with love for his vehicle.

Their washerwoman found out that morning that they were going out with Harry and would leave her to do the washing on her own. She told Nell that he'd spent nearly all of a small inheritance from an aunt on this vehicle and his family were upset about that, thinking he'd wasted it.

Mrs Compton seemed to know all the gossip in the village and no doubt that evening she'd be telling them about Nell and Mr Easton going out somewhere with Harry. She could only hope Mrs Compton hadn't noticed her feelings for Hugh. Nell didn't feel ready to face the world about that.

On his advice, she'd dressed up warmly today, wearing her mackintosh over her tweed suit, and using a long scarf he'd found for her to tie her hat on firmly.

'How fast can it go?' she asked Harry.

'Thirty or forty miles an hour on the good roads, faster sometimes.'

She stared at him in horror. 'Is that safe?'

'You'll be all right with me, Mrs Greenhill, I promise. I'm a good driver and this fine lady won't let us down.' He slapped one hand down proudly on the bonnet of his car. 'The first car built like this won the RAC trial for two thousand miles in fifteen days as far back as 1908. They're tried and tested by now, these A-Types are, though the man who owned this one didn't understand cars and got into trouble with it a few times, which is how I got it so cheaply. Now, who wants to ride in the front?'

'You ride in the front, Hugh. You know you want to talk to Harry about cars.'

'Well, if you don't mind, I would like to ask him about a few things as we go.'

She sat on the comfortably upholstered rear seat, feeling nervous at first, then getting used to travelling so fast. She held on tight to the strap though, as she listened to the two men's conversation, smiling at Harry's enthusiasm, wondering what some of the words he used meant. But she couldn't be bothered to ask. She was too excited about seeing her sister again.

'They said I'd wasted my money buying this car, Mr Easton, but I'm making a respectable living by repairing bicycles and other vehicles, and hiring my car out to people like yourself, so I don't agree. I won't let anyone else drive her, of course. And I've only just started. You'll see. They'll all see. I'm going to do much better before I'm through, whatever anyone says. I'm going to sell motor cars.'

It was lovely to hear a young man with such ambition. He was only a year or two younger than Cliff had been, but what a difference there was between the two of them. This man had a happy open approach to the world.

She held on more tightly as they got to a main road and speeded up.

'We're going about fifty miles an hour now, Mrs Greenhill!' Harry shouted back.

She'd rather go more slowly, thank you very much, and stay safe. Hugh clearly didn't share her anxiety. He kept asking more questions about the car.

Nell let them talk. As long as they were heading towards the place where her sister lived, she'd put up with the speed. She'd do whatever it took to find Mattie again. Fly to the moon, if necessary.

When they stopped on the outskirts of Swindon, she was glad to get down for a moment or two, while Harry checked everything.

'Do you want a longer break?' Hugh asked.

'No. I want to get to my sister's as soon as we can.'

'Sorry. I was so interested I forgot how impatient you'd be to see her. Come on, young Harry. Let's be off again.'

They skirted the town centre and headed south-west to Wootton Bassett, then took the Bath road.

Harry suddenly yelled in triumph and pointed to a sign saying Shallerton Bassett. He turned off the main road, and as Stan had told them, the road sloped uphill for a couple of hundred yards. The roofs of a village came into view downhill to their left, while to their right, further up the hill, stood a large house, three storeys high, with outbuildings at the rear. It was built of stone, which had weathered to a comfortable greyish colour, with a roof of large stone tiles. At the front there was a wall, with big double gates standing open onto the drive.

Nell stared at it in amazement. It was the sort of house you saw pictures of in magazines. It didn't seem possible that Mattie could own one so grand. Surely they'd come to the wrong place?

They puttered more slowly up the narrow lane and into the drive, whose gates were open. Harry stopped the car outside the front of the house. 'Here you are,' he called unnecessarily.

Hugh helped Nell out of the vehicle, and as she turned round to look at the house again, the door opened and there was a loud shriek.

'Nell!'

She ran towards her sister, sobbing and holding out her arms. 'Mattie, Mattie, Mattie!'

The two of them met and twirled round, hugging and hugging again, then leaning back to study and pat each other's faces. After that they held each other tightly, both sobbing uncontrollably.

A man came running round the side of the house, limping slightly. He stopped to stare in shock at the two women. He turned to Hugh. 'What's happening? Who's the other woman with my wife?'

'Nell. Mattie's sister.'

'Oh, thank goodness! I told her she'd find her sisters again one day, but she gets very sad about it sometimes.'

He stuck out his hand. 'I'm Jacob Kemble, by the way, Mattie's husband.'

'Hugh Easton. Nell works for me but we're also . . . um . . . getting to be good friends. This is Harry, who drove us here.' But his eyes were on Nell, who looked radiantly happy, even through her tears.

Jacob studied him, head on one side, then smiled. 'You mean, you love her. That's obvious from the way you look at her.' Then he frowned. 'But wasn't she married? To some fellow called Cliff Greenhill, if I remember correctly?'

'She was, but he was killed. And her child with him.'

By this time, the two women had calmed down a little and turned to the men.

'Jacob, come and meet my sister.' Mattie fumbled in her pocket, not finding a handkerchief.

With a laugh, her husband handed her his. 'Lost yours again, have you, love?'

Only then did Nell notice that Mattie was expecting. She couldn't be far along, but there was no mistaking the reason for the curve of her belly against her slender body. 'When is the baby due?'

Mattie beamed. 'End of March, as far as we can tell. Look at us two, standing out here weeping like fools. Let's go inside.'

'I think we should leave you two to talk,' Hugh said. 'You've got a lot to catch up on.'

Nell hesitated. 'Would you mind?'

'Of course not. I'll tell Mr Kemble what's been happening to you.'

'We can do that over a cup of tea and some of Cook's

fruit cake, Mr Easton. And call me Jacob. I'm not one for mistering.'

'I have to pour another can of petrol into the car,' Harry said. 'Though if anyone was to offer me a cup of tea and a piece of cake afterwards, I'd not say no.'

'Cook loves feeding people. You're very welcome.' Mattie was already turning away with her sister.

Jacob watched her go with a fond smile on his face. 'I like to see her happy.'

Harry agreed to drive the car round to the back of the house and Hugh followed Jacob and the two sisters inside, crossing the big hall and going through a door at the back to the kitchen.

Nell lingered to stare round the spacious hallway in awe. 'I can't believe you own a house like this.'

'I have to pinch myself sometimes to make sure I'm not dreaming. Miss Newington, who used to own it, was such a lovely old lady. We were both sad when she died suddenly. Jacob had been working for her for a while, so why she left things to me instead of him, I've never understood. Still, it doesn't really matter now we're married, does it? What's mine is his.'

'How did you meet him?'

'I got lost in a storm the night I ran away, and Jacob's son Luke found me lying unconscious in the lane. He thought I was dead and ran for his dad. If he hadn't found me, I'd have died, I'm sure.'

'Your husband obviously loves you.'

Mattie's face glowed with happiness. 'Jacob's a wonderful man, and so hard-working. He's made a big difference to this house already. He has two children from his first marriage, Luke and Sarah. They're at school at the moment.'

'Do you get on with them all right?'

'I do now, though it wasn't always easy at first. But they're nearly as excited about the baby as I am.' She hesitated, then asked, 'What about Renie? You haven't said a word about her.'

So Nell shared her news, crying again. 'My daughter was called Sarah too, like your stepdaughter. She was such a lovely child.'

Mattie pulled her into another hug. 'How dreadful for you! You've been very brave. Fancy setting off to walk across England all on your own. I'd never have dared do that.'

'I had to get away until I could come to terms with it. I didn't look after myself very well. I sprained my ankle and I was completely lost when Hugh found me.' She shrugged. 'But I'm here now.'

'You're still young, only twenty-three. You'll meet someone else, have other children. Time is a great healer.' She stopped to stare at her sister. 'Nell, you're blushing. Have you met someone already?'

'Hugh.'

'Ah. You're fond of him.'

'Yes, but things went so wrong with Cliff. And Hugh's an educated man. What can he see in someone like me? I—'

'Just a minute. I thought Cliff loved you.'

'So did I. He didn't, though. All he wanted was a woman's body and someone to do the housekeeping.' Nell couldn't help shuddering.

Mattie's voice grew softer. 'Was your marriage very bad?'

'Yes. I'd rather not talk about it. It's over and done with.'

Her sister gave her shoulder a quick squeeze in sympathy. 'All right, love. We'll talk about some good news instead. You remember how your father always used to talk about saving for his old age? After he'd died, Jacob and I found his bank book in that box he kept on top of the wardrobe. You wouldn't believe how much money the old miser had saved – over five hundred pounds.'

'No wonder. He took all our wages from the first day we went to work. Even he wasn't as mean as Cliff, though. At least we ate adequately when I lived at home.'

'Well, you won't ever go hungry again, not as long as I'm around. I'm well provided for, so I thought you and Renie could share your father's money and—'

'Actually, I don't need it. I've got quite a lot of my own because Cliff was even more mean with money than Dad. I found out after he died that he'd been saving for years to open his own business. And he'd taken out life insurance as well. I think that was in case I died, but it was one of those husband-and-wife policies, and as it turned out, I was the one to benefit. A thousand pounds I got. He'd have hated that. So if you need any money for the upkeep of this house, you should take some of Dad's.'

'I don't need it, either. We're not money-rich, Jacob and me, but we have the house and land, and he's a good manager. We've started to put a little aside, even with the repairs we've had to do. I'm glad you're not short of money, though. We'll keep Dad's money for Renie, shall we?'

'If she ever comes back.'

'We have to believe she'll turn up again one day, cheeky as ever,' Mattie said quietly. 'She will, love, I know she will.'

'I hope so.'

'Well – *you* did. I'm sure she must have had a good reason for leaving so suddenly, though I can't imagine what it was.'

'Renie's idea of a good reason isn't always the same as mine,' Nell said. 'She was a madcap sometimes, wasn't she? Do you remember that time when she was seven and she and John Gibbins were playing near the reservoir, which was forbidden. When he fell in, she had to rescue him herself because there was no one else around and he kept sinking? I never saw such a bedraggled pair!'

They both laughed at the memories of their little sister and the atmosphere lightened.

'Have you seen Cliff's family?'

Nell sighed, and told her about Mrs Greenhill screeching at her, then about Frank turning up in the village the day before. 'I can't believe it was a coincidence, as Hugh thinks.'

'Nor can I. People like the Greenhills don't go out simply for pleasure,' Mattie said. 'Anyway, forget about him. Let's go and join the men now or they'll be wondering whether we're all right. Just a minute. Let me tidy your hair . . . There . . . that's better.'

It felt like old times to have Mattie fussing over her, made Nell feel warm inside.

*　*　*

When the two women rejoined the men, who were sitting in the kitchen with the remains of a fruit cake in front of them, Harry took one look at their tear-stained faces and stood up. 'I'll go and have a stroll round your garden, if that's all right, Mr Kemble. I don't want to intrude on your family discussions. I had two big pieces of cake, so I could do to walk it off a bit.'

'That young man is a pleasure to feed,' Cook said after he'd left. 'Will your sister be staying to luncheon, Mrs Kemble?'

'I hope so.' Mattie looked at Nell and Hugh, who both nodded. 'Thank you, Cook. We'll go and sit in the breakfast room, shall we? There's a fire in there and the front parlour takes ages to warm up.'

'Have you set the world to rights now?' Jacob asked as they all sat down.

'Partly,' Mattie said. 'It'll not be fully right till we find Renie again, though.'

'Knowing her, she'll probably find us,' Nell said.

Jacob smiled at Nell. 'I just want you to know that you'll always have a home with us.'

'Thank you, but I'm all right for the moment. I've got a job and I'm needed at the farm.'

'And I very much want you to stay on with me,' Hugh said warmly.

She blushed hotly, and no one spoke for a minute or two, though Mattie gave her sister a knowing smile.

Over luncheon they talked about other things, thank goodness: what Nell had seen on her travels, Hugh's job, Jacob's plans for the land which formed part of his wife's inheritance, and which seemed to matter to him much more than the house did.

All too soon, it was time to leave and the sisters were in tears again.

'Why don't you come over to visit us?' Hugh asked, guessing Nell wouldn't feel she could be the one to invite them to his house.

Jacob frowned. 'It'd not be easy going cross country. We've not got a motor car and I'm not so sure I'd want one, either. Perhaps you could come and see us again instead? Come at the weekend and bring your niece, Hugh. She can play with my Sarah.'

'I can't ask Hugh to—' Nell began, embarrassed.

'You don't need to ask. I'd love to come again and I'm sure May would enjoy the outing. Didn't we say we needed to get her out and about more?'

She could only nod and wish he didn't fit in so well with her family. If only things were different! Whatever he said or did, she simply couldn't believe it would all work out. Or that she deserved such luck.

When they collected May from Pearl's house, she was so rude to Nell that he scolded her.

'You always take her side!' she screamed at him. 'I hate her! She's spoilt everything, taken you away from me. No one loves me any more.'

He looked at Nell aghast, but the child was sobbing so hard, looking such a pitiful lonely little figure, he had to cuddle her.

'I think you need to talk to her,' Nell said. 'I'll go and tidy my bedroom.'

Upstairs she plumped down on the bed, feeling like crying herself. What had got into May? Well, she knew, didn't she? May had lost the two most important people in her world and now she felt she was losing her uncle to Nell. And in a sense, she would be if . . .

No, it was yet another reason why this wasn't meant to be.

She stared bleakly out of the window. She'd known that from the start, hadn't she? Hugh might like being with her now, while he was living so far away from all his friends, but once he got back to London, she'd not fit into his life and he'd soon grow disillusioned.

No, she had to face facts squarely. She wasn't going to run away, though. She'd done enough running away. She'd work on here till a suitable time came to leave, but was going to tell him straight out that it was better to end their relationship now, before they tore one another apart, and before they ruined that poor child's life.

She shivered at the memory of how terrible her marriage to Cliff had been. She still had nightmares about it. Once you were wed, you couldn't escape.

She wouldn't do that to Hugh, spoil his life by tying him down to someone unsuitable. She loved him far too much.

He came up to find her, of course. 'I'm sorry. I can't get May to realise that my caring about you doesn't affect how I feel about her. As for apologising to you for her rudeness, she threw another tantrum at the mere idea of doing that.'

'There's no need. She's a child, and an unhappy one at that.'

'Nonetheless, you don't deserve to be treated like that, my darling, and—'

She held up one hand. 'Leave that for the moment. I have something of my own to say.' She swallowed the lump of anguish in her throat and said baldly, 'It won't work between us, Hugh.'

'Yes, it will! Nell, we love one another.'

'You think you love me, but once you're back in London with your fancy friends, you'll notice my faults, my lack of education. People in Lancashire laughed at the way I speak with a Wiltshire accent. And they would in London too.'

He took hold of her hands and wouldn't let go. 'Nell, I—'

'I won't let the way I feel spoil your life – and mine. And you can't force me to. Let me go.' She tugged her hands away.

He looked horrified. 'I wasn't trying to *force* you to do anything.'

'Then why will you not take no for an answer?'

'Because I know you love me and I know you're wrong about it not working out.'

'It's my choice. If you won't let the matter drop, I'll have to go and live with my sister.' She heard his breath hiss inwards as she said that, but hardened her heart, for his sake.

'Nell, don't do this!'

'I must. I've been in one unhappy marriage and I can't bear the thought of another. So what's it to be, Hugh? Will you stop pestering me, or must I leave?'

His eyes searched her face and she could have wept at

how sad he looked, but she didn't give in. 'Well?'

He spread out his hands in a gesture of helplessness and took a step backwards. 'I'll stop pestering you. But that won't stop me loving you.'

She held back the tears till he'd left her bedroom, then she locked the door and wept into her pillow, fighting to muffle the sound of her pain.

In the bedroom next door, May was wide awake, though it was long past her usual sleeping time. She couldn't help hearing the two of them start arguing. Well, she wasn't going to apologise. *That woman* wasn't going to take her uncle away from her, if she could help it.

But what she heard surprised her. It was her uncle who was asking Nell to give him a chance, and Nell who was refusing.

When May heard her uncle go downstairs again, he was walking slowly and heavily. She was glad *that woman* didn't really want him but she didn't want him to be upset, and he'd sounded so sad.

Perhaps if they went to live in London, it'd happen the way Nell said it would. He'd start seeing his old friends and forget about *her*.

May scowled into the darkness. She didn't want to go and live in London, was frightened of finding her way around in such a big city, where no one knew her.

A sound caught her attention. She couldn't at first make out what it was. It was so faint she could hardly hear it, but her mother had always said she had excellent hearing. The sound went on and on, faint and soft and sad. Suddenly she realised what it was. Nell was crying again.

But Nell had just said she didn't want to marry May's uncle, so why was she crying?

It took a long time for her to stop. May was worried now. People only cried like that when something had upset them badly. She'd cried for days after her parents were killed. And she'd heard her uncle crying too.

It must mean . . . Nell must be unhappy about what had just happened. She wouldn't have cried if she'd meant what she said . . . so she must love him after all.

Well, May was sorry that she was upset, but she couldn't have Uncle Hugh. May needed him too much herself.

Over the next few days, May watched her uncle and Nell carefully. They both looked unhappy and that made her feel bad.

He watched Nell when she wasn't looking at him, and she watched him too, sneaking glances, blinking away tears.

May heard the crying again. Every night. She didn't like to hear it.

One morning she tried to talk about it. 'Your eyes are red and puffy, Nell. Are you all right?'

'I think I've got a bit of a cold, that's all.'

May caught a glimpse of her uncle's face in the mirror on the wall, and wished she hadn't. He'd been looking at Nell so longingly.

It was all very confusing.

They were so upset, she didn't want to make things worse, so didn't tell them about the man who'd come to the school yesterday and stared at her. She knew it was her he was looking at because she always stood on her own in the playground and there was no one else near her.

He was the same man who'd stopped in a car last Sunday to look at them. She didn't like him.

Still, he hadn't done anything to her, had he? And he'd gone away again, so it was probably nothing.

She'd tell them if he came back again, though.

When May had left for school on the Friday, Hugh looked at Nell across the kitchen and risked asking, 'Are you happy with what you're doing to me, to us?'

'No, of course I'm not. But it's the right thing to do. I know it is.'

'It isn't. Only I can't think how to convince you. And if you carry out your threat and leave, I'll follow you, and keep turning up at your sister's till I've made you change your mind.'

'You promised not to pester me.'

'Is that what I'm doing? Pestering you? I thought I'd be allowed to speak to you sometimes. We've been such good friends, could be so much more.'

She couldn't answer, so turned back to the washing-up and let her tears splash down into the bowl of soapy water where he couldn't see them.

In the afternoon, he came into the kitchen and said abruptly, 'I'm going out for a walk. I need to think.' It was looking like rain, so she was a bit surprised.

When she went into the hall a little later, she saw his mackintosh still hanging on the hall stand. He'd get wet. If he fell ill, it'd be partly her fault.

Why did it hurt so much to do what was right?

Was it really the right choice to make? Should she give in and marry him? Or should she leave and go to Mattie's, end it properly?

Heaven help her, she couldn't bear to do that. She wasn't going to leave him until she absolutely had to. Anyway, they still needed her here to look after them.

Chapter Seventeen

The house seemed empty without Hugh, and when two hours passed and he didn't come home, Nell began to worry. It was a cold wet day, not the sort where you went for a long walk.

She settled herself by a side window from which she could keep an eye on the path across the fields. As an excuse for sitting there, she started a letter to her sister but couldn't settle to writing. After two failed letters, she cried out in dismay as a big blob of ink plopped off her carelessly filled pen nib. Muttering in annoyance, she screwed up the third piece of paper and abandoned the attempt. Nothing was going right today.

At the usual time, May came back from school, entering the house quietly, without her usual burst of chatter.

'Did you have a good day?' Nell asked.

'No, of course I didn't. The teacher made me do the same work as the others. Baby work! Boring!'

'It'll be better when you get to London. Your uncle will make sure you go to a good school there.'

'I'm *not* going to London! Why will you and my uncle not believe that? If he drags me there, I'll run away and come back here. Cross my heart and hope to die.' She made an 'X' sign in the air over her chest to emphasise her promise, and when Nell said nothing, yelled, 'This is my *home*!'

'It was your family home, but it isn't anymore. Your uncle's job is in London and—'

'What do you know about anything? You worked in a laundry before you got married! I shouldn't think *you* did very well at school. And you've only been to London once, so I know a lot more about what it's like there than you do.'

This rudeness took Nell's breath away and she was just about to scold May when she heard footsteps outside. 'There's your uncle coming back. Please . . . try not to upset him because he—'

The door banged open and a man burst into the kitchen. Frank Greenhill.

Nell was so shocked she couldn't speak.

'I've come for you, Nell,' he said.

'What?'

'You've got the Greenhill money. It should have come to us after Cliff died. But that's all right. You can come and live with us and we'll all—'

'You must be mad!' she exclaimed. 'I'm doing no such thing. I have my own life now and—'

He smiled, such a nasty threatening smile that she moved instinctively to stand between him and May.

He saw it, of course. 'Ah. That's the key.'

'What do you mean?'

'The girl.' He shoved Nell out of the way and grabbed May by the arm, dragging her towards him so roughly she cried out in pain.

Nell tried to free the girl, but he sent her tumbling across the floor. All the memories of her father flooded back, making her freeze. She couldn't move for a moment or two, kneeling there, terrified.

'Now listen to me. The insurance money you got belongs to the Greenhills by rights, all of it. But we can't leave you unprovided for. That'd not be fair, either. So I've worked out that you and me can get married. You had a child once, so you're not barren, and if you're acting as housekeeper here, you must be good at that sort of thing. My aunt's let things go and needs someone to help her in the house. Anyway, it's time I got some sons.'

'You must be mad! I'd never marry you.'

'You will. But if you try to delay things, you'd better start worrying about this one.' He shook May again, roughly, and she yelped in pain as she bumped into a corner of the table.

Nell tried again to get between him and May and this time he let her. 'Run away if you can,' she whispered to the girl, then said more loudly, 'You can't force me to marry you, Frank, whatever you threaten.'

'I'm sure I can. A few accidents here and there, people you care about hurt.' His eyes went back to the girl. 'And that sister of yours is expecting. A fellow at work's brother delivered some goods to her, says she's rich now. But even the rich can tumble. Be sad if she had a fall, wouldn't it? In her condition.'

She couldn't hold back a gasp of shock at this. 'I'll report you to the police.'

He laughed. 'I'll apologise for threatening you today. A man in love says foolish things. I was carried away. They won't be able to do anything.' He paused for a moment and added softly, 'But *I* will. I'll be able to do a lot of things later, things you won't like.'

She was shaken by the wild light in his eyes and said, 'You *are* mad!' before she could stop herself.

He pointed to May and mimed a slap. 'Oh, no. I'm just practical when I want something.'

Nell swallowed hard.

Frank looked at May and said harshly, 'Where's your father, you?'

'My father's dead.'

'Who's the big fellow who lives here, then?'

'He's my uncle. He's gone out for a walk but he'll be back soon, and he won't let you hurt us.'

'I saw no sign of anyone walking across the fields, so I reckon we've got time to finish our talk.' He turned back to Nell. 'Make me a cup of tea. It's cold outside.'

She hesitated, then moved across to push the kettle onto the heat.

When May would have followed her, he growled, 'You. Stay there.'

Nell made the tea as quickly as she could, pouring him a cup and carrying it across the room. When she was nearly by his side, she yelled suddenly, 'Run, May! Run!' and hurled the hot liquid into his face.

As he screamed in pain, she saw May running across the room and prayed she'd get outside safely. She tried to follow her, knocking over a chair behind her in an attempt to slow him down.

But May fumbled with the door latch and it took longer to open it than Nell had expected. By then, he'd reached them.

She barred his way, shoving May through the door and trying to fight free of Frank. But he was so big she hadn't a chance.

'You'll be sorry for that!' He threw her against the wall and her head hit the door-frame.

She cried out in pain as everything seemed to explode round her.

Hugh was walking back down the hill to the farm through the narrow path along the depression where the elm trees flourished. He heard someone scream and began to run even before he saw May burst out of the house, coatless. She kept glancing over her shoulder as she set off running towards the village, every line of her body speaking of terror. She was so busy checking she wasn't being pursued, she didn't see him till he caught her shoulder. 'What's happened?'

She screamed, then clung to him. 'Uncle Hugh, there's a man! A horrible man. He's hurting Nell. Go and save her, Uncle Hugh. Go and—'

'Who is it?'

'The man who stopped his car to look at us after church.'

Heaven help him, Hugh thought. Nell had been afraid then, and he'd dismissed her worries. 'Fetch help from the village, May. Quick as you can.'

He began running towards the farm, his heart pounding

in his chest with terror for the woman he loved.

It was agony to slow down as he approached the house, but Nell hadn't followed his niece outside, so he had to find out what was happening, not rush in and leave her open to threats. He walked quietly across a muddy part of the yard, rather than clumping over the paved part.

When he risked a glance inside, he saw a huge brute of a man staring down at Nell's unconscious body. Dear God, had the fellow killed her?

He swung round to rush inside, then stopped himself. He wasn't an experienced fighter. He needed surprise on his side. Opening the side door, he crept into the house through the laundry door, picking up the possing stick with its blunt round end as he passed through, for lack of a better weapon.

'Wake up, you stupid bitch,' the man was saying, still bending over Nell.

Hugh was behind him, so started creeping across the room. But his foot crunched on a piece of broken crockery and the man spun round, bunching up his fists.

'Get back!' he yelled.

'Get out of my house!'

He laughed. 'I'll go when I'm ready and she's coming with me. She promised to marry me and she's going to keep that promise.'

Hugh didn't dare attack him openly, so paused as if doubtful. 'She didn't. She wouldn't lie to me.'

'She's lied before. I don't know why I bother with her, but when you've lain with a woman, when she's so loving in bed, it's hard to let her go.'

'No. No, I don't believe you.' Hugh raised one hand slowly, covering his eyes as if upset.

'As soon as she wakes up, I'll take her away. You'll be better off without her, and once we're married, I'll make sure she behaves as a good wife should.'

Nell regained consciousness to hear Frank say they were engaged to be married. She hastily closed her eyes, as she remembered what had happened. She didn't want him to know she was awake.

It seemed as if Hugh believed him, because he was hesitating. How could he say he loved her one minute and not trust her the next?

Through her lashes, she saw Hugh move sideways a couple of paces. Beside her, Frank tensed as if ready to fight, then relaxed a little as Hugh continued to speak brokenly. 'She seemed to love me. I believed her. How long have you been engaged?'

'Since after my cousin's funeral. It wasn't a happy marriage and Cliff was to blame for that. I comforted her then and we agreed to marry once enough time had passed. I came here today to name a day.'

She took another quick peep and as she did so Hugh moved again. He must have seen her eyes open.

'What happened to her? Why is she unconscious?'

'She tripped on the rug and—'

Nell could see Frank's feet on that same rug, could feel it beneath her hand, and that gave her an idea. She edged back a little, leaning against the wall to give herself some purchase, then gripped it tightly with one hand. Hugh noticed and gave the tiniest of nods.

Next time Frank looked away, she was going to pull it as hard as she could and throw him off balance. She'd yell to Hugh to hit him. Frank was worse than her husband had been, far worse. But others might believe him.

Suddenly Hugh's voice rang out, 'Now, Nell!'

As fast as she could she yanked on the rug. She couldn't pull it out from such a heavy man, but she did distract him and throw him off balance.

As he'd been speaking, Hugh had raised something and now he smashed it down on Frank's head.

But it wasn't hard enough and Frank gave a bull-like roar and turned on him. She jumped to her feet, looking for something to hit him with. But by the time she'd grabbed the rolling pin, the two men were rolling about on the floor.

Hugh knew he was fighting for his life. He managed to land a punch on his opponent's jaw, but although his fist connected, Frank only grunted and shook his head.

In the meantime a giant fist slammed into his body. Hugh had time to move back a little and prevent it hitting his stomach with full force, but though he wasn't winded, it hurt. And if he didn't do better than this, he'd not save Nell.

He avoided the obvious knee thrust towards a tender part of his body, but he couldn't avoid all the blows that were raining down on him.

A voice yelled suddenly, 'I'm here, Mr Easton!' and Fred ran into the room, brandishing a chunk of wood.

There was no hope of such a frail old man hurting a huge man like Frank, but his brave effort did distract

Frank, and Nell seized the opportunity to smash the rolling pin down on their attacker's head. She felt sickened by the sound of it connecting, but he dropped like a stone.

'Get the washing line,' Hugh yelled. 'Quick!'

She ran for it, but even so, they were nearly too late, because as they were tying him up, Frank began to regain consciousness. His hands were trussed, but he still managed to jerk his body backwards and forwards, and kick out at them. There was nothing he could do to get rid of his bonds, but they didn't dare get close enough to tie his feet.

'Are you all right?' Hugh panted, pulling her back as Frank tried to slam into them.

Then they heard feet running towards the house and Pearl's husband Ronald burst into the room. Puffing along behind him were two other men from the village.

'Thank goodness! Oh, thank goodness.' Nell leant against the wall, trembling all over, feeling clammy and distant now that the worst was over.

Ronald seemed to sum up what was going on at a glance, and soon he and the others had secured Frank's feet.

'What happened?' he asked as he stood up.

'That man attacked me,' Nell said. 'He's my husband's cousin and he wants the insurance money I got.'

'She's lying. She'd promised to marry me and I came to claim her. Then they both attacked me.'

'Mr Easton?' Ronald laughed. 'He's the last man to attack anyone.'

'I saw that man attack Nell,' May said. 'He was going to hurt me and she saved me. She threw a cup of tea over him and I got away. But he caught her.'

Hugh had put his arm round Nell's shoulders. Now

he reached out the other arm and May went to stand in its shelter for a moment, then reached across him to hug Nell.

But she must have moved against an injured part because he winced. May stepped back and grimaced at the sight of her uncle's battered face, then looked at Nell. 'You should both come and sit down. My uncle's hurt and you look ready to faint, Nell.'

Ronald took over. 'I'll see to your uncle, May. You take Mrs Greenhill to sit down before she falls down.'

Leaning on the girl, Nell stumbled across the room. It seemed a long way, and although Hugh followed her, he looked very wobbly too.

'Fine champion I am,' he muttered. 'I'm nearly as big as he is but he was making mincemeat of me.'

May picked up a chair for Nell and made sure she was all right. 'I'll get some water to wash my uncle's cuts.'

'Good girl,' Hugh said to his niece, but his eyes were on Nell.

May set her hands on her hips and looked at them. 'Oh, go on, kiss her better. She deserves it.'

They both stared at her in surprise.

'I don't mind now,' May said. 'She saved me from that man and she got hurt doing it. I thought I'd lost my uncle, but I hadn't, had I? Instead I'd got someone else who cares about me as well.'

'Of course I care,' Nell said softly.

'She stood between him and me,' May told the other men. 'She's not much taller than I am, but she was so brave.'

Hugh reached out to clasp Nell's hand, giving her a smile

338

that was lopsided from a puffy cut lip. 'Very brave.'

Ronald studied them. 'You both look ready to drop. I've sent Peter for the doctor. He was at Mrs Pender's house because the old lady's been took bad. If we're in luck, we'll just catch him before he leaves.'

'I don't need a doctor,' Hugh said, but winced as he moved.

'I'd say you've cracked a rib or two,' Ronald said. 'You need him to bind them up for you. And he'd better look at Mrs Greenhill too. She looks white and wambly to me.'

Hugh kept a firm hold of Nell's hand. 'She's wonderful,' he said in a husky voice.

'Can we borrow your trap, sir? We'll take that fellow into Faringdon and hand him over to the police. My cousin's the sergeant there. I'll tell him what's happened and warn him to watch out for that fellow's lies. As if Mrs Greenhill would take up with a brute like that when everyone in the village knows it's you she cares about!'

Nell's head was hurting and she did indeed feel sick, but that remark made her smile. Had her feelings been so very obvious? Then she moved, groaning as this caused pain to stab through her head.

'I think we need to get you to bed, my little love,' Hugh said. 'I'd offer to carry you up, but I'm in no fit state.'

'I'll do that, sir. Yes, Mrs Greenhill, you do need carrying. Hold still while I pick you up. We don't want you making bad worse by tumbling down the stairs, do we?'

Hugh turned to his niece. 'May, can you fill a hot-water bottle for her?'

'Yes.'

He watched Ronald carry Nell out of the room and

winced as he moved without thinking. 'Fine hero I am!' he muttered.

'You're a hero and she's a heroine,' May said firmly. 'But it's not like the storybooks, is it? It was horrible. And you're both hurting.'

He was hurting even worse by the time the doctor had bound up his ribs, and once he'd made sure Nell was all right, he allowed them to give him something to make him sleep.

There was no lack of helpers to take care of May and keep an eye on them all.

Chapter Eighteen

The following morning, Nell woke up a little later than usual. Her head was aching and she couldn't think why until she suddenly remembered what had happened.

She found a dressing gown beside the bed, not hers, but it was obviously there for her.

Footsteps pattered up the stairs and May peeped in. 'Oh, you're awake. Good. I can bring you up a cup of tea. I put my mother's dressing gown out for you.'

'I'd rather come down for the tea. Where's your uncle?'

'He's sitting in the kitchen. He's got two cracked ribs, the doctor says, so it hurts him to move, but he'll be all right.' She looked at Nell anxiously. 'Are you sure you're well enough to come down?'

'Yes. Give me a couple of minutes.'

Hugh was sitting at the table, watching the stairs, but didn't get up to greet her, which told Nell he was hurting badly.

'Should you be up?' she asked.

'Should you?' He glanced towards the kitchen mirror.

'Ugh! I look a right old mess, don't I? But the doctor said my nose isn't broken, and it's just contusions and cuts, apart from the ribs.'

She went to join him at the table, still feeling a little wobbly.

'I want to thank you for saving May.' He reached out to clasp her hand.

'Anyone would have done the same.'

'No, they wouldn't. Especially not a little woman like you facing up to a huge brute like him.'

'May didn't get hurt, which was the main thing.'

There was a sound over by the door and May suddenly rushed across the room to throw her arms round Nell's neck, weeping loudly. 'I'm sorry. I'm sorry I was so awful to you.'

Startled, Nell met Hugh's eyes over the girl's head, patting the heaving shoulders.

'It's reaction,' he said. 'She was marvellous while we needed her, and she made breakfast for me this morning. I was so proud of you yesterday, May.'

As the child continued to weep, Nell made a shushing sound. 'Calm down now, May dear.'

When May had stopped sobbing, she reached for Nell's hand.

'I don't know how you can bear to be with me, I've been so horrible to you. I knew I was being horrible and . . . I couldn't stop it.'

'We all do things we regret.'

'Have I spoilt it all for you?'

'Spoilt what, May?'

The girl looked from Nell to her uncle and back again.

'You two. He wants to marry you and I thought I didn't want it, but I do now, because I could see how much he loved you when you were hurt. And I can see how much you love him every time you look at him.'

Hugh leant forward, his breath hissing in as he moved. 'So if I ask Nell to marry me, it won't upset you now – because you know you'll still be living with us?'

'And I'll have two people who care for me, instead of one. Yes, I know.' May brushed away a tear and turned back to Nell. 'You will marry my uncle, won't you?'

Hugh smiled. 'I can do my own proposing, young lady.'

May stared at him for a moment, then said, 'Go on, then. Do it.'

He turned to Nell. 'My darling, I know I look terrible, and you're a bit battered too, but I can't wait any longer.' Very gingerly he got down on one knee. 'Will you marry me, Nell dearest? I don't think I can bear it unless you do.'

She leant forward to kiss the cheek that was nearest. 'Of course I will. Get up, you soft fool. I never saw such a carry-on. Why couldn't you just ask me? It must have hurt you to kneel down.'

'It was worth it.'

'He had to do it properly,' May said indignantly. 'The man always has to go down on one knee to propose. I've been reading about it.'

'There you are.' Hugh eased back on to his chair, grinning at them. 'I should have added, will you take on this young lady, as well as me?'

'I can't think of anything I'd like better,' Nell said, the lump of happiness in her throat making her voice wobble.

'Hooray!' May got up and danced round the room. 'We're engaged! We're engaged!'

Hugh rolled his eyes at this, then caught Nell's hand. 'I'd sweep you into my arms, but it'd hurt too much.'

'Get on with you!'

'I didn't believe it when I read it in books, but I do now. You really have made me the happiest man in the world.'

May stopped dancing and came to stand next to them, biting the corner of her mouth.

'What is it now?' Hugh asked, recognising the signs of worry.

'London. You need to go back there, don't you?'

'Yes. I thought we could all move there as soon as Nell and I are married. I can't stay here, May. My life and work are in London.'

'I don't want to stay here now, uncle. I don't want anyone else coming to attack us. If Nell hadn't helped me escape, that man might have killed us and there was nobody near to call to for help.'

'Bad things happen everywhere,' Nell said quietly. 'We just have to cope with them as best we can, May, and be thankful for the good times.'

'Like you losing your daughter.'

'Yes. That'll always hurt, but I hope you'll be a daughter to me now.'

May's face brightened and she nodded.

Hugh waited a minute to let the emotions that conversation had raised in them all die down again. When Nell's face had lost its distressed look, he said, 'We'll send a letter to your sister and get young Harry to drive us over there next Sunday to discuss the wedding. I reckon we'll both be in a fit state to go out by then.' He chuckled suddenly. 'Fine romantic pair we are, me with my battered face and you with a big bump on your head.'

'I'd not have anyone else in the whole world,' she said.

May gave a sentimental sigh and they both smiled at her.

Then Nell said wistfully, 'There's only one thing missing from my happiness.'

'Knowing where your other sister is.'

'Yes.'

'She'll turn up one day.'

'That's what Jacob says to Mattie. I certainly hope so.'

They set off for Shallerton Bassett on the Sunday morning, after an exchange of letters with Mattie. This time an excited May was allowed to sit in the front of the car next to Harry, while Nell and Hugh sat in the back, holding hands, not saying much but smiling a lot.

As they got to the end of their lane, they met the postman, so took their letters from him to save him a ride.

'There's one for you.' Hugh passed over an envelope with childish scrawling writing on it. 'Posted in Swindon.'

Nell studied it. 'Who can it be from?'

'You'll never know if you don't open it.'

She did so, finding two sheets of paper inside, the second one with only a few lines typed on it and a mere scrawl of a signature.

Dear Nell

After I'd seen you, I got to thinking that them Greenhills shouldn't be able to stop you hearing from your Renie. So when I heard Frank was locked up, I went and had a quiet word with Mrs Greenhill about passing letters on. She's shocked at what he's done, even though she still hates you.

She handed over this letter, which they'd had for a few weeks, the miserable devils. That neighbour of your Dad's, who's been passing information to them, got hold of it and gave it to them. They'd already opened it, so I had a read to make sure it wasn't bad news. It isn't, though Renie shouldn't have gone running off to Paris like that, the minx.

Stan Telfor

Nell clapped one hand to her mouth, hardly daring to look at the second piece of paper.

'What is it?' Hugh asked.

She passed Stan's letter on to him, took a deep breath and began to read the second piece of paper.

Dear Nell,

I asked a friend at the hotel to send this to Dad if I didn't get in touch in three months.

I'm not able to tell anyone exactly where I'm going, not even you, but I promise you, I'm all right. I'm doing a favour for a friend and we'll be living in Paris for a while. Just imagine that, me going to France!

I'll send word to you when it's safe.

Love

Renie

Nell saw that May had turned round to watch her anxiously, and when Hugh took hold of her hand, she clutched his and sniffed away the tears. You shouldn't cry when you'd had good news, and she'd done enough crying in the past year.

'It's from my sister Renie. The Greenhills had this letter all the time. I still don't know what Renie's doing, but at least I know she went away willingly. I'm sure now that I'll hear from her again.'

'That must make you feel better.'

'It does. Though I shall be worrying about what she's doing with herself in Paris. Stan's right. She is a minx. Just wait till I show this to Mattie.'

He grinned. 'You'll probably both have a lovely cry over it.'

'Oh, you!' She gave him a mock punch, being careful not to hit him properly, then took hold of his hand again. His face might be battered, he was still moving carefully and his smile was lopsided, but to her he was the best-looking man in the whole world.

'They get all soppy sometimes,' May whispered to Harry.

'It's nice to see,' he whispered back.

'Huh! They're always kissing and cuddling. I'm never going to be like that.'

Keep up to date with

ANNA JACOBS

by logging on to her website
www.annajacobs.com
for book excerpts, news and articles.

Or email her at
anna@annajacobs.com

Or you can write to her at
PO Box 628
Mandurah
Western Australia 6210

If you'd like a reply, please enclose a self-addressed
envelope with an international reply coupon.

You can join Anna's announcements list
from her website, or sign up for a
monthly newsletter by emailing
annajacobs-subscribe@yahoogroups.com